A Simple Amish Christmas

A SIMPLE AMISH CHRISTMAS

Vannetta Chapman

Abingdon Press fiction
a novel approach to faith

Nashville, Tennessee

A Simple Amish Christmas

Copyright © 2010 by Vannetta Chapman

ISBN-13: 978-1-4267-1066-7

Published by Abingdon Press, P.O. Box 801, Nashville, TN 37202

www.abingdonpress.com

The persons and events portrayed in this work of fiction are the
creations of the author, and any resemblance to persons
living or dead is purely coincidental.

Published in association with the Seymour Literary Agency.

Cover design by Anderson Design Group, Nashville, TN

Library of Congress Cataloging-in-Publication Data

Chapman, Vannetta.
  A simple Amish Christmas / Vannetta Chapman.
     p. cm.
  ISBN 978-1-4267-1066-7 (pbk. : alk. paper)
  1. Amish—Fiction.   2. Christmas stories.   I. Title.
  PS3603.H3744S56   2010
  813'.6—dc22

                                    2010027885

Printed in the United States of America

3 4 5 6 7 8 9 10 / 15 14 13 12 11 10

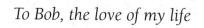

To Bob, the love of my life

Acknowledgments

I'm grateful to Mary Sue Seymour for encouraging me to write Amish fiction and finding a home for this story. I'd also like to thank Barbara Scott for acquiring it.

Donna and Kristy, you two are the most faithful first readers an author could wish for. I hope those dinners at the Cheesecake Factory are adequate compensation for your hard work.

Cathy, I wouldn't have made it through the edits without your help on the technology end. The Lunch Bunch at LISD helped me laugh through my day job, and the bell choir at FUMC picked up my spirit at practice every Wednesday night.

Amy, you were a wonderful source of help and encouragement. Thank you, dear.

Bob, for an engineer, I realize this entire writing thing is a stretch; I appreciate how hard you try.

Cody, thank you for making it possible for me to write while raising a son. I know not every mom can do both, because not every mom has a son like you.

Jordyn, Yale, and Kylie—I'm proud of each of you, and I am glad you're in my life.

Mom, you are my biggest fan. Thank you for always encouraging me in my dreams.

Baby Kiptyn, we continue to pray for you.

Finally, this book wouldn't be possible without the Lord's guidance. "I can do all things through Christ." Without him, I'm just another crazy lady with a laptop.

Note to the Reader

The setting for this novel is Mifflin County, Pennsylvania; however, the Amish community within the pages of this book is fictional. Amish rules and traditions described here have been researched faithfully. Please note, though, that there are differences among Amish communities; therefore, actions and dialogue may differ from the Amish culture you know.

A glossary is provided at the back of the book for your use.

Prologue

Mifflin County, Pennsylvania
September, 2006

*A*nnie Weaver sat in the back seat of her *aenti's* car, determined to hold in her tears. She was a woman after all—sixteen this past January. Within four months she would turn seventeen.

Which was why her *dat* and *mamm* had finally decided to send her with her aunt.

Nearly seventeen and she'd refused every boy who had wanted to court her.

Nearly seventeen and she had managed to lose three jobs.

Nearly seventeen and she was still sneaking into the barn and reading books by lamplight.

Watching the fields of her *dat's* farm slip away, she put her hand to her stomach and attempted to calm the butterflies swirling there. They had met as a family and all agreed this was for the best.

A little time with the *Englisch*.

A few months with her cousins.

A chance to clear her head and indulge her *rumschpringe*.

But what if this wasn't merely a time of rebellion?

What if she was actually different from her family and friends?

Annie brushed away the tear that slipped down her cheek, watched the last of Mifflin County fly past her window, and prayed God would settle her restless spirit and bring her safely home.

1

Philadelphia, Pennsylvania
December 1, 2009, 6:55 a.m.

*A*nnie Weaver threw her coat and scarf into her locker, slammed it shut, and twirled the lock—once, twice, three times as Jenny had shown her.

Turning to go, she nearly ran over her best friend.

"Tell me you are not headed out on the floor." Jenny's voice sounded like Annie's first-year teacher—stern and low and slightly disappointed. Sporting short blonde hair and a figure even slimmer than Annie's, Jenny looked nothing like an Amish schoolteacher.

"I'm not?"

"You are, aren't you?"

Blue eyes laughed at her, even as Annie tossed a panicked look at the clock—six fifty-seven a.m.

"*Ya.* Why?"

"Cap."

Annie's hand flew to the top of her head and met only a mass of curls. Searching, she found her nursing cap slid to the back and side of her head.

"Scope."

Looking down, she realized she'd left it—

"I.D."

Left them both in her locker.

As she turned and fumbled with the combination on her locker, Jenny re-pinned Annie's nursing cap firmly in place on the top of her long, chestnut hair.

"I'm running late," Annie explained.

"Sleep in?"

Annie shook her head. "I was up early enough, but I made the mistake of turning on the radio. The music reminded me that it's December."

"They're already playing Christmas songs," Jenny fussed. "I still have leftover turkey in the fridge."

"When I heard the music I realized I hadn't written home this week. I thought I had enough time, but then a letter to my parents was followed by another to my *schweschder*." Annie's voice trailed off. How could she explain that the Christmas decorations popping up everywhere were making her homesick?

Garlands hung from the halls of her boarding house. Colorful displays crowded the store windows lining her walk to work. Lights blinked above the streets, and Santas rang bells at nearly every door.

She longed for the simple celebrations of home.

Home.

Annie grabbed her I.D. and stethoscope, allowing her fingers to brush over the engraving, marveling that it bore her initials.

She had actually earned her R.N. degree. One year she had studied and earned her high school equivalency, then for two years she had been enrolled in and graduated from the local nursing program.

Three years of living with her *aenti*.

Three years working among the *Englisch*.

Three years away from her family.

She spun around to face Jenny. "I shouldn't have spent so long writing my *mamm* and *dat* this morning, but *ya*—I was a little homesick because of the holidays."

"Your mother and dad will appreciate the letter. Why don't you stop by my place after your shift ends? I'll make baked ziti, a giant salad, and fresh rolls—your favorite meal."

Annie blinked through the tears that suddenly sprang to her eyes, accepted the hug Jenny offered, and hurried out to the floor, glancing again at the clock as she passed underneath it.

Only one minute late.

❧

"Good morning, Annie." Jeffrey's voice was as sweet as shoofly pie, too sweet.

She'd been dodging his flirtations for weeks. Though he was a nice enough co-worker, his attention left her confused.

As did the smile he shot her way.

"*Gudemariye*," she mumbled, pretending to check her pocket for pen and stethoscope.

"Careful—you know I love it when you talk plain to me." Tall and redheaded, Jeffrey winked, then walked over to the copier machine.

"Don't tease her, Jeffrey." Shelly issued her command in a don't-mess-with-me voice. "Annie just arrived, and you know it takes her a few minutes to readjust to our ways."

Peering over her reading glasses, Shelly waited for Jeffrey to return his attention to his work, which he did. She was their shift supervisor, and she was the perfect mother hen. Dark ebony skin, tall and somewhat on the heavy side—no one doubted she could handle whatever presented on their floor.

She waved Annie toward the little boy in room 307. "Go on, honey. Kiptyn has been asking for you since his five a.m. check."

"*Danki*," Annie replied, glancing up at the status board. "I mean, thank you. I had hoped to check on him first. He rested well last night?"

"As well as can be expected." Shelly's face took on the protective look Annie had come to love so well over the past six months. "Remember, Annie, care for your patients, but don't let them break your heart."

"*Ya*. I know. You have warned me before." Annie smiled, felt in her pocket for the item that had arrived in the mail yesterday.

Christmas music played softly over the hospital sound system as she hurried down the hall toward Kiptyn's room.

She entered quietly.

The boy didn't seem to hear her over the buzzing and beeping of medical apparatus. An oxygen machine hummed beside his bed. A heart monitor beeped with the rhythm of his heart.

And cartoon characters fought to save the world on the television set.

Kiptyn didn't seem to notice any of it.

The eight-year-old boy sat staring at the wall. Annie could see, even from across the room, what an effort it was for him to breathe. She pulled in a deep breath, as if it would fill his lungs as well as her own, and cleared her throat, alerting him to her presence.

"Good morning, Mr. Kiptyn. It seems you are my first patient today. You must be very important indeed."

"Annie." The little boy's voice reminded her of a song, one that could tear at your heart while still making you smile. His blue eyes brightened as he struggled to sit up straighter in his bed.

But even from the doorway she could tell that the sixteen hours since she'd last seen him had taken their toll. The circles around his eyes were a bit darker, his skin even paler, and—though it didn't seem possible—she wondered if he might have dropped below the forty-four pounds she'd recorded yesterday.

"Let me help you, *kind*."

Moving efficiently to his side, she gently repositioned the pillows behind him with one hand and used the controls to adjust his bed with the other.

"What does *kind* mean? Is it an Amish word?"

"*Ya*. It means child. Sometimes I slip back into the plain language."

"I like when you speak Amish." Kiptyn rubbed his nose, knocking his oxygen plugs askew.

Annie reached forward and adjusted them, taking a moment to let her hand rest on the top of his shiny bald head.

She'd seen the pictures his *mamm* had brought, so she knew the boy had once had curly blond hair. Kiptyn's parents took turns staying with the child each night, then hurried off to their respective jobs early each day.

"Actually what my people speak is *Dietsch*."

Kiptyn laughed even as he fought for a full breath. "Don't you mean Dutch?"

"It's a type of Dutch," Annie agreed, slipping the blood pressure cuff over his small arm. "Actually *Dietsch* means Pennsylvania Dutch."

"'Will you teach me more *Dietsch* today?" Kiptyn asked.

"Do you remember what I taught you yesterday?" Annie took his pressure manually and noted the numbers on her chart.

The monitor could have done it electronically, but she'd noticed that he had begun bruising where the machine tightened the cuff around his arm. After speaking with Shelly, she'd received permission to take his pressure manually during the day.

Annie also felt a person's touch was more personal than a machine—anything to make his stay easier. It was her responsibility to care for these precious children.

"*Gudemariye*." Kiptyn said the word as if he were practicing for a presentation in front of a classroom.

"And good morning to you," Annie responded. She placed her stethoscope in her pocket, then tapped her chin, as if she were having trouble remembering any other words in her native tongue.

"I heard my parents talking last night. They thought I was asleep." Kiptyn's voice grew softer.

His hand crept out, and he traced the pattern of dark blue material on her sleeve, letting his fingers run down to her hand until it rested there on top of hers. "They're thinking about having another baby. Something about how a brother could help save me. How's that possible?"

"Perhaps you shouldn't be eavesdropping, *boppli*." Annie corrected him gently. She moved to check his IV drip.

"I'm not a baby, Annie." Kiptyn smiled up at her again. "You taught me that word on Monday. What I'd really like is to have a brother—someone I could play ball with when I'm well. Do you have a word for brother?"

Kiptyn's question caused a pressure to form around Annie's heart, and she felt as if tears were being wrung from it—tears she couldn't show this precious *kind*.

She sat gently on the side of the bed, taking the boy's hand in her own. Earlier in the week, the doctors had told Kiptyn's parents the chemotherapy wasn't effectively battling his cancer. They wanted to move on to a new experimental drug treatment, felt it was his only hope of survival.

"*Ya*, we have a word for brother. I have a brother, did you know that?"

"How old is he?"

"Twenty-two. He is a grown man." Annie hadn't been able to visit her family in the fall, and now for the second time since waking she was nearly overcome with homesickness. Adam would be married next year. She looked out the hospital window at the snow that had begun falling and thought of Leah, the pretty, slim girl who would soon be her *schweschder.*

"So how do you say it, Annie?" Coughing wracked his thin frame, and she reached forward to rub his chest. "How do you say brother?"

"*Bruder.*"

"Well, that's easy." Kiptyn laughed again and pulled in a deep breath. "*Bruder.* Sounds like our word."

"*Ya*, it does." Annie stood and started out of the room, had nearly reached the door when her hand brushed up against what was in her pocket. She turned back around.

"Kiptyn, remember when I asked you if it was all right to tell my *onkel* about you?"

"Your *Onkel* Eli, who builds things. Yeah, I remember."

"Well I wrote him, and he sent you something." She reached in her pocket, pulled out the wooden horse. It was handcrafted of maple wood and fit in her palm. The detail was exquisite. Walking back to Kiptyn's bed, she placed it on his tummy.

The boy reached out, picked it up, and studied it.

"Cool beans!" A smile covered Kiptyn's face, and for a moment he merely looked like a little boy instead of a cancer patient. "Could I write him and say thanks?"

"He'd like that, I'll—"

The door to Kiptyn's room burst open, and Shelly stepped through.

"Annie, could I speak with you in the hall, please?" It wasn't a question at all. The look on Shelly's face was somber, more so than Annie had ever seen before.

"Of course, I was finishing up here. Kiptyn, I'll check on you again a little later. Press your button if you need anything."

She followed Shelly into the hall, confusion and worry sending beads of sweat down the back of her neck. She suddenly wished she'd pulled her long, brown hair back into a clip, anything to help with the wave of heat washing over her.

Shelly turned as soon as Kiptyn's door closed, then reached out and placed a hand gently on Annie's shoulder.

"Annie, you have a phone call at the desk." Concern mingled with sympathy. "Sweetie, it's Vickie."

"Mrs. Brown? My landlady? I don't understand."

"She's calling about your father, Annie. There's been an accident."

2

Mifflin County, Pennsylvania
December 1, 2009, 9:30 p.m.

Samuel Yoder sat up straighter in the hard wooden chair, stared at the simple furnishings in his neighbor's bedroom, and struggled against the fatigue that threatened to overwhelm him. A glance at Jacob Weaver told him that nothing had changed in the man's condition. He still slept; his breathing remained labored but steady, his pulse beat within normal range.

Sighing heavily, Samuel unfolded his lanky six-foot frame and walked to the room's single window. He could see nothing in the darkness—the quarter moon did little to shed any light on Jacob's fields.

Samuel stared at them nonetheless.

Memories of finding Mary and Little Hannah that other December night, so many years ago—frozen and *gschtarewe* in the snow—merged with finding Jacob last night. His left arm began to shake, and he massaged it with his right, knowing the tremor would pass in a few moments.

The tremor always passed, though the memory remained.

He couldn't bring back his *fraa* and *boppli*. Their deaths were a burden he would always carry.

The man behind him could still be helped, and for that he was grateful.

If only he'd found his friend earlier.

Perhaps the cold wouldn't have settled in his lungs.

Perhaps the infection wouldn't have crept into his broken leg.

If he hadn't kept Jacob so long looking at the fields on his place, perhaps the accident wouldn't have happened at all.

A gentle tap at the door pulled his thoughts from questioning himself.

"Are you sure you won't eat something?" Rebekah peeked around the door, her voice hopeful, her round face creased with worry.

"No, Rebekah. *Danki*, but I couldn't eat now." Samuel moved back toward the bed.

"*Was iss letz?*" Anxiety sharpened her tone, and Rebekah hurried to her husband's side, her hands smoothing the blankets covering Jacob.

"Nothing's wrong, nothing more than an hour ago. I'm sorry. I didn't mean to frighten you." Samuel sank back into the chair, ran his fingers through his beard. "It's only that—"

He stopped, realizing his confession would do nothing to ease her worry. Families looked to him to be the healer—though truth was he frankly claimed to be a farmer with a minimal amount of knowledge regarding herbs and medicinal workings.

Still, his place was to ease pain.

"What is it, Samuel? We have known each other too long for you to keep things from me." Rebekah's brown eyes pleaded with him, her hands still clasping those of Jacob. "I'd rather know whatever you have to say. God will see us through, but I need to know."

"It's not about Jacob. Not really." Samuel considered again adding the burden of his guilt to her shoulders. The Bible did command people to confess and be honest with one another.

Taking a deep breath, he plunged forward with the truth.

"I blame myself. It's my fault he was traveling the main road. Jacob normally takes the back road home, but he'd stopped by my place to look over my fields. I'd been thinking about changing my western field to alfalfa hay, and I asked him to give me his opinion."

"So if you hadn't asked him to stop by, he would have come straight home yesterday afternoon." The words came out as a statement, not a question as Rebekah's expression and tone changed instantly, from concern to one he knew all too well—he'd been scolded by her often enough as a boy.

"*Ya.* I know what you're about to say, but if I hadn't kept him late talking about crops, he wouldn't have been driving the rig home in the dark."

"And when did anyone have to encourage Jacob Weaver to stay and talk?" Rebekah placed her hands on her ample hips.

Samuel cringed, knowing he was trying her patience. Perhaps he should have settled for dinner and kept his worries to himself, but she still didn't understand that he felt he was responsible for Jacob's current condition—one which might result in his being laid up until late winter or even spring. The thought of it turned Samuel's stomach sour, and all notion of eating fled.

"He won't be able to work for months, Rebekah. Who will take care of things? Who will plant in the spring? I know Adam has already purchased his own place. You won't be able to do this alone."

"And we don't plan on doing it alone. Does the Scripture not say the Lord *will provide grass in the fields for your cattle, and you will eat and be satisfied?*"

"*Ya*, but—"

"And do we or do we not believe the Scripture?"

"Well, of course, but Rebekah—"

"Don't worry about my husband's fields, Samuel Yoder. You're a *gut* man with God's gift for healing, but there are some things you don't see clearly. Our fields will be fine."

Samuel pulled in a deep breath, stood, and walked around the old wooden bed with the hand-stitched quilt. Turning Rebekah toward him, he looked down into her eyes.

Her face had been gently wrinkled by time, and despite her confident words her eyes brimmed with tears.

"Rebekah, you're going to need extra help caring for him. You listened to Doctor Stoltzfus at the hospital, right?"

She nodded, tried to speak, but he pressed on.

"The cold will settle into his lungs if we don't help him up and see that he is moving regularly. He'll catch the pneumonia. Perhaps we should have left him in the hospital."

"No. I'm glad they were able to set his legs, but he'd never agree to stay with the *Englisch*. You heard him yourself last night."

"*Ya*, but we plain folk are always in a hurry to come home when we are away. Now that he's here . . ." Samuel again turned and glanced at the dark scene outside. "He might feel differently when he wakes tomorrow."

Rebekah swiped at her tears and shook her head resolutely. "We will go back to the hospital if you tell us his condition is worse, but I'd rather take care of him here—at home."

"He's going to need constant care."

"Because of his breathing?"

"*Ya*, and his legs. One was a clean break, as the doctor explained. But the infection in the other one will require that someone change the bandages regularly."

"Plus the medicines." Rebekah scowled, not even attempting to hide her distrust.

"My herbs would not be enough to fight the infection. We want him to walk again." Samuel waited a moment, then continued. "He will need constant tending, and I don't see how you can do it and still take care of the *kinner*, not to mention running the household and your job at the store—"

He heard the front door to the house open, exclamations from the *kinner,* and then the softer murmur of voices.

Looking quizzically at Rebekah, he saw her pull in a deep breath, then draw back her shoulders.

"I've thought of those things," she said, her voice taking on the resolute quality he had heard so many times before. It instantly reminded him of working in the field, of harvest time, of bowing to the task at hand. "Which is why I sent for help."

Before Samuel could think of what to say, the door to the room pushed open, and a woman stepped inside.

She was not dressed in plain clothes, but neither was she dressed like any *Englischer* Samuel had ever seen before.

A dark blue dress hung nearly to her ankles, but there was no apron adorning it. Although it was conservative in style, it was not Amish. A small white hat sat on top of her head, and beneath the hat spilled chestnut hair—hair he was sure had never been cut. It reached well past her waist and bounced and curled as she flew into Rebekah's arms.

Her cheeks were colored a rosy pink. At first he was distracted, embarrassed by her use of cosmetics.

Then she stepped closer to his patient, never pausing to look at him, and he caught the smell of the cold December wind on her. No doubt she had run up the steps, causing the blush.

After feeling Jacob's brow, running a hand down his cheek, then trailing her fingers to his wrist, she finally turned her attention to him.

"How is my *daed*?" she asked breathlessly.

Samuel could have fallen onto the bed.

Was this woman Amish?

And why was she calling Jacob Weaver her father? Surely she wasn't—

"You will remember our Annie," Rebekah murmured softly, moving to encircle the girl with her arm. "She's been staying a time in the city, to help with her cousins there. But now she's home."

"Of course I'm home, *Mamm*." The girl's lashes glistened with tears as she again took in the sight of her father.

Samuel attempted to speak, cleared his throat, and tried again. "Your father has been seriously hurt in a buggy accident, Miss Weaver. He just returned from the hospital a few hours ago."

"Annie. Please, call me Annie."

Nodding curtly, Samuel attempted to gather his wits.

Had she joined the church before she left?

He combed his memory for any mention Jacob had made of his oldest girl. Samuel had been away at the time she'd left—helping his *bruder* settle in Ohio. Jacob had mentioned her coming home a few times since, but Samuel was not one to visit socially if he could help it.

The last time he'd seen Annie Weaver she had been a mere girl. "How badly is he hurt?" Annie asked, again holding her father's wrist between her fingertips.

"Annie will be caring for her *daed*," Rebekah explained. "Tell her everything, Samuel."

Another tap on the door revealed Adam's curly head. "Annie, come out and have some hot tea. You must be chilled from your trip."

Annie flew into her *bruder's* arms, and Samuel found himself nearly flinching at their familiarity. He'd lived alone so long now, lived alone since that other December night.

Watching this family so openly express their love for one another felt like salt poured into an open and still-fresh wound.

"You've grown more, Adam." Annie's voice trembled as she stepped back and straightened her dress.

"Doubtful, since I'm twenty-two now. Could be you've shrunk." His playful voice stopped when he turned to look at their father. "Let's go to the kitchen. Leah has some hot tea ready for you, and I'm sure you're starved."

"I couldn't eat," she confessed, her hand skimming her flat stomach. "But some tea would be perfect."

Turning to Samuel, she studied him soberly. "Will you join us in the kitchen? I need to know what you'd have me do."

Samuel nodded, motioning Rebekah to his chair. "Let me speak with your *mamm* briefly, then I'll join you."

Annie followed Adam out of the room, and Samuel turned his attention to his friend—not because anything had changed in his condition, but because he needed a moment to make up his mind about the young woman who waited for him.

⟡

Annie followed her *bruder* to the kitchen table. Her younger siblings were already in their nightclothes and situated on the stairs, but they tumbled down to the first floor the minute she walked out of her *dat's* room.

"Annie, you're home!" Charity cried.

At sixteen, she looked the most like their mother with darker hair and full, round cheeks. Annie noticed her little *schweschder* no longer looked like a girl, with her full figure and her somber eyes. How could she have changed so much in the six months since she'd last visited?

"*Ya*, I'm home." She hugged her *schweschder*, laughing that they were the same height now.

"How long are you staying?" Reba asked. She was fourteen and tomboyish. Reba still protectively cupped a hand over the pocket of her nightdress, no doubt because some critter she'd brought in from the barn was squirming in there. Annie was relieved to see that some things hadn't changed.

"Enough questions for Annie. I think your *mamm* would like you back upstairs." Leah's voice was softer than the night that had settled around the house.

She was Annie's height, nearly five and a half feet, thin as a willow, with beautiful blonde hair and a motherly disposition the girls responded to well. If anything, her future *schweschder-in-law* had grown prettier since Annie had last seen her, and even closer to the younger Weaver girls. They both hugged her, then moved back into Annie's arms.

Annie kissed each of them, promising she'd still be there in the morning when they woke.

She sat at the table and allowed the simplicity of her parents' kitchen to calm her nerves.

Unlike her *aenti's* home, the counters were mostly bare with only a few canisters stacked neatly to the left of the gas-powered stove. Her *mamm's* spice rack hung on the wall above the counter. As she stared around the room, she suddenly realized it was the only thing on the wall.

It was as if she was seeing it all for the first time.

No Christmas decorations yet adorned the room, and she smiled to think she would be here to place the candles in the windows.

A refrigerator, also gas-powered, hummed to the right side of the sink, and her *mamm's* drying rack for dishes sat to the left.

This room was where Annie had grown up.

Sitting in it, waiting to hear her father's condition, Annie wondered why she had ever left.

"What could be taking so long?" she asked.

"Adam, go and check." Leah placed a mug of warm tea in her hands, sat beside her, and pulled her own chair closer—as if their proximity could somehow ease the blow of the terrible news.

Annie laced her fingers around the warm mug and was staring down into it when Samuel stepped from her parents' room.

He was nothing like she remembered him, and of course she did remember Samuel Yoder.

The last time she'd seen him, he had been tending to a *kind* who had cut open his arm on the school playground. She had been out of school already, but she'd stopped by to deliver a book she'd borrowed. She'd stared in fascination as he'd sewn up the boy's arm just as her *mamm* mended a tear in a skirt.

While the teacher had turned pale and pretended to have other duties to attend to, Annie had been completely absorbed by the procedure.

She'd had so many questions, none of which she'd dared ask.

What type of string did he use?

How did he cleanse the wound?

Where did he purchase the special needle?

Was the procedure something she could learn?

The picture had stayed in her mind as she'd worked first at the dry goods store in town, then at the small diner owned by her mother's *schweschder*, and finally with the animals on their own farm.

At the first two jobs her employers had gently suggested she try something more suited to her temperament. Since the owners were members of their church, they preferred not to fire her, but they couldn't keep her on when her ineptitude for the work was so painfully obvious to all.

Annie was relieved when the jobs came to an end.

Working for her *dat* had been no better.

Nothing had satisfied the desire born in her heart that day on the school grounds—nothing until she'd stepped into the halls of Mercy Hospital.

Samuel walked across to their kitchen table and accepted the warm mug Leah handed him. "*Danki*," he muttered, his voice low and vibrant—sending Annie's stomach tumbling.

When he raised his eyes to hers, Annie wondered if he even remembered that day so many years ago. From the surprised look he'd given her when she'd walked in, probably not.

No doubt she'd changed.

She studied him as he sipped the tea and spoke with Adam about the cold winds rattling their windows.

In the past three years, he'd grown more handsome.

Annie's cheeks colored at the thought, but it was true.

His hair remained coal black with no streaks of gray, though he probably neared thirty years now. Samuel was six feet tall, thin but not skinny—if anything he'd filled out since that day so long ago, but it wasn't his slight change in weight that captured Annie's attention as he conversed with her *bruder*.

It was his eyes.

They were without a doubt his most startling feature—reminding her of a mare her *dat* had once owned. The horse was an amazing blue-black color, the color of the sky at night.

In the shadows thrown by the gas lamps, she could see worry lines radiating out from those compelling eyes, lines he was too young to sport. It occurred to her that Samuel's burden of grief had only grown since she'd last seen him so many years ago.

Certainly the blow he'd received as a young man had been heavy.

She had been twelve at the time his *fraa* and *boppli* had died, and she could still remember standing beside the grave with her family while the two boxes were lowered into the ground side by side.

As the December wind shook their windows, she tried to remember the details of the accident, but couldn't. Something about a snowstorm and the horse losing its way.

Does a heart not heal from such a terrible tragedy as he had suffered?

The question had barely found its way from her heart to her mind when he cleared his throat and began questioning her.

"Annie, do you realize the seriousness of your *dat's* condition?" The question came out like an oral exam she'd once been given by a professor.

"*Mamm* told me both legs were broken and he'd lain injured a while in the cold before he was found."

Samuel's cheeks colored and he stared down into his tea. "*Ya*, that's right. The breaks are quite bad. It looked to me as if his buggy might have been hit by one of the *Englisch*."

He eyed her clothes and his voice hardened a bit on the last word. When she didn't respond, he continued.

"The horse had to be put down."

Annie's hand flew to her mouth. She turned to Adam.

"It was the older mare *Dat* was so fond of, but Samuel's right—it had to be done. There was no other option."

Folding her hands in her lap to still their shaking, Annie nodded. Losing a horse was a tragedy for any family, but her father had survived. Best to focus on what they had to be grateful for.

"Your father was unconscious when I arrived." Samuel met her gaze fully as the impact of his confession slammed into her.

"I don't understand. Why did you—"

"All the men were out looking, Annie." Adam reached over, placed his warm hand over Annie's trembling ones. "We're fortunate Samuel found him first."

"He'd been lying in the cold too long, though." Samuel's voice remained detached, as if he were briefing her on a patient she might encounter on her morning rounds—not her father lying in the next room. "It settled into his lungs, and I'm very worried about that. One of his legs is a simple break. It should heal with no problems. The other has infection already."

Annie pushed back from the table, began pacing between the stove and the chairs. "Then we should take him to the hospital—"

"He's been to the hospital," Samuel said. "Doctor Stoltzfus saw him, set both his legs and prescribed antibiotics."

Realizing how serious it must be for her *dat* to agree to go to the hospital, Annie tried to grasp all that Samuel was saying.

In all the years she'd lived at home, she'd never known either of her parents to go to the hospital. She and each of her siblings had been born at home with the help of a midwife. It wasn't that they didn't believe in hospitals; her *dat* hadn't ever felt the circumstances had warranted either the expense or the trip to one.

This situation was different.

It was grave.

Her father's life must have been in jeopardy. Her pulse began to thunder, and she had trouble staying in the room.

She wanted to rush back to her *dat's* side.

She wanted to call a driver and take him back to the *Englisch*.

She realized for the first time that he wouldn't live forever. She'd always known that intellectually, but it was an entirely different thing to consider while sitting at the kitchen table.

"How is he now?" she asked. "I don't understand why he's here. Why he's home."

"It was your *mamm's* decision to make."

"But if it's as serious as you say, then he came home too early."

"Rebekah believes—and so do I—that we can handle him here at this point."

"But it's not *your* father lying in there, is it?" Her voice rose as she turned on him, ready to fight, ready to claw the admission out of him.

"Peace, Annie." Leah stood and walked around the table. Stopping beside Annie, Leah trailed a hand down her hair, down her back, rubbing in soft circles. "Samuel wants what is best for Jacob as well."

"Indeed I do. I count him as one of my closest *freinden*." Samuel also stood, moved toward the stove as if to warm his hands, but in fact stepping closer to Annie and lowering his voice. "I won't leave him with a girl who isn't mature enough to handle the pressures. His recovery will be long. He'll need constant attending, and your *mamm* needs someone who will stick with this job."

So he did remember her.

Annie felt her chin come up even as the air left her lungs. "You needn't worry about me, Mr. Yoder. I won't be leaving my *dat's* side until he's well enough to drive the buggy again. Now if you'd like to leave your instructions."

And not waiting to see if he followed, she turned and marched into her father's room.

3

*A*nnie woke the next morning unsure why she felt so comfortable, so right.

Then she heard her *dat's* roosters crowing before the sun had lightened the sky. Gratitude washed over her, through her heart, and into her morning prayers as she contemplated her day.

She could not feel thankful for the tragedy her father had suffered, or the fact that she would have to endure Samuel Yoder's insufferable, patronizing directions.

Replaying the conversation in her *dat's* room—the one after she'd lost her composure in the kitchen—she questioned whether she should have admitted to Samuel that she was a nurse. She hadn't even admitted that to her family yet. How could she explain it to Samuel? Her *mamm* and *dat* thought she'd spent the last three years living with her *aenti* and acting as a sort of live-in governess. Annie had never lied to them, but she was old enough to know a lie of omission was a lie nonetheless.

Rolling out of bed, Annie found her clothes neatly folded on top of the chest at the end.

The memory of last night's discussion caused her cheeks to burn anew even as she dressed in the darkness.

Samuel might not realize she had medical training, but he still spoke to her as if she were a child younger than Reba—a child who couldn't be trusted to change a Band-Aid correctly let alone a dressing.

"Is *Dat* worse?" Charity asked, sitting up in alarm.

"He's fine. Go back to sleep. I'm used to waking early."

"Earlier than on a farm? That's hard to imagine." Charity turned and burrowed deeper under the covers.

Annie tiptoed out of the room, carrying her shoes with her until she'd descended the stairs to the kitchen. Though it wasn't yet five in the morning, her mother had already rekindled the fire in the potbellied stove that heated the living room and set water to boil on the stove in the kitchen. The two-stove system would have looked strange to anyone from her *aenti's* house, but to Annie it immediately spoke of home.

She looked longingly toward the kitchen—a cup of hot tea would start her moving—but she decided to check on her patient before indulging herself.

Lacing her shoes, she moved quietly across the living room, noticing again that her *mamm* had begun none of the Christmas preparations. Her heart sang at that realization. No doubt the nativity scene had been cleaned off and lay ready in the barn. Perhaps they would set it out in front of the house on the weekend.

She stopped at her parents' room and knocked gently on their door.

"Come in." Her *mamm's* voice was like a sweet balm over chapped skin.

In that moment, stepping through the doorway, Annie fully realized how much she had missed being home, being with her family, being with the people who loved her.

Rebekah sat beside the bed, knitting by the light of a kerosene lamp.

"How is he?"

Her *daed* lay sleeping, same as before. She'd yet to see him open his eyes. His quietness unsettled her. She was used to seeing him working, always working.

"He woke about an hour ago. Adam and I helped him to the bathroom, since he isn't to put any weight on the leg yet. And I managed to coax a few spoonfuls of tea with honey down him. Go and make your own breakfast while he's sleeping." Rebekah reached up, accepted her kiss, and then returned to her knitting. "Go on now. You'll have enough of this room by the time this day's done."

Smiling to herself, Annie made her way back into the kitchen. She'd worked quite a few twelve-hour shifts in the last six months, but she wasn't quite sure how to explain those days to her mother.

And what good would it do?

The important thing was that now she was home.

Slipping the teabag into the cup and pouring the hot water over it, her thoughts returned to her prayer of thanksgiving— the one she'd uttered on rising.

She was grateful to be back in Mifflin County, grateful that she would be home for Christmas.

This was where she belonged.

Her heart had nearly stopped when Shelly had said her father had been in an accident. So many terrible things had passed through her mind.

Her *dat's* condition was serious to be sure, but she had seen much worse.

Kiptyn's face flashed in her memory, then Laquisha's, Stanley's, Logan's. She had managed to stop by their rooms and tell them goodbye before she left, and she'd promised to write to Kiptyn. It had seemed to her the boy's color looked better by the time she'd cleaned out her locker, hopefully owing to the fact they had started the new medications the day before.

Hugging Annie goodbye, Shelly assured her she would watch over her patients and drop her a line as to the children's status.

So much suffering in the world.

While Mercy Hospital—and facilities like them—provided a needed sanctuary for the sick, she preferred to nurse her father here.

Slicing a piece of her mother's raisin bread and a red apple, she looked out the window to see if dawn was yet claiming the sky, driving back the night's blackness, but it was too early.

A vision of Samuel Yoder's brooding eyes pierced her calmness, but she pushed it away. She wouldn't need to see him often, and there was another prayer of gratitude she would be offering up when she knelt by her bed. The Lord knew she had enough work, and enough men in this household, without adding one with a sharp attitude to the mix.

❧

The morning passed as quickly as any she had spent on the ward at Mercy Hospital.

In the first hour, four heads popped around the corner of her *dat's* door, in descending order. First Adam, coming in from the barns, then Charity on her way out to help Adam. Next came Reba—still yawning, and still protectively holding one hand over the pocket of her apron.

Each of her siblings whispered, "*Gudemariye,*" cast a worried eye toward their *dat*, and affirmed again how glad they were she was home.

Only her *mamm* motioned her outside the room. "He still hasn't wakened?"

Annie shook her head. "I believe the herbs Samuel gave him are helping him sleep."

"But it's so unlike him—"

"Sleep is what his body needs." Annie placed a hand on her mother's arm, easily falling into the role of comforter—though it did strike her as ironic that she was consoling her mother.

It seemed as if just yesterday she had stood in this room explaining how she'd been asked to leave yet another job, and her mother had been the one promising everything would be all right.

"He's never been in bed this late." Rebekah's voice creaked like the swings on the playground at school. "Not even the time he had the measles."

Annie smiled at the story they had all laughed over so many times—laughed because it had ended well and the thought of her father tending the stock while he was broken out in the red bumps must have been a sight.

The measles weren't a laughing matter among her people though. Since many in their community did not immunize their children, it remained something they had to vigilantly guard against.

"Rest is what he needs now. Go on to the store. We'll be fine."

Rebekah nodded, pulled herself up straighter as she tied the strings of her prayer *kapp*. "Your *bruder* is working here today. David Hostetler has agreed to help out, and Adam is going to show him what needs to be done."

For a moment, Annie thought of confessing to her mother exactly what she'd been doing during her *rumschpringe* years. Perhaps if her *mamm* knew she'd been at school rather than running wild, she'd relax.

Pushing her hair back from her face, she decided while it might ease her own conscience, it likely wouldn't help her *mamm* a bit. Rebellion was precisely that in the eyes of the Amish people—didn't matter that it was schooling she had pursued while she was away.

The point was she sought that which was forbidden to them.

Best to leave it alone.

Her *mamm* had enough to deal with this morning.

"I'll shout for Adam if I need anything."

"Or ring the bell."

"*Ya*, or I'll ring the bell. I haven't forgotten how we do things, you know."

"Of course you haven't." Rebekah stopped gathering her things and pulled her close. "*Danki* for coming home."

Annie wanted to say so much in that moment. Instead she merely returned her *mamm's* hug, forced back her tears, and nodded. "*Gem gschehne*. Now go, or you'll be late and the *Englischers* will be lined up outside the store waiting to purchase Mr. Fisher's fine things."

❧

Two hours later, Annie was checking her *dat's* vitals when his hand reached out and covered hers. The sight of his weathered hand lying gently over hers caused tears to sting her eyes. She drew in a deep breath, willed herself not to cry, and reminded herself that she was a professional.

"Please tell me you're hungry."

"*Ya*. Seems like you don't feed your patients much around here." His voice was weaker than she remembered, but those blue eyes opened with a twinkle, and a smile pulled his beard that was streaked through with gray.

Annie forgot for a moment that she was a registered nurse.

She threw herself into her father's arms, buried herself in the smell of him—a smell that still held the barns and the fields, though he hadn't been there in over forty-eight hours. It wasn't until he patted her clumsily and began wheezing that she pulled back, wiping at the tears streaming down her face.

"Did I give you so big a scare?" Jacob asked, his voice cracking.

"You did. I suppose you did." She flew to the pitcher of water, poured him a glass and held it to his lips as he struggled to sit up.

Drinking even a little tired him, and he lay back against the pillows with a sigh. Looking out at the daylight, he shook his head, plainly unhappy. "Must be nearing nine in the morning."

"Don't worry about the farm. Adam's here, and David Hostetler is coming."

He nodded, but looked no happier.

"What do you feel like eating? Maybe some bread first, or tea—"

"Wait." His voice stopped her more quickly than the hand that reached out to grasp her wrist. "I remember the hospital and a doctor. . . ."

"Doctor Stoltzfus set your legs." Annie said it gently, not sure if he realized yet the extent of his injuries.

Jacob nodded, not looking down at the covers—bunched high from the casts covering both his left and right legs from knee to ankle.

"*Ya*. He spoke with me when I first arrived. I don't remember anything of the procedure though."

"Your left leg is a simple break, according to Samuel. It should heal quickly."

"Samuel was here?" Jacob turned his attention from the window to her.

"He found you, in the snow late that night, then rode with you to the hospital."

"Yesterday?"

"Day before yesterday. You've been sleeping quite a bit."

"I don't remember any of that."

"What about the accident?" Annie didn't want to tire or upset him, but she'd learned with patients that often their first memories were their clearest. "The police have no leads."

"Why are the police involved?"

"You don't remember anything?"

Confusion clouded his face now, and Annie was sure if she felt his pulse she'd find it had accelerated. He shook his head and attempted to sit up straighter.

"Let me help you." She plumped his pillows, positioned them behind his back and head.

"The first thing I remember is waking up in the hospital, with Dr. Stoltzfus and your *mamm* standing over my bed."

Annie thought of waiting until her *mamm* had returned to tell him, but she knew there would be no putting her *dat* off. She also suspected he wouldn't rest until he'd had the entire story.

"Someone hit your rig when you were driving home from Samuel's. Someone in a car. You're lucky to be alive. You lay there in the cold for hours, which is why we're worried about pneumonia. It's why you have such a heaviness in your chest."

Jacob frowned but didn't interrupt her.

"The mare was still alive when Samuel arrived, but maimed. He had to put her down. Then he stopped a motorist and borrowed a cell phone to contact Dr. Stoltzfus. He called an ambulance and met you at the hospital."

"And my legs?" The question came out harshly, like a rock dropping onto the ground.

"The left one will heal quickly. The right is a more complicated break and has grown infected."

Jacob clenched his jaw, the lines across his forehead creasing as he did. It was an expression she had seen occasionally as a child, and it never signaled anything good.

Jacob had been a kind, gentle father—but he'd also had an extremely stubborn streak. Rebekah had often teased his genealogy could be traced back to Noah himself because Jacob was stubborn enough to build an ark during a drought.

Annie saw that stubbornness in her father now. She wanted to reach down and kiss his weathered cheek.

Instead, she poured him more water.

He drank it, then asked, "How long until I can work again?"

"Samuel says it will be later winter, maybe spring before you're even walking."

She had returned the cup and pitcher to the stand, straightened his covers, and walked to the door—determined to bring him something to eat—when he finally spoke. His words didn't startle her, but neither were they exactly what she expected.

"Samuel Yoder is a *gut* friend, and I consider him a smart man in such matters."

"*Ya*, I expect he is."

"But smart men are sometimes surprised by things they haven't lived long enough to see, things they can't understand."

Annie thought she heard a desperation behind his words, but then again perhaps it was the exhaustion speaking. She nodded, went into the kitchen, and prepared him a simple breakfast.

In the early afternoon, he woke again and reached out for her hand.

"What is it, *Dat*?"

"Are you home, Annie?"

"Of course. I'm right here." She checked his forehead, wondering if fever had set in, if the infection had worsened—but his skin was cool to her touch.

"I mean are you home for good? Are you here to stay this time?"

She looked into his blue eyes, crinkled with concern, and ran a hand down his brow. "*Ya*. I'm home to stay."

"So you've put your *rumschpringe* behind you?"

Annie understood then what he was asking. She also understood she wasn't only answering because he was ill, or from a desire he rest and not worry.

She *was* home to stay.

Wearing her plain clothes, surrounded by her family, among her community—this was where she belonged.

She had known it all along. Why had she ever left?

There were things she had longed to learn, yes.

She knew them now, and she would find ways to use them.

God would show her ways to bless others.

"I have put my *rumschpringe* completely behind me."

Jacob closed his eyes, satisfied at last. "Your mother will be *froh*. Now all you need to do is choose one of the fine boys from the area to marry."

"Back less than twenty-four hours and you want to be rid of me?"

"We need *bopplin* in the house."

"Babies will be coming soon enough from Adam and Leah."

"They're a blessing, Annie—children are an inheritance from the Lord." Jacob began to nod, then fell into a light slumber.

"Indeed they are," Annie whispered.

Her father's words made her smile. He was always one to say exactly what was on his mind. But his talk of *grandkinner* also renewed an ache in her heart she had struggled with for the past year.

Most of the girls she had grown up with had wed already.

She had been home in the summer and bumped into both Mary and Elizabeth. Her *freinden* had been so *froh* to see her, folding her in their embrace—clumsily because they had both been heavy with child. *Freinden* from her childhood, married less than a year and about to be mothers.

The glow about them was undeniable.

And yes, she had felt a pang of envy.

At the way they talked of their husbands and their homes. At how their hands would fall to their stomachs in a protective way. But more for the fact they knew with no doubt what they wanted in life.

Why was it so easy for them?

And why did she feel so torn?

Tears again threatened to fall, and she closed her eyes against them. Perhaps she was more tired than she had realized. Or maybe her emotions would settle down after a few weeks at home.

Walking around her father's bed to straighten his covers, she glanced out the window and saw three men walking toward the house.

They walked resolutely against the cold December wind, dark coats flapping, posture slightly bent, and each holding one hand to his black hat in an effort to keep it firmly atop his head.

It might have been a comical sight any other day, but today it struck her as bittersweet.

Her *bruder* Adam occupied the middle spot.

To his right, she recognized David Hostetler. They'd grown up together in school, but she hadn't seen him since she'd moved to the city. David wasn't the reason she felt her heart slam against her chest though.

To the left of Adam strode Samuel Yoder.

Now what had made her think he would trust her to take care of his patient for a full day? She pulled in a ragged breath, squared her shoulders, and told herself to be grateful for his concern.

He was here to see her *dat*.

It had nothing to do with her.

Best to put up with his questions, and then be rid of him as quickly as possible. Hopefully the man had enjoyed a *gut* night's sleep and would be slightly less arrogant than the evening before.

Thinking of her father's earlier comments, Annie shook off her melancholy mood and smiled.

Samuel Yoder was one man she would not be considering for courting from the local group. The man had spoken to her as if she didn't have a brain cell in her head.

She had no doubt God would provide her a *gut* husband and from her Amish brethren, but it would be a man who was loving, kind, and had a respect for women and their intellectual abilities.

From what she had seen so far, Samuel didn't receive points in any of those categories—though no doubt he knew how best to take care of his patients.

4

Samuel stepped into Jacob's house and resisted the urge to walk straight to his patient's room. Instead, he stamped his boots dry on the mat and set his medical bag inside the door. Jacob wasn't exactly his patient.

And he wasn't a doctor!

He'd been reminding the *gut* people of Mifflin County that for the past ten years. They remained hesitant to take the time to see the *Englisch* doctors.

Fortunately in this case, Jacob and Rebekah had understood the necessity straight away. Jacob's injuries were far more serious than anything Samuel could handle. He could, however, keep an eye on him since the man refused to remain in the hospital. Which was exactly what he planned on doing—in spite of the confrontation he'd had with Annie Weaver last night. Trouble was he hadn't figured out exactly how to approach today's visit.

Then she stepped out of Jacob's room, and all of the cold from the December wind suddenly left his limbs.

Annie was wearing plain clothes—possibly the same blue dress as the night before, but with a black apron covering it. A white prayer *kapp* covered her chestnut curls, which had been corralled into a proper bun. She looked far more lovely than a young girl should.

Seeing her standing in the bedroom doorway quickened his pulse, confused him in a way he didn't understand.

"Adam. Samuel, *gut* to see you again. David, welcome." Her voice was like a warm spring breeze caressing his skin, though she remained on the far side of the room.

"*Danki*, Annie. It's been a long time." David stood at the door, holding his hat and smiling like a fool.

Samuel had the oddest desire to smack the kid on the back of the head. "Come in out of the doorway, David. We need to shut out the wind or Jacob will have to battle a cold as well as his injuries."

Samuel heard the harsh tone in his voice and winced, but he couldn't stop himself from lecturing.

"*Ya*. I'm letting in all of December's bluster." David laughed as he pulled the door closed. "Confused me seeing Annie there, all grown up and prettier than the winter birds singing in the fields."

"David, you haven't changed a bit—still writing poetry in your spare time." Annie moved to the stove and began heating water as she set out five mugs. "Would you like tea or *kaffi*? It looked like a bitter wind as I saw you walking across from the barn."

"Tea sounds great to me," Adam said.

Samuel and David agreed.

"How's *Dat*?" Adam asked, peering toward his father's room.

"He's fine. You can go and see for yourself. He's been sleeping for the last twenty minutes or so."

"I'm awake now," Jacob called from his room.

Adam grinned and moved toward the bedroom door. "Better come with me, David. He'll have instructions for you since you'll be picking up most of the work around here."

"I'll be back for that tea, Annie."

David grinned at her again as he trudged across the room, and Samuel once more felt a twinge of irritation with the lad.

He'd never spent much time with the younger Hostetler boys since he was out of school by the time they were in, but he certainly had no reason to feel such agitation with David. Not to mention that the boy was doing a fine thing by offering to come out and help while Jacob was unable to work.

Unless he was doing it in order to be close to Annie.

As he stepped toward the kitchen area, Samuel wondered where that thought had come from. He'd barely had time to examine it when Annie turned from the stove and looked at him quizzically.

"Something on your mind, Samuel?"

He stepped back and bumped into the cabinet holding Rebekah's dishes, causing them to rattle.

Annie merely raised a delicate eyebrow and waited.

"Why would you say that?" he asked gruffly.

"You seem unusually quiet, that's all."

"Man has a right to be quiet, doesn't he?"

"Sure."

When she didn't add anything else, he twirled his hat in his hands and tried to remember why he had stopped by again today. After all, the day was wasting, and he had a barn wall badly in need of repair.

"Something important in your medical kit?" Annie asked as she placed tea bags in each mug, then added hot water.

Watching her move gracefully around the room distracted him. When had she changed from a girl to a woman?

"What?" Samuel sat, pulled his cup toward him, gulped the tea, which hadn't yet steeped, and grimaced when the weak brew scalded his throat. Frowning at the mug, he tried to remember what she had asked.

"The black bag you set by the door. I was wondering if there was something in it you meant to bring for my father."

There was an outright sparkle in her eyes now, and if Samuel didn't know better he'd guess she was laughing at him. Thumping the mug down, he pushed back from the table and stood up. What he needed was to be done here and hurry back to work. He felt disoriented because he was sitting around sipping tea during the middle of the day.

Walking to the door, he picked up his leather medical kit— once a shiny black but now faded and weathered from years of use. He brought it to the table and set it next to his mug.

Last night had not gone well when he'd tried to give her instructions on how to change Jacob's bandages. He knew Annie was a bright girl—correction—woman. But she seemed to have trouble paying attention. She'd barely listened to him at all, though he'd gone through the complete procedure twice.

He wasn't confident this would go any better, but he owed it to Jacob to try.

Perhaps today she would be willing to listen.

"Annie." He cleared his throat, did his best to sound teacher-like and patient, though he knew he was neither. "Last night I told you I was worried about your father's breathing and about the infection in his leg. Do you remember?"

She actually leaned back against the kitchen counter and studied her own mug of hot tea.

"Of course I remember."

"Did you take his pulse each hour?"

"*Ya.*" Now she hid behind her mug, and Samuel was certain she was trying not to laugh at him. What could she possibly find funny about this situation?

Samuel said a silent prayer as his frustration with her grew, then pushed on with his questions. "Did you change his bandages last night and again this morning?"

"I did, and I wrote the notes on the pad as you showed me." The smile spreading across her pretty face caused her eyes to twinkle and a smattering of freckles to pop up across her cheeks and the bridge of her nose.

"This is very serious, Annie." His voice was nearly a growl now. He reached into the bag and pulled out his extra stethoscope and blood pressure cuff.

"I'd like to show you how to take your *dat's* blood pressure. I realize this is a lot for you to learn at once, but it's important we know how he's reacting to the medicine. I have this one extra stethoscope and cuff, and I'm willing to leave it with you—if you'll pay attention and treat it carefully."

He looked at her and waited for her reply, but of course what she said next was nothing he would have ever guessed.

❧

"Samuel, I don't need your things." Annie stepped toward the table, motioned for him to put the items back into the bag. She felt her smile slip as the teasing mood she'd been enjoying passed.

Samuel looked at her sharply, as if he must have heard her wrong.

She had hoped he would be less condescending this morning, but if anything he was more so. For some reason, instead of making her angry, it had hit her funny bone.

It might have been the way he had glowered at David earlier. Suddenly she realized Samuel Yoder didn't have issues conversing with her—he had issues speaking with anyone five or more years younger. Oddly enough, he seemed perfectly at ease when talking with her parents. The realization had helped to ease her tension.

Perhaps Samuel had spent too much time at home after his own personal tragedy.

Perhaps he'd become old before his time. After all, the man hadn't yet reached thirty.

So she'd teased him a little—her *dat* had always said she could tease paint off a barn.

Then Samuel had pulled out his extra stethoscope, with that somber expression on his face and a rumble in his voice—as if he were pulling gold from a safe.

The stethoscope had changed her mood instantly.

Annie knew the importance of supplies among their community. Samuel had to scramble to purchase all he had—there was no fund to reimburse him. Neither did he request payment for the medical assistance he offered. He was, by trade, a farmer. The few supplies he had were paid for with donations, and the time he missed from work—well, she didn't know how he made up for those precious hours.

Annie moved closer to the table.

With the medical bag resting between them, Annie realized it would be wrong to keep the truth from him any longer. She didn't have to tell him everything about her time with the *Englisch*, but she should tell him what was in her apron pocket.

Before she had a chance, though, Adam and David clomped back into the room.

"Helped *Dat* to the bathroom. He seems much better than last night. Still weak, but better." Adam sat down and reached for a mug of hot tea, then pulled the basket of breads left over from breakfast toward him.

"*Ya*, your *dat's* able to boss me around just fine." David laughed good-naturedly as he joined Adam at the table. "He'll have no trouble instructing me how to handle the fields."

Samuel threw a challenging look at her. "Excellent news. Let's go see our patient, then, and I can show you how to use this properly."

Before Annie could respond, before she could think of how to correct him, Samuel turned and walked out of the room.

Samuel stood beside her *dat's* bed, already deep in discussion with him when Annie joined them.

"I don't think it will take me until spring to find my way out of this bed," Jacob muttered, then began coughing as the congestion that had settled in his lungs battled its way clear.

Samuel helped him through the coughing spasm, then reminded him in a firm but kind tone, "Jacob, both of your legs are broken. If you hurry your recovery, things are going to be much worse than if you follow Doctor Stoltzfus's instructions."

"*Ya*. I understand. Am I looking stupid? I only meant it doesn't seem to me like it will take four months for a body to heal. Already I feel much better than I did yesterday."

Glancing up at her, Samuel frowned and shook his head. "We can thank the antibiotics the doctor gave you for your improvement—"

"And Annie's care." Jacob reached out and patted her hand.

Samuel pulled back the bed covers to inspect her bandages. "You're blessed to have three *dochdern*," he agreed.

"That I am, and I love each one dearly, but it did my heart *gut* to wake up this morning and see my Annie sitting beside my bed—as if Christmas had come early."

"You're going to make me blush, *Dat*." Annie walked around to see what Samuel was scowling at. "Something wrong with those bandages?"

Refastening them, he tucked the blankets around Jacob's leg and fixed her with a stare. "Everything looks fine—surprisingly fine."

"I'm glad you're pleased."

He looked anything but *froh*, however, and she still hadn't settled on a way to tell him about the stethoscope in her pocket.

Resting his fingers lightly on Jacob's wrist, Samuel glanced down at the watch on his arm.

"No need to do that," Jacob said. "She's been bothering me regularly with such nonsense."

Annie picked up the pad of paper she'd been keeping her chart notations on and handed it to Samuel. "Maybe we could talk about this outside. I'm sure my *daed* would like to rest—"

"But how did you—" Samuel flipped from the first page to the second, then glanced up at her.

Annie felt the heat rise in her cheeks. Fortunately, her father seemed oblivious to the exchange taking place between them.

"Actually, I wouldn't mind a piece of your *mamm's* bread if you'd like to send Adam in with it." Jacob resumed his coughing but fought his way through it. "Now that I'm awake, I am rather hungry—another sign I'm healing faster than Doc Stoltzfus thought I would."

Samuel let the pad rest against the bed and turned to stare at Annie. "I don't understand."

"Let's step out into the living room." She adjusted her *daed's* covers, then turned and fled the room, trusting Samuel would follow. Once in the kitchen, she placed some bread and fruit on a separate plate. "Would you take this in to him for me, Adam? If you don't mind, I think I'd like to take a five-minute break outside."

"Sure thing, Annie." Adam looked at her curiously, but accepted the plate.

David pretended to study the latest issue of *The Budget*.

Annie grabbed her coat and practically ran outside. She couldn't talk to Samuel about her time with the *Englisch* in the kitchen—not with David and Adam there, not with her *dat* in the next room.

She wasn't ashamed of what she'd done.

In many ways she was proud of her work in Philadelphia, but it was complicated. Her family had long practiced an attitude of grace toward *rumschpringe*, believing once the years of rebellion were over the less said about them the better. Adam had spent two years traveling away from Mifflin County, then he'd come home, joined the church, and was now engaged to Leah.

Everyone assumed Annie would do the same.

She would.

Wouldn't she? Suddenly an image of the sick *kinner* at Mercy Hospital popped into her mind, and she wasn't so sure.

The front door opened and Samuel followed her out into the bitter cold, still holding the tablet she had used for a chart.

She walked around the corner of the porch, where they'd be protected from the worst of the wind. He followed, stopping less than three feet from her.

"I suppose you have questions," she said tentatively.

"I do." His voice was flat and hard, like the road that led to her *dat's* farm.

Annie pulled her coat tighter and nodded. "All right."

Samuel's dark eyes pierced hers. Even from a distance of three feet they reminded her again of the horse she had loved so as a child. Samuel remained cold and aloof, though. Why did the man have to be so disapproving of her instead of a help?

Didn't she have enough to deal with these first few days of settling back into her old life?

Rather than ask her about the chart, he sank into the oak rocker, placed the tablet on the porch floor, and began massaging his temples.

He looked so tired, so vulnerable with his head bowed. Annie's heart went out to him, and she again remembered the man had been through much these past eight years.

"Let's start with the bandages," he finally said.

Annie moved to the rocker across from him. "I know they were done perfectly."

"That's my question. You barely listened to a word I said, so how could you possibly change a bandage so professionally?"

Annie tried to meet his gaze, but she found herself glancing at the wall, then the porch railing, then the bare fields beyond.

Where should she start?

How much should she tell him?

How much did he need to know?

"And what about this?" Samuel picked up the tablet and shook it, leaning toward her. "What are these blood pressure notations?"

Reaching into her pocket, Annie pulled out her stethoscope. When she did, Samuel jerked away, as if the instrument were a snake that might coil and strike.

"It's only a stethoscope."

"Did you take that from my bag?" His voice held a tone of accusation, and his frown deepened even more.

It rankled on Annie's nerves that he would accuse her. "Of course not. It's mine."

Samuel shook his head, still not comprehending.

"Look, does yours have this logo?" She pointed to the pink breast cancer symbol on the side, then the engraving. "Or my initials?"

"All right, so you have your own scope because . . ." His voice trailed off as he waited for her explanation.

He massaged his temples one last time, then drew himself up in a stiff posture. "I have chores to finish, and I don't have time to spend guessing what's going on here. Do you want to explain yourself or not?"

"As you know, I was with my cousins the last few years."

"You were on your *rumschpringe*." He didn't say the word gently, but Annie chose to ignore what sounded like condemnation.

"Correct. While I was living with my *aenti*, I received some medical training."

"How much?" His eyes glared into hers.

"Enough to know how to change bandages and take a person's blood pressure."

Samuel launched out of his chair and began pacing up and down the porch. "But you're only a girl."

"I am not. I'm twenty years old."

"A girl with an eighth-grade education."

"What are you saying, Samuel? That I'm not intelligent enough to understand how to conduct simple medical procedures?" Annie was up now and standing in his path.

"Do your parents know this?"

Once again his eyes stared down into hers, causing her stomach to tumble and turn. She ignored it and crossed her arms. "Not exactly."

"It's a yes or no question."

"And it's none of your business."

He pushed his hat down more tightly on his head. "It is my business who is tending to Jacob. I count him as a very close friend, and I won't be leaving him with you if you plan on taking off again when the urge hits."

Annie fought to control the fury coursing through her veins. "Who cares for my *dat* is not your decision, Samuel. My *dat* is the one lying in there with two broken legs, and I will be the one taking care of him."

She stepped closer, glared up into his face, and dared him to challenge her.

When he only clamped his jaw shut, she took one final step forward and he stepped back.

"Now if you find a single thing wrong with the way I care for him, I'd count it as a favor if you'd let me know. Until then, maybe it would be best if we stayed out of each other's way."

"Maybe it would." Black eyes snapped at her, and she knew he was fighting against his temper.

Annie jerked her tablet from his hand and stomped to the door. Reaching it, she remembered there was one item she hadn't set straight, so she turned back around—caught him staring blankly out over the fields.

"And for your information, Mr. Yoder, I am here to stay." She fought to keep her voice low and even, knowing if she had to shout to make her point she wouldn't prove a thing to him or to herself. "You needn't worry about me running back to the *Englisch* or anywhere else for that matter. I'll be here until my *dat's* better. In fact, I'll be here until he's old and surrounded by more *grandkinner* than he can shake his old man's cane at."

Seeing his scowl deepen, she felt a small bit of satisfaction and turned back toward the front door of the house.

"For your information, the Amish view medicine differently than the *Englisch* do." He was behind her before she realized it, his palm against the door, and his voice in her ear.

"But then you should know that, since you are Amish. You do remember what it means to be Amish, don't you, Annie? Try to keep in mind you aren't in the city anymore. Try to remember there lies a vast space between the knowledge you possess and what folks are willing to tolerate, what they'll interrupt their workday for you to do. Takes maturity to know the difference between tending to someone and caring for them."

And with those words in her ear, he turned and stormed off toward his buggy.

5

$\mathcal{A}$nnie battled and won the internal fight she insisted on waging with Samuel Yoder, but it took her another two days to do so. By that time she had fallen into a rhythm as steady and exhaustive as the winter weather outside the tight farmhouse.

She cared for her father all day, tending to as many of the household chores as she could when he napped. Once her *mamm* returned home each afternoon, she took a short walk outside—or in the barn if the temperatures were too cold. Grooming the new black mare worked out her restlessness from being confined inside all day.

"Do you like the name Blaze?" Reba asked. The girl would have been happy to spend the entire day in the barn, and she often went straight there when returning from school.

"I do," Annie admitted, rubbing the white spot between the mare's eyes. "It's a perfect name for her."

"I took her out yesterday. Let her run. You should see her, Annie. She's fast—faster than *dat's* old mare," Reba's voice caught and sputtered like the *Englischer's* cars on cold mornings. "Not that I'm *froh* about what happened."

"Of course you're not, sweetie. God finds ways to bring blessing out of every tragedy. Perhaps Blaze is our blessing."

Reba nodded, straight dark hair tumbling over her shoulder as she did.

"How are things at school?" Annie eyed her sister curiously. They'd had little time alone since she'd been home.

"I like it. I'll be glad to be finished this year. All day I count the hours until I'm back here, back with the animals." Reba's voice became wistful, reminding Annie of the sound of the wind through the trees in the fall, when the leaves still whispered their song.

"If you're to work with animals, God will find a way, Reba."

"Do you think so?"

"I know so, but if we don't both hurry back into the house, Charity will be out here looking for us."

"With Charity, it's like having two *mamms* around to boss you."

Looping arms together, they walked back toward the house, and Annie was flooded again with the warmth of being home among her family and her people.

So why did a vague feeling of restlessness continue to disturb her?

What was still missing from her life?

She felt as if she should be grateful and content, but in those rare moments when she was honest with herself she realized she was not.

In order to ignore those moments, she threw herself more forcefully into the household work.

After helping with dinner, she again checked on her father, then sat with her sisters and mother, sewing or reading. Above all, she made sure she was away from the house if Samuel stopped by, which he had again on Friday.

She told herself she wasn't avoiding him, but she turned down an invitation to go to town on Saturday. Instead, she spent the morning in the barn, cleaning off the large, wooden nativity scene they'd created as children.

She paused only long enough to talk to the bishop when he came for a visit. They agreed she would be baptized into the church the following Sunday, since there would be no service the next day—it being their off week.

Annie was grateful she'd have a few more days to prepare. Not that the thought of being baptized and accepted into the church made her nervous; she actually was looking forward to it.

But the idea of Samuel watching?

Ach! It made her scrub even harder with the soapy water, rubbing away on the large wooden cut-out figures.

"I believe the dust is all gone from that one," Rebekah said, entering the barn and studying the silhouette of the virgin Mary.

"*Ya.* I suppose it's clean enough." Annie laughed at her own absentmindedness, then stood and helped her mother carry the four-foot carving out of the barn and place it among the other pieces.

"*Mamm.* Tell Reba to keep her mouse out of the infant's cradle. It's not proper." Charity marched forward with an armful of straw and dumped it into said cradle.

Reba's screech could have been mistaken for a mouse. "Careful, Charity."

"He's a mouse. He lives in straw, when he's not in your pocket, which is disgusting, by the way."

"Girls, you both helped build this nativity scene, when you were very young. Do you remember?" Rebekah's question— calm, wistful, and tinged with only a touch of disappointment— was enough to stop Charity and Reba's bickering.

Charity stepped closer to Reba, and Annie heard her ask, "He's all right, isn't he?"

"*Ya.* Only a little scared."

"Maybe you should give him some of that cheese you carry around."

The two girls turned and walked back into the barn to collect the last of the wise men.

"I remember when we made them," Annie admitted. "Adam and I practically ran home from school the entire month of November that year."

"Your *dat* had the idea. Charity was struggling with the concept of the virgin birth, and Reba was certain the infant Jesus had forced some poor animal to lose its dinner by sleeping in the trough." Rebekah slipped her arm around Annie's waist and walked with her back toward the house. "Jacob decided having you children build the nativity scene would help everyone understand the Christmas story a bit better."

Annie waved to Jacob who was sitting on the porch, wrapped in blankets. "I'm glad he's well enough to sit outside and watch. That's nothing short of a miracle, *Mamm.*"

"Never doubt the Lord. He will take care of your *dat*, and he'll take care of whatever's bothering you too."

Annie nodded and squeezed her mother's hand, and her thoughts returned to Samuel.

Too often she found herself picturing his coal-black hair and haunting eyes—on rising each morning, while doing her chores, even as she slipped between the cold sheets each night. She did not have any trouble falling into a deep sleep, though. She'd discovered the key to forgetting Samuel's caustic words and claiming a good night's sleep.

All she needed to do was stay up as late as her mother each night and rise with Adam each morning. She dressed, then prepared breakfast for her younger sisters so her mother would have a few moments to spend with her father.

By the time everyone left for work and school, she had been up three hours and was as wide-awake as the winter birds searching for food outside the window. Caring for her father was remarkably easy on her nursing skills—she'd never done a stint as a private nurse.

And it was remarkably hard on her patience.

As Samuel had predicted, there were many things her father grew less tolerant of the stronger he became.

"Annie, you checked my blood pressure not an hour ago. I can't see as it would have gone up since you haven't allowed me out of this bed." Her father's face took on the expression of their *Englisch* neighbor's old bull—stubborn and ornery and looking for a fight.

"I explained to you last time, Samuel wants hourly notations so he can be sure the medication isn't affecting you adversely."

"There's another thing I'd like to talk to him about. Why am I still taking the *Englischer's* medicine? I don't believe I need it. A *kind* could tell the infection has gone out of my leg."

"In six days?" Annie snorted. "It's better, *ya*, but not healed. As for your pestering, a child could see through it. You're simply trying to find a way out to the barn."

"What's wrong with that?"

"You'd be likely to re-break one or both your legs, that's what's wrong." Annie sank onto the hardwood chair beside her father's bed and studied him. The stern approach she used with the children at the hospital was not working with her *dat*.

Samuel's parting words of caution still rang sharply in her ears, and the memory did not improve her mood this morning one bit. Surely she could outwit a crotchety old Amish farmer and a crotchety young one combined.

Standing up, she moved to the window and looked out over the snow-covered fields, toward the barn where she knew David was working. "Reba told me she'd taken the new mare out for a run."

"The girl does have a way with animals."

"She's using the old lead rope, though. I'm a bit afraid it might break on her."

"I had Adam buy new rope." Jacob's bored and petulant voice took on new interest.

"*Ya*, but did you show David how to properly weave the rope together into a lead halter?"

"'Course I did," Jacob grumbled.

"I don't mean to criticize him," Annie turned back toward the bed. "He's a fine young man—shows up for work on time every day, always has a pleasant word. Certainly isn't his fault if he doesn't know how to weave a lead rope."

"I showed him how in this very room last week."

"Mark my word, Blaze will break the old one. The thing really is in tatters."

Jacob struggled to sit up straighter now. "That mare runs off, we won't catch her before she reaches the next county."

Annie studied him a minute, her finger tapping her chin. "I could sneak the rope in here, let you do it. I'd have to tell David it was some sort of physical therapy to start you moving."

"Tell the lad whatever you want, but go fetch me the rope. I should have thought of it myself. Man's hands aren't useless when his legs are broken in a buggy accident. Now hurry and finish with Samuel's medical contraptions, so as you don't interrupt me later."

Annie slipped the pressure cuff on, noted that her patient's color and disposition had improved, then grabbed her scarf, coat, and gloves from the living room.

"I'll be back in ten minutes. You're sure that you'll be okay alone?"

Her father waved her away as he studied the latest issue of *The Budget*, the same issue he'd read yesterday.

✑

Scurrying through the snow to the barn, Annie found herself wishing she could escape across the field.

She loved nursing, loved everything about it.

But on days like today—when the sky was blue, the wind was low, and enough snow covered the ground to make things interesting, she could stand for a long walk across the hills.

"Annie, I don't see you out here often." David stood, brushed his hands on his pants.

She was still surprised to find she had to tilt her head a bit to look up at David. His hair was a light sandy brown, the color of wheat in the fall. His eyes, the same color, were gentle, usually laughing. He reminded her very much of the boy she'd known in school—only taller, much taller.

"I need your help, David." Annie walked around the portion of the barn that served as a workroom. "My *dat* is becoming a bit restless."

"*Ya*. I noticed his list of instructions grows longer the more he'd like to be out of his bed." David chuckled good-naturedly.

Now here was a reasonable man with a reasonable temperament. Perhaps he could ride over to Samuel Yoder's house and give him a lesson or two.

"Was there something specific you wanted me to do, Annie?"

"*Ya.*" Annie felt her cheeks flush as David's voice brought her thoughts away from stewing over Samuel. "I'm looking for some projects for my *daed.* I might have, well, hinted that you weren't braiding the lead rope correctly for the new mare."

David had been about to sit down at his workbench, but with Annie's confession, he stopped mid-seat and stared at her. "Say again?"

"I'm sorry." Annie's confession gained speed as her explanation tumbled out of her. "I know you're competent. You've been *wunderbaar*, helpful in every way. But he's driving me crazy in there. I told him you couldn't figure out how to braid the lead rope, and I suggested maybe he needed to do it himself."

David began laughing softly, then he couldn't seem to stop himself. It was a *gut* thing he was near the workbench, because he plopped on it, placed both hands on his knees, and laughed so hard Annie saw tears glistening in his eyes.

"It's not that funny," she said, suddenly irritated with him, Samuel, and her father. Perhaps the entire male race needed temperament classes.

"Oh, but it is, Annie. My own *mamm* and *dat* used to say I couldn't braid as well as a child. They'd make me practice on my *schweschders'* hair at night." He stood and walked over to her. "Now how would you be knowing such a thing about me?"

"I didn't, of course. I was just trying to think of something, anything, to keep him busy. So you're not angry?"

"Not at all." David walked to the workroom's far side and retrieved the rope. "I have learned to braid better than when I was a *kind*, and the new mare won't break her rope whether your father makes it or I do. I'd be *froh* to show you sometime—maybe you'd like to go for a buggy ride with me or to a church social."

Annie felt the heat creep up her neck, past her cheeks, to the very roots of her hair. "I appreciate the invitation. It's very, um, sweet. I haven't really thought about . . . that is to say, I don't know yet when I'll be able to—"

"It's all right, Annie. You needn't be deciding now." David handed her the rope with one hand, touched her shoulder with the other. "Take the rope. I'll keep my eyes open for other projects I could use his help on. Your father's a skilled farmer. I'm sure lying up in the bed is taking its toll on him."

"And on me," she mumbled as she turned and headed back toward the house.

Rebekah arrived home from her work at the store to find her bedroom filled with several projects from the barn. When she stood in the doorway, hands on hips, and cleared her throat, both Annie and Jacob began explaining at once.

"Now, Rebekah. Don't be thinking I spilled any of this tool grease on your lovely quilt."

"Indeed he didn't. I took your lone star quilt off and stored it on the chest by the window." Annie jumped up from the chair and set her needlework down in the basket. How had she not heard her mother's buggy pull up? "I covered *Dat* with an old blanket we found in the closet."

Stepping past her mother, she whispered, "I'll explain more when you take your tea."

Rebekah removed her coat and sailed into the room. "Looks to me as if someone couldn't go to the barn, so they managed to bring the barn into my bedroom."

Annie couldn't hear the rest as she fled to the kitchen, set the kettle on the stove, and began pulling out bread and fruit.

"What's going on in there?" Charity asked, leaning back against the counter.

"Nothing. David brought in a few things for *Dat* to work on is all."

"What do you two talk about?" Charity asked dreamily, playing with the strings of her *kapp* and stepping closer to Annie.

"Me and *Dat*?"

"No, *gegisch*. You and David. It's obvious he's sweet on you."

"Charity Weaver. David is in the barn all day working. We don't talk about anything."

"Then why are you blushing?"

"I am not blushing."

"Who isn't blushing?" Rebekah asked, walking into the room.

"Annie. All I did was ask her about David, and she started blushing as if she'd been standing over the stove for an hour. Look at her cheeks and tell me they aren't red."

Annie raised her eyes to the ceiling and prayed for patience.

"Stop teasing your *schweschder*, and take some of this fresh bread and fruit to your *dat*."

"Sorry, *Mamm*."

Drawing a deep breath, Annie turned and smiled at her *mamm*, offered her the hot cup of tea.

"*Danki*," she said.

"Does David make you blush?" Rebekah asked.

"David confuses me. He seems like the same boy I went to school with, except taller . . ." she hesitated, suddenly realized that her thoughts had careened toward Samuel whenever she was around David.

"And?" Rebekah studied her over her steaming tea.

"And today he asked me to go on a buggy ride with him."

Rebekah grinned, reached out, and squeezed her hand. "What *gut* news. Did you say yes?"

"I don't know if it's *gut* or not, and I didn't say anything. It was like being asked by your *bruder*. I've never thought of David in that way—in any way other than as a friend."

"Things change, but sometimes our perception of them stays the same."

Annie selected an apple from the bowl of fruit, rolled it back and forth in front of her.

Rebekah cleared her throat and changed the subject. "Care to tell me why your father's looking so *froh* in there, working as if he were in the barn?"

"He was driving me crazy this morning, so I went outside and asked David if he could find a few projects."

"Looks as if he did."

"*Ya.*" Darting a look at her mother, Annie was relieved to see her smiling. "You don't mind?"

"I've been married to your *dat* for twenty-five years. I've never seen him stop working and can't imagine how you kept him in that bed for nearly a week." Rebekah finished her tea and stood up. "Just try to keep the animals out of the house."

6

*I*n addition to the nativity scene, they had placed a single candle in each window—battery-operated, of course. Annie smiled at the simplicity of their decorations. Her *Englisch* friends would look at their home and be aghast.

No tree?

No knickknacks?

No gifts?

Annie knew Adam would be cutting sprigs of greenery to bring in as First Christmas grew closer—what her *Englisch* friends had referred to as Christmas Day. For the Amish, First Christmas was only the beginning of the celebration. It was the day they focused on the spiritual aspects by attending services, reading Scripture, and singing hymns. Second Christmas they gave gifts to each other, though those were quite simple compared to the lavish things she'd heard her co-workers speak of.

Though they didn't decorate a tree, evergreen boughs placed around the house signaled that the celebration was near. As for knickknacks, they didn't need them to clutter the room. And as for the gifts, she understood better than anyone that small presents were being worked on each evening—she was busy embroidering as fast as possible.

She'd just turned off the last of the Christmas candles and was climbing up the stairs for bed when a knock at their front door splintered the quietness of the evening.

Adam paused, his hand on the gas lantern, about to extinguish its light. He turned, hesitant as their *mamm* walked back into the living room.

Rebekah, Adam, and Annie all stared at one another, each wondering if they'd perhaps imagined it, when the knock sounded again.

"Hurry and answer the door, Adam—before whomever it is freezes to the front step." Rebekah's voice brooked no nonsense.

Annie reversed her way down the steps and moved toward her mother.

Young Joshua Hooley stepped into their living room, stamping his feet and setting a battery-operated lantern on the floor. He wore a thin coat, hardly enough covering for a fall day and nowhere near enough protection for such a cold winter night.

"Joshua, is everything all right?" Rebekah hurried across the living room, pulling her nightgown more tightly around her.

"*Ya.* I mean, no. It's not." He sounded as if he'd run the entire way in the darkness, though now that she listened, Annie could hear his horse outside the house. "I'm here to fetch Annie."

"Me?" Annie's voice squeaked like a mouse caught in a trap.

"Come farther inside, Joshua. You must be frozen." Rebekah walked over to the boy.

He couldn't have been eighteen by Annie's reckoning. When he pulled his hat off his head, brown hair stood out in all directions. He warmed his hands at the potbellied stove Rebekah opened up, and nodded to each of them in turn.

"Mrs. Weaver, Adam, Annie. Sorry to barge in so late. My *mamm* sent me over, asked me to bring Annie back." A shiver passed over him as warmth began to flood through his body.

"Put some water to boil, Annie. We need to make Joshua some tea." Rebekah pulled a blanket off the couch and wrapped it around his shoulders.

"Can't stay but a minute, ma'am. Folks will be expecting me back. They asked me to hurry."

"Hurry for what, Joshua?" Adam's boots echoed as he walked across the living room floor. "Why do you want Annie to go with you?"

Joshua gazed another few seconds into the fire. When he looked up, he stared straight at Annie, his eyes imploring her. "It's my *bruder*—little Daniel. He's suffering with the fever real bad. If you could come and look at him—"

"Annie isn't a doctor, Joshua." Rebekah placed a hand on his shoulder.

"*Ya.* We know that." Joshua started to say something more, but he stopped himself, closed his mouth, and waited.

"What is it, Joshua?" Annie walked over to the lad, who stood no taller than she was and couldn't have outweighed her by much. He was still a boy really. "Why don't your parents take your *bruder* to the hospital?"

"My *dat* doesn't think things are so bad yet, but my *mamm*— she's real worried. She sent me here to ask you to come, and *Dat* agreed it would be okay."

"If you don't want to go to the *Englisch*, Samuel should be the one to look at your *bruder*." Adam plunged his hands into his pockets, obviously unhappy with the boy's explanation.

But Joshua only resumed staring at the floor's smooth boards.

"Joshua?" Annie waited until he looked up, until his blue eyes looked directly into hers. "Tell me why your parents didn't send you to Samuel's."

He licked his lips, but didn't hesitate with the truth, didn't look away from her. "I can't say for sure, but I suspect it's because they weren't able to pay him anything the last time or the time before that either."

"Samuel doesn't require payment for his services," Adam insisted.

"Doesn't matter though, does it?" Joshua looked from one to the other now. "He might not require it, but most folks give something. Even a child could see it's the way things are done. My *dat*—he won't be going back until he can pay what he owes, and that won't be until spring."

He sank onto the couch, ran his hands through his hair. "They argued about it yesterday, and again tonight. My *mamm*, she heard from the ladies in town that you had some medical training."

Annie looked at her mother.

"Probably true. I mentioned in town that you were helping with your *dat*."

"We hoped maybe you could do something, or at least talk some sense into my *dat*."

Annie turned, headed upstairs.

"Where are you going?" Adam asked, his voice a low rumble.

"To change. I can't go with Joshua like this."

Adam shook his head in disapproval, but didn't bother arguing with her. "You're not going with Joshua at all. Their place is more than ten miles away, toward the northwest edge of our district. I'll be taking you."

"I'll find extra blankets for you both."

"Should I wait for you or go on ahead?" Joshua asked.

"At this hour? I want you to wait. We're safer traveling together. The last thing we need is another buggy accident." Adam shrugged into his coat and headed to the barn.

⌒∽

Annie had changed and was on her way out the door when her mother stopped her.

"Take this," Rebekah said, pushing a quilted bag into Annie's hands.

"What is it?"

"A few supplies—some aspirin, Tylenol, bandages, a thermometer, and the supplies you keep beside your *dat's* bed." She tucked a stray curl into Annie's *kapp*. "The Hooley family is hard-working though a bit poor, and as Joshua mentioned they are somewhat proud. That child might need some of the items in here."

Annie nodded, slipped the bag under her coat, and kissed her *mamm's* cheek. "I feel like Florence Nightingale."

"You're a *gut dochdern*, and it's a fine thing you're doing. Just be careful."

"If I'm a good daughter, it's because of the way you raised me, and of course I'll be careful. There's no need to worry. Adam will be with me, remember?"

The cold wind slapped at her when she stepped out into the wintry night.

As they rode in the buggy toward the Hooley house, Annie prayed for wisdom.

She knew her own knowledge was quite limited. She wasn't a doctor. She was a skilled nursing practitioner, more than capable of carrying out a doctor's orders.

The problem was there was no doctor here to assess the situation, and she was breaking several laws if she were to even attempt to diagnose this child.

But she'd be breaking moral laws to leave a child ill in the night if she could help him.

So as they moved through the snow and cold, she prayed, and tried to remember everything she could about high fevers—but she couldn't help wishing Samuel would be there with her.

         ⟿

Samuel didn't at first notice the lights of the approaching buggies. He was busy replaying the scene he'd left at Stephen Umble's farm. By the time he realized he wasn't alone on the country road, the two buggies were nearly upon him.

He clucked softly to his mare and pulled her to a slow trot, then a stop as the first, then the second buggy pulled up alongside his.

Young Joshua Hooley's face stared out at him, pale and cold, eyes settling somewhere to the left of Samuel's shoulder.

"Joshua, fine night to be out and about."

"Ya, it is, Mr. Yoder." The boy's voice was respectful but clipped, as if he didn't want to reveal more than was necessary.

"Little late though."

"Ya, it is."

Samuel unfolded himself from his buggy, walked to where Adam Weaver sat holding the reins hitched to his new mare. "Adam, Annie."

"Evening, Samuel." Adam's tone was warm and friendly, but Annie confined her greeting to a single nod and stiffened her spine a bit straighter.

"Little late to see two buggies out following one another. Some social gathering going on I wasn't aware of?"

"I wasn't aware you attended social gatherings," Annie said.

Samuel and Adam turned to stare at her.

"Not that I would have noticed if you attended or not." Annie reached up, tucked a loose tendril of hair into her *kapp*.

Samuel felt a smile tugging at the corner of his mouth as Annie's cheeks colored rosily.

She'd avoided him each time he'd stopped by the Weaver place. Obviously, she was still angry at him about the scolding he'd delivered four days ago, which she had deserved. But he would have thought she had better control of her tongue.

Then again, her feistiness brought some sparkle back into his evening.

"Can't say as I am in the habit of attending social gatherings. Can't remember the last time I participated in any sledding or such. Didn't realize it went this late or ever included a mere two buggies." He stared at her pointedly. "Is that what this is about?"

"Actually, no." Adam shushed his horse and took control of the conversation. "Joshua needed a hand at his place, so Annie and I are on our way over to help him out."

Samuel stared at Annie a moment longer, but she suddenly was preoccupied with straightening the blanket around her lap.

Turning his attention back to Adam, Samuel nodded toward Joshua's buggy. "Maybe there's something I could do. I just finished putting stitches in Stephen Umble's hand and was headed back to my place. I'd be *froh* to follow you over—"

"No!" Annie and Adam shouted the word at the same time.

"What we mean is, it's kind of you to offer, but probably we have this covered." Adam picked up his hat, then settled it back on his head. "You must be tired what with working all day and then driving the long distance out to Umble's place. How's the room coming along he was trying to add on?"

"Going well. His youngest son wandered in while Stephen was nailing up some shelves. He glanced down at the boy and nailed his hand instead of the wood. Didn't hit anything major, but it bled quite a bit."

Samuel studied Annie who was again staring out over the snow-covered fields. "Something you might have been interested in seeing, Annie. I seem to remember you were quite fascinated by the process of stitches and how it was done when you were a younger girl."

Annie threw him a look much like a hammer slamming into a nail. Samuel wondered why it made him want to laugh. Usually he preferred solitude, but meeting these two on the road tonight had perked him up quite a bit.

Plus there was the mystery of what they were really doing out on this cold winter night.

"We best be going if we hope to be done and back home at a decent hour," Adam said.

Samuel felt his eyebrows rise, looked over at the moon silhouetting the fields. "I'd say you've already passed that time. Most folks are in bed by now."

"True. All the more reason for us to move on. Nice talking to you, Samuel."

"And you as well. Evening, Adam. Evening, Annie." He didn't have to call her by name, but when he did, manners forced her to return the parting.

She turned those brown eyes to gaze into his, and Samuel received a little more than he had bargained for. There was the anger he'd come to expect, but there was something else in addition. A pleading he didn't quite understand.

A concern quite out of keeping with their bantering.

So he stepped out of the way, gently slapped the horse's rump, and watched them as they trotted off into the night following Joshua's buggy.

Why were they headed toward the Hooley place so late in the evening?

More pointedly, why was Annie headed there?

And why did he care?

Samuel walked back to his buggy and continued in the opposite direction, back to his home, which would be silent and dark. He'd realized of late that he avoided his own place, but what was to be done about it?

Life was difficult—didn't the *gut* Book say as much?

His lot was still better than many of those he ministered to. He wouldn't complain about it.

But as he allowed the mare to walk leisurely toward home, he no longer thought of Umble and his hand, or even what he needed to do around his farm the next day. Instead, he thought of a young lady in a buggy, blankets wrapped around her lap, cheeks reddened by the cold—and he wondered who had summoned her and for what purpose.

Mostly though, he thought about those brown eyes and the sparkle they'd held.

7

When Annie stepped into the Hooley household, three small heads popped up from the corner of the living room to stare at her. They were lying on a pallet on the floor, covered in quilts. Their hair shot out in all directions, reminding her of tiny haystacks, and their eyes stared at her as if she were a stranger from a faraway land.

"Back to sleep, *bopplin*. Miss Annie is here to see your *bruder*." Martha Hooley walked across the room to greet Annie, took her coat, gloves, and scarf, then peered past her into the darkness. "Is Joshua coming?"

"He's in the barn with my *bruder*, Adam, and your husband." Annie moved to the stove to warm her hands. "They were tending to the horses."

"And I suspect they'll stay there for a while. The house is a bit crowded, and since I moved the little ones out here there's less room for reading or socializing."

"I wouldn't worry about the men, Martha. They'll be fine in the workroom." Annie glanced at the makeshift bed and the three boys, then back at Martha. "Why did you move the younger children to the living room? Are you afraid Daniel is contagious?"

"I don't know." Martha swiped at her graying hair, rubbed at her eyes, and sank into a chair at the kitchen table. "I honestly don't know. It seemed the safest thing to do, and then with Daniel waking up and needing my attention, they weren't sleeping much in their bedroom."

Annie nodded as the small stove's warmth chased the cold from her arms and legs.

"I remember when you were a little girl," Martha said, her voice mingling with the quiet crackling of the fire. "I'd see you at school when I walked down to pick up Joshua. Now you're a grown woman and a medical practitioner too."

Annie crossed the room, pulled out a chair next to Martha, and covered the older woman's hand with her own. "I remember you as well. I'm not sure what you've heard, but you know I went away a few years to live with my *mamm's schweschder.*"

Martha swiped again at her hair, looked into Annie's face with hope.

"I had a bit of medical training while I was there—nothing more. I won't be misrepresenting myself, Martha." Annie paused and waited for the woman to accept what she was saying. "If I can help your *kind*, I will. But if I think he needs to go to the *Englisch* doctor, then I'll be telling your husband myself it's what needs to be done."

"*Ya*, and I would expect you to do as much. You have your mother's directness."

"I understand your situation with Samuel, but he certainly has more experience than I do."

"I've tried to tell Simon the same thing." Martha's voice cracked for the first time since Annie had entered the home. "He won't budge on that, though. Don't judge him too harshly, Annie. Simon cares for his children, and though pride is a sin—"

A coughing from the adjoining bedroom interrupted their conversation.

The three children in the living room again popped up, glancing first to their mother, then to Annie.

Martha stood, motioned for Annie to follow her.

Annie started into the adjoining room, then turned, and walked back to the front door, and picked up her mother's quilted bag. Pausing again in the kitchen, she stopped at the sink and washed her hands.

By the time she reached the bedroom, Martha was sitting close to the bed.

Glancing around, Annie could tell that this was normally the room all four children shared. Like the front room, no Christmas candle decorated the window. In fact, the room could be described as sparse, even for Amish folk.

Four hooks positioned on the wall opposite the bed held clothing. Under that was an extended cubby for shoes, and above the hooks ran a shelf for hats.

Joshua must sleep up in a loft, and no doubt the parents' room was next door. It was a small, snug home—simply built and clean.

Suddenly Annie remembered the Hooleys had all boys— someone had made a joke at one of the Sunday meetings about the fact that Simon Hooley would one day need more land— with five strapping boys able to do so much work, and one day bound to marry and build homes of their own on the family place.

Looking at the exhausted little boy lying spent under the covers, Annie tried to picture him out working in the field, playing in the sun, taking a girl for a buggy ride—she tried and failed.

Instead, watching the small form in the bed, Annie immediately thought of Kiptyn at Mercy Hospital and the letter she had received Saturday. She thought of how hopeless his situation had been. Yet he was improving—only slightly—but still, improving. She thought of Kiptyn and drew courage.

Stepping forward, she set her bag on the table beside the bed.

"When did he first become ill?"

"Three days ago. He came home from school, didn't want any dinner. I knew something was wrong, but I was tired—didn't pay attention right away. It wasn't until the other children came to bed and noticed he was already here, sleeping and sweating, that they came and alerted me."

Annie pulled out her notepad, started a case history, and took Daniel's pulse. His skin was fire-hot to her fingertips. She didn't need a thermometer to know his temperature was over one hundred and two, but she pulled one out of her bag anyway.

"Hold this in his mouth for me, Martha. Careful he doesn't bite down on it."

Martha moved to the far side of the bed. With one hand she held the thermometer steady in Daniel's mouth, with the other she wiped the sweat from his face.

"It's my fault. I should have paid closer attention. Should have noticed."

"Wouldn't have made any difference. You know that. He would still have whatever it is he has." Annie slipped her blood pressure cuff over the boy's arm. "How old is Daniel?"

"Eight. He turned eight last month."

Daniel didn't wake as Annie continued assessing his condition. He remained basically unresponsive although he coughed a few times, and twice he tried to turn and curl up on his side.

"Any signs of rashes?"

"No."

"Any vomiting?"

"The first night. He hasn't eaten since."

"Any diarrhea?"

"No."

Annie took the thermometer and noted the temperature of 104.8 on her tablet.

The entire time, Martha stared at her child, her eyes as frightened as those of the boys in the other room.

"Martha, I want you to look at me. There are many, many things Daniel might have. I'm not a doctor, and I'm not going to pretend to be able to diagnose him. Some of those things are fatal, but those things are also rare."

Martha clutched Daniel's hand, but nodded, focused on Annie's words.

"In all likelihood, he has a case of influenza—the flu."

"*Ya*. Many kids catch the flu each year. Three of mine had it last winter."

"True, but what worries me most about Daniel is his fever and his dehydration. We need to coax some liquid in him and we need to bring his fever down."

"I've tried to get him to drink. It's no use."

"I want you to find some ice chips. Even if you have to send Joshua or Simon out to the meat house. Have them fetch a bucket of ice and ask one of the men to start chipping it into tiny pieces. I also want some juice. We'll feed it to him by the spoonful if we have to."

Martha nodded, but didn't move.

"If Daniel were in the hospital, they'd start him on an intravenous drip, a line into his veins that would carry fluid through his body."

Annie let her hand trail down the boy's arm. "If we don't see this fever come down in the next few hours, I'm going to strongly suggest we call a driver and transfer him to the hospital. First, we'll try to break the temperature here, but I want your word. If this doesn't work, we'll go to the *Englisch*."

Martha straightened the hand-stitched quilt covering her son, then returned Annie's gaze. "*Danki*, for helping us."

"No need to thank me."

"And you have my promise." Her words came out hard, firmer. "We'll give this till morning, then we'll take him to the *Englisch*—if I have to put him in the buggy and drive him myself."

While Martha was outside setting the men to work chipping ice, Annie inventoried what her mother had slipped into the quilted bag. She nearly shouted for joy when she came to the chewable children's Tylenol.

Going to the kitchen she retrieved a spoon and saucer and began to crush two of the pills. Then she added a few drops of juice and created a paste. Lastly she retrieved a dish towel and a basin half filled with water, then carried everything back into Daniel's room.

Martha returned slightly out of breath, but also refreshed from her short walk outside. Annie wondered if the woman had stepped outside the house at all in the past three days.

"They're working on the ice, and I told Simon to have the buggy ready—that we might be needing it to go and fetch a driver come first light."

"Excellent. Now I need you to sit behind Daniel and prop him up. I've crushed some children's Tylenol."

"He won't swallow that. I've tried and the child won't open his mouth for anything. I'm surprised we were able to put the thermometer in."

"Move behind him and prop him up in a sitting position. *Wunderbaar.*"

"He's even hotter than earlier—like having a stove pressed against you." Martha's face creased with worry.

Annie wanted to stop and allay her fears. Right now, though, she needed to focus on Daniel.

Dipping the towel in the basin, she began running it across Daniel's face, over his lips, down his neck—then dipping it into the basin again.

She repeated the process two, three, and then four times.

Finally Daniel slipped his tongue out when she passed the cloth over his lips. "*Gut*, Daniel. You're doing well."

Glancing toward the door, she saw Simon standing there, holding a small bucket in his hands. He was a big man, a big version of Joshua. When his eyes met hers, he didn't look away. She read his fear there, and something else.

She hoped it wasn't shame, but she worried it might be.

"*Danki*, Mr. Hooley. You can bring the bucket in and set it here beside the nightstand."

"How is he? How's Daniel?" He stepped toward the bed, set the bucket on the handmade rug, and then took two steps back.

"Daniel just showed the first signs that he knows we're here."

Simon nodded, began to turn away.

"Mr. Hooley? Could you do one more thing?" His expression changed then, as if she'd offered him a newborn calf.

"Would you bring Daniel a fresh glass of water, and another spoon?"

"*Ya.* 'Course I will."

He was back in less than a minute—the mug of water large enough to make three cups of tea. Annie thanked him, dipped the spoon in it, and slipped the little bit of water between Daniel's lips.

The boy swallowed once, and his tongue darted out again.

Martha looked at Annie and the smile they shared, the victory they shared, was unlike anything she'd experienced on a hospital floor before. It was more intimate, like something passed between friends.

Was Martha her friend?

She was certainly more than the mother of her patient.

"That's *gut, ya?*" Simon stood at the door, clasping his hat in his hand.

"Yes, Simon. It's very *gut.*" Martha smiled up at her husband, then turned back to her son. "His fever is very high, though. It's over 104."

"Is there anything else I can bring? Anything else I can do?"

"You can pray." Annie paused as she once again dipped the rag into the basin. "We can all pray his fever breaks by morning."

Simon nodded, then turned and trudged back out of the room, out the front door, out to the barn.

8

*D*aniel's fever didn't break then, though Annie and Martha managed to coax the spoonful of Tylenol down him. They continued to bathe him with the cool rag and place ice chips in his mouth, and once an hour Annie took his blood pressure and temperature—recording the numbers on her pad each time.

At four a.m., as she began to worry they would have to send one of the men in the buggy for a driver, send Daniel to the hospital with the *Englischers*, he began to sweat heavily.

Martha stirred from her place beside him in the bed, wiped the sweat from her son's face. "It's *gut, ya?*"

"It's very *gut*." Annie squeezed Martha's hand, then hurried to the kitchen for more fresh water.

She was refilling the basin when she heard Daniel begin to cry.

"Everything is fine, *boppli*. You've been very sick, but now everything is fine."

It was the first time Annie had seen Daniel's eyes open. Though they were still sunken and tired, their color was a warm golden brown, much like Joshua's.

Then the boy said words that caused Martha's tears to spill over. "*Mamm*, I'm hungry."

She pulled him to her and rocked him and laughed and cried at the same time. Finally, she wiped a hand across her eyes and declared, "I'll go and heat him a little broth."

Within minutes she was back and insisted on feeding it to Daniel herself. The boy wasn't able to take more than a dozen spoonfuls, but it was enough to ease Annie's worries. Once he'd fallen back into a more restful sleep, she pulled Martha into the kitchen and reminded her of all she would need to do.

"It's important to continue with the Tylenol regularly for the next two days, or the fever might rise again." Annie pressed the bottle of children's Tylenol into her hands.

"I can send Simon to the store for some in a few hours. Of course, we have the kind for older children, but I never thought to have the chewables on hand."

"It's all right. Take mine. *Mamm* gave me this, and I'm sure she has more. Remember to mix it with the juice as you saw me do earlier until you're sure he can chew up the tablets."

Martha placed the bottle in the pocket of her apron.

"Be sure he's taking plenty of liquids. We want him up and using the bathroom regularly. Color should come back to his skin, and you should see elasticity return within the next six hours." Annie showed her how to test for dehydration on her own arm, and the difference when she touched Daniel's skin.

"So it was the influenza?" Martha asked.

"I believe so, but we may never know for sure. Keep the other children away from him until twenty-four hours after the fever's gone. Be sure no one drinks or eats after him."

Martha walked her to the door. They both stopped and looked out the window, where the eastern sky was beginning to lighten with dawn's first glow.

"Annie, I owe you more than I can say. If you think of any way I can repay you—"

Annie stopped her, wrapped her arms around the woman's thin shoulders. "I'm very glad I could help. Take care of your *kinner*, and find a way to grab some rest yourself."

"I will, and the children will be fine. They're all a help to me."

Hugging her one last time, Annie stepped out onto the porch of the small house. Walking to the barn, she couldn't help thinking again of Kiptyn and of the letter among her things back home.

Kiptyn, too, had made a turn for the better—though for how long, God alone knew. Annie realized suddenly that his parents would give much to be able to keep him in their home, to be able to care for him in his room as Martha was doing.

Had Martha placed her child at risk by not rushing him to the hospital? Or had she done the right thing by keeping Daniel in the one place she knew she could care for him—safely surrounded by his family and community?

Annie was too tired to puzzle it all out.

After delivering the good news to Simon and Joshua, she climbed into the buggy with Adam.

She wanted to talk to Adam, wanted to ask him what he thought she was to do, now that she was home. And whether Samuel was right in his criticism of her. Did she have any business trying to help people like Martha and Simon with their child?

But her eyes were too heavy and she couldn't fight the fatigue that washed over her like a wave as they made their way through the brightening morning. She pulled the blanket around her, cornered herself into the buggy's seat, and fell fast asleep.

Each night that week, Annie was called on by her neighbors—that first time because they couldn't pay Samuel, twice because he was tending to someone on the county's far side, and once because the woman lived alone and felt better seeing another woman.

Each time, Annie reminded her neighbors that she'd had minimal training, and each time they looked her in the eye, thanked her for her honesty, and asked her to help them with whatever ailed them.

Plain people might prefer simpler ways, but they weren't ignorant as far as what constituted an outright emergency. When the young boy on the farm adjacent to theirs cut his arm in a long gash on an old farming tool, his father sent one sibling running for Annie, and another running to the nearest neighbor with a phone.

By the time Annie arrived to bind up the wound, a driver was there with a car to transport him to the hospital—the boy would need a tetanus shot and a long row of stitches.

Annie feared the biggest battle they would face over the next few months would be influenza. In only a week, her mother's extra medical supplies had dwindled to nothing. When Friday arrived, Annie didn't turn down a chance to ride into town and replenish them.

Stepping from the general store into the light snow flurries, she clutched her bag of purchases to her, bent her head against the cold north wind, and walked straight into the man she had been avoiding—Samuel.

"If it isn't Annie Weaver. *Gudemariye* to you."

She should have been thankful for the way his form blocked the wind, but looking up into his teasing face she couldn't work up any gratitude. A small voice inside her head told her to return his greeting and step around him, but she had not yet learned to listen to that voice.

So instead she stopped, cocked her head, and looked up at him, wondering if his attitude had improved at all in the last week. "Samuel, how are you this morning?"

"I'm fine, and I suppose your patient is fine since you're in town today."

Annie fought against the blush staining her cheeks. "My *dat* is now able to spend a few hours each day in the barn with David, you'll be *froh* to know. He's healing quite well."

"He seemed to be last time I checked on him. You do realize I check on him. Don't you?"

Annie rolled her eyes and glanced toward the winter skies. She hadn't rolled her eyes since she was a young girl in school, but Samuel Yoder had a way of making her crazy. Pulling in a deep breath, she pushed past him on the sidewalk.

To her surprise, Samuel turned and matched her step for step. "Funny thing, I haven't seen you either of the times I've been by your *dat's* place. If I didn't know better, I'd believe you were avoiding me."

She turned on him in a flash, causing others on the sidewalk to have to swerve around them.

"And why would I want to avoid you?" Her voice rose in spite of her best attempt to remain unfazed by him. "Possibly because you're rude or arrogant or unpleasant to be around?"

Tugging her scarf closer around her ears, she spun away and marched down the walk toward Mr. Fisher's shop where her mother worked, pleased with the image of him standing there in the middle of the sidewalk, his mouth half-open in surprise.

The man *was* rude and arrogant and unpleasant to be around.

Jerking open the door to the shop, she stepped inside. Handmade quilts, scarves, and needlework adorned the left side of the store where several *Englischers* browsed as Mr. Fisher tidied the display in the window. A small café area had been set up to the right, and the smell of *kaffi*, tea, and cinnamon muffins immediately surrounded her, calmed her.

Rebekah waved from behind the sales counter and pointed over to the small café area. Waving back, Annie turned to the right and chose a table near the window. Sitting with her back to the door, she set her bag of purchases in the middle chair.

Which was when she heard the bell over the door tinkle, turned in her chair, and saw Samuel duck into the shop.

He slid into the chair across from her and removed his hat, setting it on top of her bag of purchases.

"What are you doing?" she asked.

"I might sometimes come across as rude and arrogant, but I don't think I'm unpleasant to be around. Some people actually like being around me."

"Why did you follow me in here?"

"Can't a man walk into a shop and order something warm to drink?"

Flustered that she should be in this situation, Annie tried to catch her mother's attention, but suddenly Rebekah was busy restocking a shelf, though she did sneak a peek and beam broadly at her.

"Problem?" Samuel asked.

"I'm meeting someone," Annie hissed.

"Oh. Well, there's a third chair, I can put my hat in my lap."

"That's not the point."

"What is the point, then?"

"You're insufferable."

"You have a long list of adjectives. Did you learn them from the *Englisch*?"

Annie stared at him, wondering if the man had gone mad. Where was the quiet, reserved Samuel Yoder she'd known all her life?

"I was beginning to think you'd hightailed it back to the city." He drummed his fingers against the table and waited for her answer.

As if she would reply to such an accusation. She wanted to pick up the small vase of plastic flowers and chuck them at him.

Was he actually smiling?

Yes, she could see the corners of his mouth tugging his beard upwards as heat again flooded her face.

And why was she the one blushing? He was the one acting completely inappropriate in a store full of shoppers.

Just as she had determined to snatch her bag of purchases out from under his hat, her *mamm* showed up at the table. "Samuel, how nice to see you. I can't remember the last time you stopped into the café."

"And I've been remiss. I should come in more often."

"I'm glad you did. I was supposed to have a sip of tea with Annie—"

"I'm sitting right here, Mother."

"Hello, sweetie." Rebekah placed a hand on her back, studied her a moment. "Why do you still have your coat and scarf on? You are staying. Aren't you?"

"Of course. It's just that—"

"Take them off, then. Let me help you. We'll set them on this chair until I have a break." Rebekah's voice had taken on a purring quality, and her face was positively beaming. "Unfortunately, several shoppers have decided to come in at once. I asked Charity to bring you both some hot tea. Is tea *gut*, Samuel?"

"Tea would be *wunderbaar*."

"Excellent. We have apple cinnamon this afternoon, but I know sometimes men prefer our straight brew."

Annie listened to her mother discuss flavors of tea with Samuel, and she felt the beginnings of a headache pulsating in her temples.

⌘

Rebekah scurried away.

Samuel leaned back in his chair and smiled. Why was he smiling so much today? The sadness still lurked in his blue-black eyes, but somehow provoking her had become a larger pleasure than basking in his own tragedies.

The thought had barely formed when she realized how uncharitable it was.

She glanced away quickly—across the room, down at his hat. Her eyes finally settled on the little menu her *mamm* had placed in front of them.

Survive the next few minutes and perhaps he would go away.

⌘

Samuel realized he shouldn't be playing games with little Annie Weaver, and he told himself he wasn't.

Then she had stared into his eyes for those few seconds.

What had she seen that caused her eyes to blink rapidly, caused her to look away? When she did, he lost all his resolve.

"See something that bothered you?"

"Excuse me?"

He leaned forward in his chair, lowered his voice. "I thought you might have seen something that bothered you, when you glanced at me then looked away. In fact, you suddenly look a little *naerfich*."

"I am not nervous," Annie declared, picking up her paper napkin and beginning to shred it into tiny pieces.

"Humph. Usually when people shred things, it's a way of dealing with uncomfortable situations."

She jerked her hands into her lap. "Oh, so you're a psychologist now, are you?"

"No. I've observed a bit of human nature in my years is all."

"Samuel Yoder, you act as if you're fifty years old, and I imagine you're not a day over thirty."

Samuel tugged on his beard, accepted the tea Charity brought them.

"Samuel, Annie." The girl actually giggled when she looked at Annie. "Nice to see you *both* here. *Mamm* asked me to bring over this basket of sweets for you, in case you wanted an afternoon snack."

"*Danki*, Charity." Samuel's stomach growled so he reached inside the checkered cloth and pulled out a warm, miniature honey bun. "I'm usually not one for sweets, but suddenly I'm starved."

"Harassing me must work up an appetite."

Samuel's laughter rang out through the café, causing a few *Englischers* to stop and look their way.

"I believe that's what I enjoy about your company, Annie. You don't mind speaking what you're thinking—fairly rare these days."

"Perhaps it's only rare around you."

"*Ya.* I think you might be right." Samuel popped the honey bun into his mouth and sipped his tea.

"Why do you think that is?" Samuel asked, when the conversation seemed stalled.

Annie merely stared at him, not rising to the question. But now Samuel had waded too far into the pond to back out.

It wasn't like him to stop a woman outside a store and speak to her—a brief nod would be more his style.

And he'd never followed one into a café and sat down beside her.

He didn't have to worry about making a fool of himself in front of little Miss Annie—he could check "task completed" in that column.

As the sounds around them faded into a comfortable blend of peripheral life, he leaned forward and asked one of the questions that had lately troubled him much, one she had inadvertently touched on.

"Why do you think it is people are so reserved around me?" He picked up another honey bun but didn't eat it, opting instead to unwind the miniature roll of dough. "I don't mean they're rude. Plain people are among the most polite, in my opinion. But it's as if an invisible barrier exists between myself and others."

He set the sticky bread down, dabbed at his fingers with his napkin. "It might be that I irritate you—*ya*, I was listening to your words and your body language—but at least with you, the barrier is gone for a moment."

Annie looked directly into his eyes again, and his pulse kicked up a notch. He waited, but instead of responding, she sipped her tea, looked out the window, sipped her tea again. When he'd about given up, she cleared her throat.

"I noticed the reservation you speak of between *Englisch* doctors and patients too."

He sat back and waited, knowing there was more.

"There's a respect, but also a distance."

Samuel nodded. "I suppose you're right—though it could be my rude, arrogant, unpleasant personality."

Annie smiled now, looked up at the ceiling. "*Ya*, I suppose it could be that too."

"Or?"

"Or it could be—"

"Annie. Samuel. I'm sorry to keep you both waiting." Rebekah pulled out the chair, still beaming at them both.

Samuel helped her set Annie's things and his hat at a nearby table.

The conversation changed, and he had a second cup of tea.

He was surprised to find he actually enjoyed their company, as he wasn't usually one to linger and sip tea in the middle of the afternoon.

But then it could have been that he was gazing across the table at Annie of the beautiful chestnut hair, and though she no doubt took great care to pin it beneath her prayer *kapp*, wayward curls insisted on escaping.

They finished their tea, spoke of the cold weather, even talked of the upcoming holiday. He stayed far longer than he'd planned.

As he said his goodbyes and made his way back out into the lightly falling snow, he couldn't help wondering what it was that Annie had been about to say—and she *had* been about to say something else.

Why did she think people maintained a distance from him?

Annie was young, but she had a degree of perception that was unusual.

If he were looking for a wife, which he wasn't, he'd be tempted to court young Annie. And wouldn't he be earning himself a tongue-lashing then? He could just imagine the list of adjectives she'd come up with should he ask her to go on a buggy ride.

Somehow though, driving home through the cold winter afternoon—the idea became less humorous and more something he had trouble putting away.

Not that he'd ever act on it.

9

Saturday, Annie helped the rest of her family give the house and barn a thorough cleaning. The Sunday service would take place at their home the next day—ironic since she was being baptized. It did rotate to their place once every twelve weeks. Still, Annie couldn't help smiling as she beat out the rugs.

Things had worked out better than she could have imagined when she was walking down the streets of Philadelphia, cringing at the brazen holiday decorations.

Then her mind slipped to thinking of Samuel, and she beat the rug a bit harder.

It wasn't in her nature to avoid a man or a confrontation. But neither did she enjoy disagreements, and the truth was he did make her a bit uncomfortable.

She'd been nervous around doctors before.

Her first rotations had left her more jumpy than Reba's kitten. The doctors at Mercy Hospital had expected as much though. They'd been patient and kind. They'd also been older, reminding her more of her father than of someone she might consider going on a buggy ride with.

Is that what she was struggling against?

An adolescent crush?

The thought made her blush more than the winter breeze did.

Her father had been back to see Dr. Stoltzfus that morning. The danger of pneumonia had passed. Though the two casts remained, he was now able to move around on crutches.

And though she still needed to check on him, he wasn't a full-time job for her anymore.

She broached the subject with her mother that afternoon as her *dat* hobbled off to the barn, Adam helping him over the snow so he wouldn't slip and fall.

"Perhaps I should see about finding a job in town."

"Why would you say that, Annie?"

"*Dat* doesn't need me around here all day. The bandages only require changing at night and in the morning. I love working around the house, but more and more I find myself with time on my hands."

Rebekah stopped kneading the loaves of bread she was preparing for Sunday's meal and studied her. "You've changed, you know."

"How so?"

"There was a time when you avoided work, and it hasn't been so long ago."

Annie laughed. "I suppose you're right." She fiddled with a napkin on the table. "So what do you think I should do? Is there someone in town who is hiring?"

Rebekah began kneading the dough again. "How many times last week were you called to families' homes, to help them with their sick ones?"

"Three, no, four times."

"It would be difficult to continue helping others as much as you are and also hold a job. If I remember correctly, two of those times you were gone nearly all night. Adam is becoming quite used to sleeping in people's barns while he waits for you—not that he minds, but if he didn't sleep he'd never be able to do his job the next day."

"*Ya*, but that's my point. Adam has a job. He contributes. Charity has a job. I'm not contributing to the family. I should be bringing in some income."

Rebekah gave the bread a final thump. "You've been home less than two weeks. I don't see as our expenses are any more than they were before you returned."

"But *Mamm*, you know *Dat* feels everyone should work, everyone should contribute."

"Has your *dat* brought this up with you?"

Annie shook her head.

"'Course not, because it's not bothering him. If it was, he would have mentioned it to me."

"And still I feel I should be adding something tangible to the household, what with you and *Dat* feeding so many mouths."

"And you are adding something to our home—our community." Rebekah reached across the table, covered Annie's hands with her own, dusting them with the flour from the bread. "Your *dat* is very proud of you, Annie, and so am I. You are helping people in a way that few among us can. So you aren't paid for it. Why should such a thing matter?"

"I should be earning something," Annie insisted stubbornly.

Rebekah pulled a pan of vegetables toward her and began slicing them for a stew. "Perhaps God will provide a way you can do both—earn some money and help others."

Annie shook her head.

"Have you talked to Samuel about this?"

"No."

"Does he know what you're doing? About your visits to the other families?"

"I don't know. He hasn't brought it up and neither have I." Annie squirmed in her seat, feeling suddenly like a small *kind* with her hand caught in the jar of oatmeal cookies.

"Hmph. He's a *gut* man, Annie. It might be he'd have some ideas on the subject."

Annie stood, paced back and forth between the kitchen and living room. They'd removed the partition between rooms for the next day's service and it gave her plenty of room to walk, but somehow it didn't ease her restlessness. Finally, she stopped beside the table.

"I didn't tell you what happened when I first came back, what Samuel said to me." She drummed the back of the chair with her fingers as she thought back to that day, to the cold and distant man Samuel had been.

Which was the real Samuel Yoder? The one who had scolded her like a child on the porch? Or the one who had spoken to her like a woman while sitting with her at the café?

The way he had initially questioned her commitment to her family still rankled when she thought about it. And his rebuke that her family had a right to know about her nursing degree still irked her.

"There's actually quite a lot I haven't told you," Annie murmured. Then she turned, grabbed her coat, and walked out of the house.

❧

Annie told herself she wasn't running away, but sometimes she feared she'd go crazy unless she broke free of the house's four walls. Fortunately, today the weather was unseasonably warm. Clouds hung low over the fields.

At breakfast the men had discussed a heavy snowfall that had been forecast—it was due to arrive before Monday. All the more reason to walk out to the garden now and have a look at what might be.

She'd been in the small fenced-in area less than ten minutes, pacing around and doing her best to remember spring, when her *mamm* joined her there.

"I come here a lot myself." Rebekah sounded as if she were discussing where to plant the radishes in April, not questioning why her daughter felt the need to rush out into a snow-topped garden on a Saturday afternoon. "Mostly, I walk out this way when I start feeling like I could outrun one of the horses in Jacob's barn."

Annie stole a peek at her mother. "I thought you were always perfectly content."

"No one's always perfectly content, dear." Rebekah brushed snow from the top of the fence post, then moved past her into the garden area. "Secrets aren't always bad, Annie. Unless they weigh heavy on your soul—like the clouds pushing down over our fields."

Looking out at the land, Annie realized her mother was right.

She'd been carrying this burden around far too long—not just since she'd come home, but since she'd left over three years ago.

"When I went to stay with *aenti*, I continued my schooling. I couldn't seem to stop. Learning more made me want to learn even more." She moved closer to her mother, near where the vines would flower and bear fruit in the spring.

"I became a registered nurse, *mamm*. I worked in a hospital with sick *kinner*."

Rebekah reached out, touched her face as gently as the breeze touched the vine they stood beside. "And I'm expecting you'd be missing those children some days."

"That's it?" Annie's voice rose in disbelief. "That's all you have to say? I must miss the *kinner*?"

"Well, don't you?"

"Of course I do."

Annie's thoughts tumbled over one another, as she tried to grasp the gentleness in her mother's voice, the compassion on her face. "That's not the point, though. I thought. That is . . ."

She finally gave up and sat down on an upended milking pail.

"Are you so surprised I would have guessed what you were doing, Annie? You're my oldest girl. I've watched you for twenty years. I know you better than anyone does."

"But, what I did was wrong. It goes against our teachings, our ways. Tomorrow I'm to be baptized, and I hadn't even told you of this. I thought you'd be angry with me. I thought . . ." Her voice fell away like so many leaves scattered in the wind.

"That you needed to hide who you are—what you are—from your parents? Oh, Annie." Rebekah leaned forward, folded her in an embrace that was softer than the downiest quilt. "We love you because you are our *dochdern*, because you are a beautiful person God has shared with us. And we're proud of you."

Taking Annie's face in her hands, she looked her straight in the eyes, as if this was the most important thing she'd said all morning, perhaps in many years. "Baptism is a committing of yourself to God, to our church and our community. We will speak with Bishop Levi before the service. He already knows of your time with the *Englisch*, but if he thinks a confession is necessary then so be it."

Annie nodded, brushed at her tears.

"As for the gifts God has given you, I have no doubt he'll provide a way for you to use them in our community, among your Amish *schweschders* and brethren. God has a reason for everything, dear one, even our *rumschpringe*."

Annie stood, walked to the fence, and plucked at the dried leaves of the vine.

"Doesn't mean it will be easy, finding a way to fit your *Englisch* gifts into our community," her *mamm* continued. "Plain folks can be stubborn regarding any type of change."

Swiping at her nose, Annie attempted a laugh. "And so our conversation has come around full circle. If we're talking about stubborn Amish, you must be referring to Samuel Yoder. I've never met a man more mulish."

Arms linked, they turned and began walking back toward the house.

"I won't deny that, but tell me about the night you came home—about what Samuel said to you."

So she did.

They discussed the evening Annie stepped into her father's room and saw him lying in his bed, and how Samuel had challenged her willingness to stay and care for him. By the time they'd gained the porch steps, the sky had grown darker, though it was still early in the afternoon and the temperature had not yet turned.

"Annie, I wish you could have known Samuel before. He was quite a different person."

"Before what?"

"The accident. Before his *fraa* and *boppli* died. Samuel was more like Adam then—maybe not as quick with a laugh, but always smiling, always with a light in his eyes."

Rebekah sat down in the rocker, and Annie sat beside her, curious to hear the entire story, though some part of her wanted to turn away from it.

"It wasn't his fault, but he blamed himself. He was out on a call, and Mary tried to drive the buggy over to a neighbor's.

She made it to the Lapp's and should have stayed the night."
Rebekah's voice came from a distant place—one full of heart-
ache, one people knew existed but preferred to forget about
until life thrust them into its path again. "No doubt Mary
thought there was time for her to make it home."

"There was a storm?" Annie asked.

"*Ya*. It had been threatening all day, but we all thought it
might hold off until morning. When it hit, well, it had the fury
of a hard, driving rain—only it was snow."

Annie waited, barely daring to breathe.

"Later they realized the horse must have lost its way."

Silence surrounded them as Rebekah sank into the memory.
Finally, she sighed, shook herself from it.

"They weren't found for a day. It broke that man's heart.
He'd helped so many, but he couldn't help Mary and little
Hannah. Samuel wasn't the same afterward. It was as if he
became frozen."

"I remember a little of it, a bit of the funeral."

"You children were very young. The community turned out
for them, but I doubt Samuel noticed. His grief was a heavy
burden, still is, I imagine. After the accident, being around
other families became a difficult thing for Samuel. I think it
reminded him of all he'd lost."

"Is that the reason he's sometimes so angry?"

"I don't know if *anger* is the correct word. You know our
ways, Annie. After watching you these two weeks, I believe
you've accepted them."

Annie began to interrupt her, but Rebekah held up a hand
to silence her.

"I do believe you've put your *rumschpringe* behind you and
fully embraced our faith."

"*Mamm*, I'm joining the church tomorrow morning."

"True. But occasionally sons and daughters will do so to please their parents. With you, I believe it's more. With you, I believe it's a true reflection of your heart."

This time Annie didn't interrupt, merely nodded and watched her mother intently, waiting.

"So I think you understand that we believe in giving ourselves up to what happens in life, to what God allows to happen."

"*Ya.* It's not always easy, like *dat's* accident."

"Or seeing small children fall ill, like the ones you worked with when you stayed in the city."

Now Annie couldn't speak, had to swallow past the lump in her throat as she thought of sweet Kiptyn. He was still receiving the new medication, still improving, but every day was a miracle.

"I know Samuel well," Rebekah continued. "He was able to accept what happened to Mary and Hannah, but over the years it seems he's simply forgotten how to act around others. He tended to his farm and cared for the medical needs of others, and somehow life slipped past him. Make no mistake, Annie—Samuel's a lonely man. But he's like a cat who wants to be petted, then when you do, he swipes at your hand."

Annie smiled at the image.

A cat described Samuel perfectly, and she had the scratch marks to prove it.

"It all happened so long ago, though. I don't mean to sound disrespectful, but what does it have to do with me?" She sighed, stood, and walked to the porch railing. "I don't know how to act around him."

The low-lying clouds had begun to drop their burden of snow in giant fluffy flakes, though they melted when they hit the still-warm ground.

"Maybe it doesn't matter," Annie continued. "It's not as if we need to see each other very often."

"You're the only two people within our community of Amish folk with any medical training. I'd say that alone is enough reason for you to learn to tolerate one another." Rebekah joined her at the railing, rubbed her back in small circles, then kissed her on the cheek. "And there is His admonition to do unto others as you'd wish—"

"I know the Scripture, *Mamm*."

"I expect you do. Most of us know it. The knowing is easy. It's the doing that gives us trouble."

10

Samuel had seen the process a hundred times—probably more.

Water ladled from a bucket, poured out into Bishop Levi's hands.

The bishop sprinkling the petitioner once, twice, three times.

It was the holiest of occasions.

Annie sat there with one hand covering her face—indicating her submission and humility to the church—the other hand calmly holding a handkerchief in her lap.

The bishop spoke openly of Annie's time with the *Englisch*, of her pursuit of additional education, of her nursing degree. Since she hadn't been a member of the church at the time, he was not requiring a confession from her, but he encouraged the members to pray for her—that she would find humility, find a way to use what she had learned during her time of *rumschpringe*, and find her place among the community.

Samuel thought of the young lady who had stood up to his rudeness out on the front porch, the young woman who had met his gaze across the café table, and he felt a lump rise in his throat. This was like watching the birth of something special, which indeed it was.

He committed himself to praying for her, as even now they all prayed for her.

Sitting straighter on the backless wooden bench, he focused on the final hour of instruction and hymns, and wondered if he should have a talk with Jacob about young David Hostetler. Samuel's skin prickled at the thought of the boy courting Annie, not that it was any of his business. Still, her *dat* should know it could be happening in the near future, especially given the circumstances of David's working on the farm every day.

Wasn't it his place as a family friend to at least broach the subject?

Certainly David was a fine young man, though awfully young now that Samuel thought of it.

He brought his mind back to the sermon and pushed thoughts of Annie away. He'd talk to Jacob later. It would be the neighborly thing to do.

∾

After the baptism, Annie returned to her seat with her *schweschders* and *mamm*.

The entire baptism process had brought to mind one of her earliest memories, being wrapped in one of her *grossmammi's* quilts and carried out to the buggy for the trip home. Her grandparents had lived only a little way down the road and the ride had been short, but the evening had been a very cold one. She'd awaken, seen the familiar stitching of the quilt, and felt warm and safe.

God's mercy, Bishop Levi's words, the water cascading down her face, and the murmured prayers of her family and friends had held the same warmth as that old quilt.

Now the room quieted, and the bishop stood once again.

As it did, a peacefulness filled Annie's soul.

She had missed her family when she was away in Philadelphia, missed the beauty and quietness of the farm.

But her heart and soul had ached for these simple Sunday services.

Of course, she had attended church while staying with her *aenti*, and even found a place to worship close to the hospital where she worked. But she'd never come to feel at home there like she did here among people she'd grown up with.

She joined in singing with the others. Her mother, Reba, and Charity sat so near she could smell the light scent of soap they'd used earlier that morning. Sunshine poured in, warm, yellow, and comforting, like a shawl upon her shoulders.

Annie reached up to swipe at the tears stinging her eyes.

She truly was grateful to be back where she belonged.

And this *was* where she belonged.

There were no doubts in her heart or her mind about that—Mifflin County was home.

As she focused on Bishop Levi's words reminding them of *gelassenheit*, Annie felt as if God had prepared this message especially for her. No doubt she had heard the lesson many times as a child—a call to calmness, composure, and placidity.

But never before had she realized how much she needed His calmness in her life. She wanted His quiet spirit to fill her heart. And yes, she knew God's serenity would be the only thing that would bring her joy—not the things she could or couldn't accomplish on her own.

Peacefulness was not something that came naturally to her; perhaps it never would. But she knew, in that moment—surrounded by the community God had blessed her with, the family He had provided—that peace was something He meant her to have.

Regardless what lay ahead, for these few moments, that knowledge was enough.

⁓ℯ𝒬ℯ⁓

Temperatures plummeted, and the snow continued to fall throughout the afternoon and all through the night. The cold front settled around them.

When Samuel woke on Monday, it was to a winter wonderland.

After so many winters and so many Christmas seasons, he should have been accustomed to the sight, but a part of his mind insisted on calling up the memories of Mary and Hannah, how they had looked that last day, the touch of her hand on his face. He remembered and ached still for what he had lost.

But a tiny part of him, a part he had kept buried and hidden for a very long time, considered taking a sled out and inviting a certain young lady for a ride.

He didn't, of course.

He had animals to tend and a barn to close up tight. Between chores and staying warm, he was exhausted by day's end, which was when the buggy arrived from Faith and Aaron Blauch's place.

Aaron's brother Micah banged on his door. A young man of nearly sixteen, he was all hands and feet, awkward even as he waited on the porch.

"Come in, Micah. You must be near frozen."

"True, I am, but there's no time. Faith has the pain down low, and Aaron told me to fetch you now."

Samuel wiped his hands on the dishtowel he'd been using and motioned the young man inside. "I've been by a few times to see Faith, but she's a bit early. Are you sure it's real labor?"

"*Ya.* She says the pains are real."

"All right. My understanding was that Belinda, the midwife from Pine Grove Mills, would be assisting with the birth."

"I tried calling from the phone shack, but I couldn't reach Belinda. Finally called her neighbors—the Smiths. They said she'd been gone for hours. Turns out she's on the road in that little car of hers, and the road is closed in several places because of the snow."

"Is she coming?"

"No. She did call me back, but only to say she's gone to the far side of the district on an emergency birthing. Told me to come and ask you."

A sort of you're-our-last-resort tone crept into Micah's voice. "Faith won't go to the hospital—she's determined to have the babe at home. I'm not sure how we'd move her there at this point anyway. The roads are fairly impassable and snowplows won't be out before morning. Aaron said to ride out, plead with you to come."

"All right. Of course I'll come. Do you know how far apart her pains were?"

"Couple an hour."

"*Gut.* We have time. I'll follow you in my buggy, but I need to put a few extra things in my bag first."

Samuel went to his supply room, grabbed the medical bag he kept ready, and the emergency labor supplies stacked on a shelf to the left of the door. Putting it all together, he shrugged into his coat, made sure he banked the fire in his stove, then went out to his barn to hitch up his buggy.

Night had fallen, but the snow hadn't let up any.

The drifts looked to be at least four to five feet high, and his mind insisted on returning to that other night. He forced his attention back, though, watched Micah's buggy, thought of the woman waiting and the *boppli* about to be born.

Perhaps God didn't intend to bless him with a *fraa* or *kinner* of his own, but he could at least be a part in helping others. As he pulled the blanket and his coat more tightly about him, he told himself ushering life into the world would have to be enough.

It seemed ironic, even to Samuel, that the last farm they passed on the way to Aaron and Faith's was the Weavers'.

He thought of Annie and was grateful she was tucked safely inside, surrounded by her family, protected from the harshness of the storm.

❧

Aaron Blauch's place was another twenty minutes past the Weavers'. He had built his home a few hundred yards back and behind his parents' smaller log cabin. The older Blauchs had passed a few years ago. Samuel remembered attending both their funerals, but the house still stood—a sturdy presence against the winter blizzard.

Both places were tucked against a hillside, quite off the county road. Both families were staunch Old Order Amish. They preferred the remote location and rarely came into town. The Blauchs enjoyed their solitude.

The younger Blauchs took care of what trading needed to be done, but they'd inherited much of the older Blauchs' attitudes. Samuel knew Faith was determined to have her child at home.

Given the weather's worsening condition, he'd have a hard time moving her to the *Englisch* hospital anyway. Unlike some of their congregation, Aaron had never petitioned the bishop for a phone in the barn—though he might have for his work or because of his remote location. Calling a driver in this weather would be difficult. In fact, there were no neighbors closer than the Weavers to run to for assistance.

⁂

Pulling up to the front of the house, Samuel gathered his supplies from the seat, handed his reins to young Micah who had already tied his horse's lead rope to the post, and strode up the front steps.

On entering the house, the first sound to greet him wasn't the occasional cries of a first-time mother in labor. Instead, he could make out small, incoherent whimpering sounds from the front bedroom.

"Aaron?"

A young man in his mid-twenties stepped out of the room. Worry creased his eyes, and by the looks of his dark beard and hair, he'd spent quite a bit of time tugging on both. His hair cropped out in odd angles.

"She's in here, Samuel. *Danki* for coming."

"Of course. When did the pains start?"

"Two days ago."

Samuel stopped, pulled the man back into the living room. "Did you say two days ago?"

"*Ya.* At first Faith thought it was the backache she gets sometimes, but now we're thinking it was the child." Aaron's eyes darted from Samuel's face to the darkness beyond the windows, then back again. "She's in a bad way. I've stayed by her the entire time, tried to help as best I could."

Samuel strode past him, into the bedroom, alarmed now.

Faith lay there, sweat matting her blonde hair against the pillow. She was a small woman, perhaps five foot four inches, and right now she was all belly. Blue eyes stared up at him, pleading, even as her hands sought to comfort the child fighting for life in her womb.

"How are you, Faith?"

"Not so well. *Danki* for coming." Another spasm hit her, but where she should have cried out with the pain, she only squeezed her eyes shut, curled into a ball on her side, and whimpered like a pup in need of its mother.

Samuel reached for her wrist, noted her pulse, which was weak. He also checked her for fever and was relieved when he found none.

"Have the pains been this intense for two days, Faith?"

"No." She breathed deeply, tried to pull in enough air to answer his question. "The worst started this morning."

Samuel looked to Aaron for confirmation.

"*Ya*, she's right. The first day was just an ache where she'd hold her lower back. She was still up walking around the house, cleaning and preparing for the *boppli*. Then this morning, she hollered out and collapsed in the front room by the rocker. I had to pick her up and carry her—she couldn't walk."

"I need to check you, Faith." Samuel laid out his supplies on the nightstand. "Aaron, I want you to start boiling water—lots of it. And I'll also need more light in here."

"There's another lantern in—"

"Bring it."

Samuel began to gently turn Faith on to her back, when another spasm hit her, this one harder than the last. He could see the muscles across her stomach contract.

She curled again into a fetal position and gasped, and tears streamed down her face.

Samuel placed his hand on her stomach, waited for the muscles to relax. The minute they did, he moved her on to her back, positioned the room's single lamp at the foot of the bed.

"Have you lost the *boppli's* water, Faith?"

"A few hours ago." Her voice was a broken whisper.

She dozed while he did a vaginal exam, confirming what he'd suspected the moment he walked in the room. The infant was in the wrong position. She wouldn't be pushing him out unless Samuel could turn him a bit, or convince her to go to the *Englisch* hospital for a Caesarean birth.

Aaron walked back into the room with an additional lamp as Samuel re-covered Faith with the quilts.

Samuel kept his voice low, not wanting to wake Faith. She'd need every ounce of strength she could find for the next few hours. Even these small naps between contractions were her body's way of preparing her for what needed to be done.

"I'll be honest with you, Aaron. The baby is positioned wrong."

"That's why she's having so much trouble?"

"*Ya.*"

"Then we should pray."

"Praying would be a *gut* thing; so would taking her to a hospital."

"No. Faith wants to have the baby here."

"I know she does." Samuel stepped closer, fighting to keep his voice even and patient. "She might not make it, Aaron. You might lose Faith and the baby. She's weak, and the baby can't come this way."

Aaron put both hands into his hair, tugged, then turned and walked to the wall. Placing his palms against it, he stood there a moment, head bowed. Finally he pivoted, looked Samuel in the eye.

"There's no easy way to the *Englisch* hospital, even if she'd agree to go. Roads are all snowed under, and besides she can't ride in a buggy this way. No phones—you know I don't abide phones here. What else can we do?"

Samuel looked at the exhausted woman on the bed, woman and child.

Why this night?

Why during the worst storm of the year, one so like the other?

He would not lose another woman and child to a snowy, winter night.

"She's a few weeks early, so I believe the baby is small. If I can turn the baby even a little, there's no reason it can't be born posterior first." As he spoke, resolve steeled his voice like a pond freezing over. "But I'm going to need a few things."

"Anything. Tell me what it is, and we'll get it for you."

"More hot water, towels, one more lantern—"

Aaron must have thought he was done, because he was already walking out of the room, when Samuel realized what would help him more than anything else, what could make this interminable night bearable—and she was less than twenty minutes away.

A nurse.

"Before you bring any of those other things, help Micah hitch up the buggy again. Send him to fetch me Annie Weaver." He walked across the room, grasped the young man by the shoulders. "Tell her there's no time for Adam to hitch up his buggy. She needs to come with Micah. She needs to hurry."

⌖

Annie had just fallen into a deep sleep.

She began to dream immediately—one of those dreams that made no sense but was filled with images. Warm sunny days, her *dat's* fields, sheep all around her, pressing up against her legs. She bent down to touch one and instead was grasping spring flowers.

A knocking echoed through the air, and that made her laugh.

How could there be a knocking sound in the middle of a field? She looked around for the woodpecker but saw no large trees.

Then she was tumbling, tumbling down a big hill, and she was a child again. Charity and Reba were beside her—and they all squealed as they rolled down the meadow. She could smell the fresh grass, feel the warm wind brush her face.

It practically called her name.

"Annie, you need to wake up. Annie. Can you hear me?"

Blinking, she looked into her mother's eyes.

Spring vanished as lantern light threw shadows across the bedroom floor.

"What is it? *Was iss letz?* Is it *Dat?*" She struggled to sit up, throwing off the comforters and reaching for her robe.

"Your father's fine. Samuel has sent for you."

Annie froze, one arm in her robe, one arm out.

"Samuel?" She peeked out the window, saw darkness, and plopped back down on the bed. Perhaps she was still dreaming.

"It's Faith Blauch—she's having her baby, and it's not going well."

Annie stood and began throwing on clothes as her mother explained the small amount Micah had been able to share. Within moments, she was dressed, down the stairs, and pulling together her own supplies.

"Don't you think Samuel will have all he needs?"

"I don't know, *Mamm*, but there'll be no second chance to come back for more." Closing the quilted bag, she gave her mother a quick hug, then stepped out into the night and into Micah's buggy.

They practically flew across the snow, and it was as if she hadn't awakened, as if she were once again tumbling down the hill in her dreams.

Except the warmth of spring—the wildflowers and laughter—all of that was gone. In its place, winter's cold gripped them. Instead of being a *kind* playing a child's game, she was a woman, doing what God had equipped her to do.

She prayed it would be enough.

She prayed for Samuel as he ministered to Faith even now.

And prayed for an infant, struggling to be born.

11

Micah hurried to the barn to bed the horse, and Annie flew up the steps of Aaron and Faith's home.

The living room was deserted, but the bedroom door stood open. She heard voices coming from that direction, followed by a low whimpering sound.

Annie strode in, pulling off her coat and scarf as she did.

Aaron Blauch looked nearly as exhausted as his *fraa*— nearly, but not quite.

Faith lay spent in the old, oak bed. She didn't open her eyes as Annie entered the room.

"Annie, *danki* for coming." Samuel exchanged a quick look with her—a look conveying more than a thousand words could have. Faith and the baby were in danger.

"Of course, Samuel. Aaron, would you like to take a break for a minute?"

Aaron had been so attentive to his *fraa*, he seemed confused to glance up and find Annie in his room. She touched his shoulder, nudged him gently from the bed.

"I'm here now, Aaron. Maybe you could go and make us some hot tea."

"*Ya*. I suppose I could if you're sure you don't need me here."

"Micah's putting the horse in the barn. You might check on him as well."

"Should I . . . what I mean is, would it be all right for me to leave for that long?" His voice sounded like a broken and wounded thing. Annie wondered how long they had been at this, what it had taken for the man to sit here and watch his wife suffer so, see his child fight to be born.

"It will take Annie and me a few minutes to ready things, Aaron." Samuel turned him toward the bedroom door, coaxed him into leaving the room. "Go to the barn and check on Micah. We need him in here boiling water, sterilizing instruments. And Annie's right—strong tea would be *wunderbaar* as well."

Aaron nodded, looked back once at his wife, then left the room. Annie waited until she heard the front door shut before she began asking questions.

"What's her status?"

"Blood pressure is low, pulse weak. She's been in labor at least forty-eight hours. Water broke early in the evening."

Annie bathed the young woman's face while Samuel spoke. Though Faith murmured softly, she didn't wake until the next pain claimed her—then she moaned and curled onto her side.

"Pains are approximately three minutes apart." Samuel knelt beside the bed. "Faith, don't push. Can you hear me? I don't want you to push the baby. Open your eyes and look at me."

Annie pulled Faith's hair back from her face, rubbed the lower part of her back where her muscles had grown rigid.

"Breathe out like I showed you. Remember? One, two, three, four . . ." Samuel counted, and Annie rubbed until the spasm passed.

Though tears were tracking down her cheeks, Faith immediately fell into a light sleep once it was over.

"Did your training include an ob/gyn rotation?" Samuel rose from the bedside, walked over to the dresser.

"*Ya.*"

"Faith's baby is breech."

"What type of breech?"

Samuel had been laying out his supplies, but he jerked his head up at her question, his eyes met hers, and something passed between them.

From the look in his eyes, it seemed to Annie as if for the first time he realized she wasn't a young girl but a registered nurse. Surely he knew that, since he had sent for her, but her question seemed to catch him by surprise nonetheless.

"Frank breech."

"If you use forceps—"

"I'd rather use my hands. I'm not as comfortable with the forceps."

"There's no chance of moving her to a hospital?"

"I tried earlier—between the weather and the closeness of her pains, I think we should do this now."

Annie nodded, began looking through the stacks of sheets Faith had piled neatly in the corner. Picking the oldest, she tore some in strips, tied them around the top corner posts of the bed, and went in search of extra pillows to put at the bottom.

By the time they had the bedroom ready, Aaron and Micah were back.

Annie heard Samuel explaining to both men what was about to happen. When Aaron walked back into the room, he looked better for having had a few minutes away—afraid though, still very afraid. Annie stepped over to him and put both hands on his shoulders.

"Aaron, we are all going to help your *fraa*."

"It's been a long night."

"*Ya.* I'm sure it has and waiting is hard, but now things are about to move very quickly. I need to go and help Samuel scrub up. I want you to stay beside Faith until I come back. Do not let her push. Remind her to breathe like Samuel showed her."

She waited until Aaron nodded his understanding, then she rushed to the kitchen. Micah stood beside the stove, a large wooden spoon in his hand, and all the burners covered with pots. He looked for all the world like a master chef. Too bad water was the sole item on his menu.

Annie was a little embarrassed to realize she was hungry.

Patting him on the shoulder as she walked past, she murmured, "Warms towels too, Micah. We'll want to wrap the *boppli* right away."

She moved next to Samuel.

Some of the tiredness had left his eyes, and he actually smiled as he rolled up his sleeves past his elbows. Bottles of disinfectant sat beside the sink, along with two brushes and a bottle of soap. He'd laid out a surgical gown and mask.

They both realized in addition to helping Faith's *boppli* into the world, her next biggest risk would be infection.

Infections were rare with home births, but Faith would be tearing, and they'd have to take extra precautions.

"Room enough for two at this sink?" Annie asked.

"Actually, there is."

She stood beside him, scrubbed while he scrubbed, shoulder-to-shoulder, sort of. A full foot and a half shorter, her shoulder didn't actually reach his.

Then she helped drape him, standing on tiptoe to tie the scrubs at his neck. When she pulled the mask up and over his mouth, his eyes twinkled back at her.

"Little Annie Weaver—all grown up."

"Surely you are not teasing me about my height, Samuel Yoder."

"I wouldn't even think about teasing you." Holding his hands up and away, he turned and walked back into the bedroom.

She followed him, reminded Micah, "Keep an ear out for us, Micah, and keep the water boiling nice and hot."

He nodded and looked a tad less frightened as he turned back to the stove.

Hopefully their bantering had eased some of his tension. It had certainly eased hers. Samuel would do his best, and that was all anyone would expect from him. As she stepped back into the bedroom, she prayed it would be enough.

Aaron knelt beside Faith, counting.

Faith's eyes were wide open now, reminding Annie for all the world of a frightened deer.

When the contraction had passed, Aaron wiped the sweat from his face. "That one was worse. It was longer than the others."

"*Ach!*" Faith cried out instantly.

"All right, Faith. Listen to me." Samuel continued to hold his hands up, but stood near her. "The pains are closer now, because your *boppli* is ready. Annie and Aaron and I are going to help you, but it will be hard work. You need to concentrate on exactly what I say. Can you do that?"

Faith nodded, clenching her teeth together as tears streamed down her face. This time when the contraction passed, she panted instead of falling asleep.

"Quickly, Aaron." Annie showed him how to position himself behind his wife. "I want Faith to be able to push back against you."

"Faith, hold on to these straps, honey." Gently guiding her hands to the loops of sheet she'd tied to the headboard, Annie let her fingers linger on the woman's wrist, noted her pulse was stronger than when she'd first arrived.

"We're at ten centimeters," Samuel confirmed.

"Here comes another . . ." Faith gasped as the pain rippled through her.

"Last one to breathe through." Samuel positioned himself near the foot of the bed while Annie placed Faith's feet against the pillows she'd stacked there. "When this one eases, I'm going to turn your baby a little, Faith."

Annie peeked out into the living room. "Be ready with those warm towels, Micah."

Moving to the bed, she placed her hands on top of Faith's stomach.

"Eight, nine, ten . . ." Aaron's voice in his wife's ear was as soft as a prayer.

"Her contraction's easing, Samuel." Annie kept her hands on top of Faith's stomach.

"All right," Samuel sounded as calm as if he were considering what to plant in his field next spring. "Pant, Faith. I need one more minute."

"Another contraction should start . . . now."

"Push, Faith. Push into your bottom." Samuel stood up, his right hand completely inside Faith, guiding her baby, his left now on top of her knee.

In that moment it was as if Faith let out all the energy she'd been conserving for two days, or possibly for nine months. In that moment Faith somehow knew her child's life depended on what she was able to do.

"Excellent. Very *gut*." Samuel's voice was smooth, soft, filled with wonder. "We have a baby boy. One more push, Faith."

Annie looked down, saw the *boppli's* bottom, then his body, his hands raised up and cradling his beautiful face, and a mass of wet hair.

Hurrying to the door, she grabbed a warm towel from Micah's outstretched arms, then placed it under the baby at the same second Samuel lifted him clear. Annie used the DeLee's suction to clean out his air passage, and his first joyful cry pierced the room. Samuel lifted him high so Aaron and Faith could see their son.

Faith began crying, and Aaron dropped his head to her face, kissing her and speaking to her softly.

At the same moment that Annie placed the baby on Faith's stomach, Samuel reached forward and clamped the cord.

Holding the scissors up, he asked, "Who wants to do the honors?"

Silence filled the room, then Faith nodded and Aaron smiled. "We'd like Annie to do it."

Even as she accepted the tool from Samuel and looked into his dark eyes, she knew it was a moment she would never forget.

The first time she'd severed the sacred bond between a mother and child.

She cut the umbilical cord and glanced again at Samuel, a smile spreading across her face.

Something passed between them then, a current of life as their hands rested on Faith's newborn child. For a moment all that existed was the two of them and this precious miracle.

Samuel blinked, turned back to the new mother and father.

"A few more pushes, Faith. Then Miss Annie will have your little *boppli* all cleaned up and ready for you to hold."

Annie took the babe over to her makeshift newborn center, while Samuel helped Faith deliver the placenta.

She administered the drops to his eyes and performed the apgar test—another first for her, at least in a home setting.

Young Blauch scored a solid seven—a *gut* score, especially given his difficult entry into the world.

When Samuel glanced her way, she held up seven fingers and though he still wore his mask, she saw the smile by the way his eyes brightened.

Did she know him so well now?

Before she could dwell on that question, baby Blauch began crying in earnest.

"Micah, I'll be needing more warm blankets now."

Micah, apparently too timid to enter at the baby's first cries, now thrust his hands inside the door, loaded down with small, neatly folded blankets that had been tucked inside bigger blankets and heated in the stove.

Annie cradled the baby in her arms, carried him to the doorway, and let Micah have a peek.

"You're an *onkel*."

"What?" Though he was a grown man, his voice echoed off the walls like a young boy waking to his first snowfall. "Is it, I mean is he a he or a she?"

Annie laughed, accepted the pile of blankets. "Young Mr. Blauch would be a he, and I'm sure Faith would be *froh* for you to come in as soon as she is cleaned up." Shooing him back out, she added, "A cup of weak tea might be *gut* for the new *mamm* in a.few minutes."

She snuggly swaddled the *boppli,* then carried him over to Faith and Aaron.

Samuel had finished sewing up the tears in Faith's perineum and was making notations in his patient logbook.

One part of her was aware that he stopped and watched as she approached the bed with the baby.

"Mr. and Mrs. Blauch, I have a little miracle here who would sorely like to meet his *mamm* and *dat*."

Faith reached out, accepted the baby as she would a price-less treasure—which he surely was. Aaron's eyes remained fixed on his *boppli*, but Faith kissed the infant once, then looked up at Annie.

"He's all right, isn't he? It seemed to take such a long time."

"*Ya*, he's perfect. As Samuel explained, your baby insisted on coming out bottom first, but he's fine. You'll notice some light bruising on his hips I suspect, but it's nothing serious."

"All his fingers and toes?" Tears started down the young woman's face as her baby started rooting for her breast.

"Ten of each. You can check if you like."

Faith shook her head, swiped at the tears.

"You'll need to show him how to nurse at first." Annie moved to her side, showed her how to guide the baby toward her breast.

The next hour passed without Annie being aware of it. By the time she looked through the bedroom door, the sky was beginning to lighten.

She fussed over Faith, straightened the room, made sure anything the baby might need was close at hand.

An hour after that, Samuel insisted she take a break.

She had just made arrangements to stay at the Blauch home for at least a day so she could help Faith.

Faith's sister was due to arrive from the next district, but with the snowstorm and the baby's early delivery, it might take her a little while to get there.

A sudden knock at the front door stopped their conversation mid-sentence.

Standing on the porch, clutching a small overnight bag, were Faith's sister and brother-in-law. They'd heard from the midwife's neighbor that Faith was in labor. By the time they'd received the message and driven through the snow, daybreak had come—but they had arrived. And they planned on staying to help with their new nephew.

"Annie, Faith would like to speak with you." Samuel touched her arm as she was bundling into her coat and scarf.

"Sure thing." As Annie slipped back into the bedroom, she marveled at the completely different scene from when she'd arrived.

Faith's hair was combed and she wore a fresh prayer *kapp* and clean bedclothes. She now lay propped against a bed with unsullied linens, obviously exhausted, but with a smile playing across her face.

The first rays of morning sunlight peeked through the curtains, which were partially open. A blue sky sparkled outside the window.

"How are you doing?" Annie asked.

"We're fine. I wanted to say *danki*."

"You don't have to thank me, Faith."

"I know I don't, but it meant a lot to me, having you here. I was terribly frightened last night, Annie." Faith gazed down at the child sleeping beside her, bundled anew, fist resting near his mouth.

Annie realized Faith's next words were something rarely shared between women. She'd worked with enough mothers to know that it was natural to ignore such fears, to turn away from them and not acknowledge how close death had come.

Faith spoke softly at first, but she gained strength as her words expressed and healed what was in her heart. "Trying to have him here might have been a mistake. And not sending for help sooner, well, I know now that that was certainly a mistake. I don't know, Annie. Perhaps living out here so remotely—perhaps that decision in itself is a mistake."

Faith reached out, traced a finger down the face of her son. "But at three this morning, it was too late to right any of those errors, *ya*?"

Annie squeezed her hand.

"When Samuel came, I was in and out with the pains. I could tell he was concerned. I knew he'd do his best, but I realized something wasn't right. A woman knows when a man is holding something back. I could see by the look in his eyes he wasn't telling me what worried him."

"It was a complicated birth, Faith."

"I'm not blaming, Samuel. Not at all. I'm trying to say, I could tell a difference the minute you walked in. He needed you, Annie, and so did I. So I suppose I'm saying that I'm thankful the Lord sent you."

Annie tried to speak, but her throat was suddenly clogged— stuffed with the answers to her doubts if not her questions. Words couldn't make their way past. So instead she reached forward and hugged her new friend, gently touched her babe.

Then she turned and walked out into the fresh December morning.

12

Samuel expected Annie to be tired. He expected her to sleep a little on the buggy ride back to Jacob's place.

But then Annie Weaver rarely did what he expected.

The first few miles they rode in comfortable silence.

"What are you thinking about?" he asked.

She snuggled into the blankets. "How Faith's baby reminds me of the Christmas child, and how that reminds me of the cross. I believe the bishop mentioned the connection between the two, but I don't think I really understood it fully until just this morning. Life—birth, death, our heavenly resurrection—it's all a marvelous circle, isn't it?"

"I suppose it is." He glanced at her, surprised at the path her thoughts had taken.

They passed a small herd of deer foraging in the early morning light, and she drew in a small gasp, reached out, and clasped his arm, turning to him with the smile he was learning to like . . . learning to need.

He shook his head and clucked to the horse, "Get on, Smokey."

"Why did you shake your head?" Her voice was teasing.

She snuggled down into the blankets and seemed to study him as he attempted to focus on the horse and the snow-covered road. Drifts lined it on each side, but the morning light revealed that the snowstorm hadn't been as bad as he'd feared.

Much of last night had not been as bad as he'd feared.

"Did I shake my head?"

"You know you did."

"It's just that you seemed so surprised by the deer." He glanced her way, then quickly back to the road. "It's interesting how you take such joy from the sight—like a child would."

Instead of becoming prickly, she laughed into the blankets. "I feel like a child sometimes, as if everything here is new to me again. There weren't a lot of deer on the streets of Philadelphia."

"I suppose there are advantages to going away for a time," he admitted. "Certainly on returning it would cause you to appreciate your home."

He began to squirm when her stare became over-long. "Do I have some snow on my face?"

"No, but I believe the long hours may have altered your personality. You're actually being kind. Where is the other Samuel Yoder, the one who growls and snaps like a bear?"

Samuel laughed—the sound round and full and foreign even to him. "Now, Annie. I haven't been as bad as you describe."

"I suppose not. You weren't a bear last night." Her voice grew soft, thoughtful. "Without you, Faith's baby wouldn't have survived."

Samuel didn't respond, but the compliment passed over him like a welcome breeze on a hot summer day.

"I'm not merely saying words, Samuel. People in our community very much depend on you. Perhaps you've done this so long that you've forgotten, but they do."

Samuel allowed the horse to slow, then stop to rest as they gained the top of the hill. The sun was risen fully now, and he wanted to enjoy the sight of undisturbed snow stretching for miles in front of him.

The Weaver place lay directly in front of them—a tidy frame house rising up out of the snow's whiteness, barns painted red, large shade trees that had been planted long ago surrounding the buildings and marking the lane.

From where they sat, the home looked like the center of a wheel. Spreading out in every direction were fields, like spokes, growing wider as they moved away from the house—all well-tended and cared-for, ready to receive the spring planting.

One farm, surrounded by others that stretched off further than he could see—all connected like a patchwork quilt his *mamm* had once made. He hadn't thought of the old quilt in quite some time, but he supposed it was still in the house somewhere.

"Did you hear me, Samuel?"

"*Ya*, I heard you. And I appreciate what you're saying." He clucked to the horse, though he allowed her a slow pace. "I suppose you're right. To tell you the truth, I don't think about it much. I've been farming and tending to our people for ten years now, Annie."

He turned, looked her in the eyes, and fell a little deeper into the warmth of her honey-brown gaze. "I was younger than you are now when I started."

She nodded, but didn't interrupt him.

"I learned as I did my apprenticeship. Slowly, doctoring became a part of who I am, so as I don't think about it anymore."

A small flock of birds flew out in front of their buggy.

"I'm glad things turned out well for young Aaron and Faith and their *boppli*, but it doesn't always." He cleared his throat, pushed on. "That's the hard truth of trying to give medical assistance to our people."

Annie looked down then, traced a pattern on the hem of the rough blanket covering her lap. "Even with our medicine at Mercy Hospital, it didn't always turn out well. There were children who didn't make it, despite our best efforts."

"We can't always understand the Lord's will."

He pulled the horse into her father's lane. "Have you thought about focusing your skills to midwifery?"

Annie jerked her head up. "Belinda takes care of our district's midwifing needs."

"As you saw last night, it's a big district. She can't always be where folks need her. She's mentioned to me before that she'd like an apprentice." Samuel pulled the horse to a stop, set the brake on the buggy, then walked around to her side.

He opened her door of the buggy, but paused—studied her a moment. "Think about it. You did a fine job, and we could use your skills with the women and *bopplin*."

Then he reached up and helped her out of the buggy.

It was the first time he'd touched her, other than a casual brush of fingertips. When their hands clasped together, he thought of his mother's quilt again, of how the squares were sewn together and had remained so all these years.

A surge of energy flowed through him, a warmth that came from more than the rays of sunlight splashing across their entwined fingers.

"*Danki*," Annie whispered.

"Annie—"

"There you are." Adam opened the door to the house, bounded down the stairs. "I was about to drive out to the Blauchs' and see if there was anything you needed. How is she? How's the baby?"

Samuel stepped back while Annie updated Adam, and though they both insisted he come inside he politely declined.

As he turned his mare toward home, he looked back once— saw them walking arm and arm up the stairs. Something inside of him ached then, but he was suddenly too tired to examine it.

Breakfast, then some rest.

No doubt he'd be back to his old self afterwards—his old, grumpy-bearish self. He couldn't help smiling at the image as he drove the rig toward home.

～✺～

Annie was surprised when Samuel stopped by to check on her *daed* the next evening. He was carrying this Jacob-is-my-patient excuse much too far.

He found her in the barn, grooming Blaze. They spoke of the weather and the upcoming school Christmas pageant. Samuel mentioned that her *mamm* had convinced him to stay for dinner. The chicken and dumplings would be ready in ten minutes.

Then he admitted that he'd been by the Blauchs to see Faith and the baby.

"They've picked a name." He smiled as he helped her put up the grooming supplies for Blaze.

"Are you going to tell me, or are you going to make me ask?"

"I thought I'd make you ride out there and find out for yourself." He sidestepped her swipe, but barely.

"I've no time to drive out to Faith's this week. It's all I can do to keep my *dat* from breaking his leg again on this snow. If

I were to leave him for a full day, he'd probably be out there digging up the garden with a snow shovel."

Samuel tugged on his beard. "Giving you a bit of trouble, is he?"

"I'll say. David and I have taken every possible project we can find into the house."

"Might be a few things around my place I could use some help with. 'Course I'd have to pay him—"

"Samuel Yoder. My father is not going to accept payment from you." Annie put her hands on her hips and by the time the words popped out of her mouth she not only sounded like her mother, she felt like her too.

The realization had her drowning in a fit of giggles.

Samuel cocked his head and stood staring at her, waiting for an explanation, but she didn't even try. Pushing him out of the barn, into the cold, she closed the barn door.

"It's best you don't know." She hollered as they both ran for the porch.

A light sleet had begun to fall. Eleven days until Christmas and winter was still settling in, so why was she longing for spring?

When they reached the steps to the house, Samuel reached out and steadied her arm. "Careful, Annie. We don't need two Weavers with broken legs."

"All right, all right. I'm fine."

She turned on him as if she were a child on ice skates. "Now tell me the *boppli's* name or you'll have to go home with no warm dinner, Mr. Yoder."

"You would send a poor Amish farmer home hungry?"

"I would." She darted in front of the door, blocking his path.

He rubbed his chin, as if considering which more important, his secret or Rebekah's cooking.

"It's dumplings remember, and I made peach strudel for dessert."

"Well if you made the strudel, I best be telling you, then." He stepped closer, close enough for her to smell the soap he must have used that morning. "Noah. They named him Noah, and they asked me to tell you hello. As soon as the weather clears Faith wants to see you."

"Both are doing well?"

"They are. Her *schweschder* is still there. *Boppli's* nursing well, and Faith is healing fine."

"That's *wunderbaar*, Samuel. I'm very glad to hear it."

"I knew you would be."

They stood in the cold, smiling at each other, and Annie knew they should go on into the house.

"Okay, then. I suppose you've earned your dumplings and your strudel." She turned back toward the door.

"Annie?"

Swiveling, looking up into those eyes she thought of each night before sleep claimed her, Annie felt her breath catch in her throat.

"How would you like to come and help me on Saturday?"

"Help you?"

"It's third Saturday of the month."

"*Ya*."

"That's always my busiest Saturday. Folks come to the barn with whatever ails them. It would help them a lot . . . that is, it would help *me* a lot if you could be there."

Annie thought back to their first discussion, here on this porch, just after she'd arrived home. She'd wanted his approval so badly, wanted him to approve of her nursing.

He'd put his hand on this same door, and lectured her on how little she knew about helping the Amish. He'd dismissed her as a mere girl.

What had changed since then? Was it that she'd earned his trust? More importantly, was she going to let that memory, which still rankled a bit if she allowed her mind to wander to it, was she going to let the rudeness they'd first shown to one another stand in the way of doing what she enjoyed?

And doing it with Samuel.

She looked up into his eyes, even as she heard the door behind them open, heard the laughter of her family and Reba calling them in to dinner.

"Will you come by on Saturday?" he asked again.

"I'd like that very much," she said, then turned and walked into the comfort of her parents' home, knowing he would be following her.

13

Saturday morning dawned crisp, clear, and cold.

Perfect.

For once, Annie had allowed herself to sleep in until near sunrise, since Samuel had said she didn't need to be at the barn until nine. He had to take care of his own chores before opening what folks insisted on calling "Doc Samuel's" side of the barn.

Farmer Samuel to the left.

Doc Samuel to the right.

The jokes were quietly offered up, along with payment and items-given-in-lieu-of-payment left on a table near the door.

Charity had told her all about it when she'd questioned her on Wednesday evening.

"How does it feel, Annie?"

"How does what feel?" Annie tugged at the thread that had knotted on her embroidery and willed the blush away from her cheeks.

Her *mamm* was in the bedroom, settling her *dat* for the evening, and Reba had gone to bed early, suspiciously eager to turn in with one hand held protectively over her apron pocket and the other clutching an empty shoebox she'd found in the bottom of Annie's closet.

Though darkness had settled around the fields over an hour ago, Adam had returned to the barn in order to work on a mysterious gift for his bride.

Which left Charity and Annie alone by the warmth of the stove, sewing last-minute Christmas presents.

"How does it feel to be *in lieb*?"

"Charity Weaver. You cannot be talking about Samuel." Annie pulled harder on the knotted thread, tugged it through the broadcloth linen, and stuck her finger with the needle.

Popping it in her mouth, she glared at her sister.

"Don't glare at me. I wasn't careless with the needle. Is it bleeding?"

"No, it's not bleeding." Annie examined her finger under the light. "But it's sore, and you distracted me. Now tell me about Samuel's clinic."

Charity raised an eyebrow as her needles clicked away on the blue and gray scarf she was knitting for Reba. "In the winter, he takes the large tack room and puts wooden benches inside along one wall. Then he curtains one or more of the stalls for privacy, and that's where he sees people."

"There in the barn?"

"*Ya*. And he always has his sign up. It's only a handwritten sheet of paper, but I've never been there when it wasn't on the wall and on the table where people signed in."

"What does it say?" Annie let her sewing rest in her lap.

Why couldn't she remember any of this?

She'd been to see Samuel herself when she was young— once when her throat had swollen and she couldn't swallow a thing. He'd made her say "Ahh," shined his light down her throat, and sent her right on to Doctor Stoltzfus, who had prescribed antibiotics.

But she remembered nothing about his barn or home. Her visit there must have been when Samuel first began practicing, maybe a year or so before the accident that killed his *fraa* and *boppli*.

Charity dropped her voice an octave, imitating Samuel's tone and serious manner. "This is not a medical facility. Neighbors help neighbors, but I am not authorized to dispense medicine. Please go to the *Englisch* facility if you think you need a licensed medical doctor."

Annie smiled and resumed sewing. "You do a fair imitation."

"*Danki*. In the summer, buggies line the yard and folks sit around under the shade trees, waiting until he calls them in. It's easier on the *kinner* if they can be outside."

"At the *Englisch* hospital where I worked, we had a playroom with toys."

"Do you miss it?"

Continuing with her row of stitches forming a neat hem on Adam and Leah's linens, Annie didn't reply right away.

"I miss the *kinner*," she finally said, her voice low and honest like the cry of a bleating lamb. "But the city was not for me. I couldn't have stayed there much longer. It pulled at me, made me *naerfich* deep inside."

Charity's knitting needles paused. "I didn't think anything ever rattled you. You were always the rock that didn't budge—like *Dat* or Adam."

Annie's laughter bubbled up, causing her to slip a stitch. "I suppose I had you fooled so you'd mind me when you were small."

They both glanced over at Rebekah as she opened her bedroom door. "Is there room by the fire for one more?"

"*Ya*. Especially if you bring the plate of cookies," Charity teased. As Rebekah sidetracked to the kitchen, Charity leaned toward Annie. "Are you positive you're not a little *in lieb* with Samuel? You act like one of Reba's new kittens when he's around. Is that how love feels?"

Annie's heart beat faster and her palms began to sweat so much that she feared she'd stain Adam and Leah's gift.

She stopped to blot her hands against her apron, met Charity's quizzical gaze, but before she could answer her question, before she could deny such an absurd thing, Rebekah had joined them, and they turned the conversation to the Christmas meal, which was exactly a week away.

⚬⚭⚬

But she thought of Charity's comment later that evening as she readied for bed and again the following morning. She did feel like a new kitten when she was around Samuel—clumsy, warm, alive. Was she in love or could she be coming down with the flu?

But she didn't feel sick, she felt excited.

So she enjoyed breakfast, checked the supplies in her quilted bag—even though she knew Samuel would have everything she'd need—and thanked the Lord for sunny weather. Driving the buggy to Samuel's place would be no problem.

Chaos ruled in the house at the moment, but instead of annoying her, the activity energized her even more. Her *dat* stumped around the living room in an attempt to show Rebekah he'd be fine spending the entire day in the barn with Adam.

"I believe my legs are stronger, from having to carry these casts around so long." He limped across the room's entire length again, the longer cast making a hollow thumping sound echoed by the crutches he now used.

"Catch her!" Reba called sharply.

"I am not picking up your rat." Charity pulled on her gloves and walked toward the door. "Mother, tell her she can't ride with us if she insists on carrying rodents in her pockets."

"Come here, Priscilla." Holding a small piece of cracker out to the field mouse—which she had apparently named—Reba coaxed the mouse out from under the stove. "Don't be afraid of Charity—she's all bluster."

Annie wasn't a bit surprised when the creature crawled into her *schweschder's* hand.

Quicker than a raindrop falls to the ground, Reba slipped the mouse into her apron pocket and fastened the button over it against any further escapes. Reba was the only person Annie knew who had sewn button straps over her pockets. With a huge smile on her face, she pulled on her coat and turned to Charity.

"I'm ready."

"Oh no, you're not. I told you before, no mouse is riding with us."

"*Mamm*—" Reba turned toward her mother, a petulant look on her face.

Adam burst through the front door, and all conversation stopped.

"We have a transportation problem."

Everyone froze in the midst of pulling on coats, gloves, and scarves.

"What are you talking about, son? I checked the buggies myself last night." Jacob hobbled over to the door on his crutches.

"Problem isn't the buggies, *Dat*. It's the horse." Adam pulled off his gloves, strode to the table, picked up one of the fresh cinnamon buns, and began eating it. When Annie slapped him gently on the back of the head, he moved out of her reach but continued eating.

"What? These smell heavenly. Can't a man eat?"

"He can after he explains the problem. We're all ready to go our various ways." Her impatience surged through her.

"Your *schweschder's* right. I was headed into town in one buggy with Reba and Charity," Rebekah said. "Annie was taking the other to Samuel's to help him with Saturday patients."

"And I was coming out to the barn to work for the day, alone, with no women-folk around." Jacob scowled and thumped nearer to the table.

"Hold on." Adam set his sweet roll down on the table and brushed his hands off on his pants. "I didn't say anyone had to cancel. I said we had a problem. The older mare has something wrong with her shoe. I noticed her favoring it last night. Now she won't stand on it."

Annie groaned and plopped down on the couch. The older mare was the one horse she trusted herself to drive.

"Still have two buggies," Jacob reasoned. "Charity's harnessed Blaze to the smaller buggy a few times. No reason Annie can't drive her."

All eyes turned to Annie.

"Oh, no. I love your new horse, *Dat*. I brush her nearly every night, but I'll not be driving with her harnessed to the small buggy. I'd end up in the next county by the time she tires."

"I wouldn't mind trying," Rebekah said slowly, "But I'm headed into town—probably not the best destination for her first formal trip."

"Charity can handle her." Adam reached for another cinnamon bun, stepping even farther away from Annie as he did so. "And don't slap me for eating. A man thinks better as he eats."

"'Course I can drive Blaze," Charity declared in her no-nonsense way. "But I was headed into town with *Mamm*."

Annie sailed across the room to her. "You wouldn't mind coming with me, would you, Charity? Just this once. I'm sure we could use an extra hand, and think of the people you'll be helping."

Charity reached into her coat pocket even as she shook her head in exasperation. "Here's my list for the store, *Mamm*. At least I won't be riding with a mouse!" Then she opened the front door and trudged off in the direction of the barn.

Annie glanced from Adam to her father. "Are you sure she can handle Blaze behind the buggy? I don't want to end up in a ditch."

"Your *schweschder* can handle the mare without any problem. She's a strong hand about her when it comes to horses." Jacob chuckled. "The man will be lucky who snatches up Charity."

"Man maybe, animals not so much." Reba scooted out the front door before either parent had a chance to correct her.

Soon they were all climbing into their respective buggies, and Jacob and Adam were waving them off. Annie would have waved back, but her fingers clung to the seat for dear life as Charity gripped the reins and clucked to the horse, and Blaze galloped away.

⁓❧⁓

"I thought you could control her," Annie managed to gasp.

"I am controlling her. We're right side up, aren't we?"

"Barely. Can't you slow her down?"

Charity rolled her eyes and jerked on the horse's reins. When she did, Blaze stopped hard, throwing both girls forward and nearly off their seat.

Annie reached out an arm to break her *schweschder's* fall, much as their *mamm* used to do when they were small. The reaction was so instinctive, and so unnecessary given they were grown women, that it threw them both into a fit of giggles.

Blaze first tossed her head, then proceeded to nudge through the snow looking for something to nibble.

Charity wiped at the tears springing from the corners of her eyes. "Hold these reins, *mamm*," she teased. "I need to have a talk with my horse."

Annie would have refused the reins, but Charity had already tossed them into her hands and climbed out of the buggy without waiting for an answer. Walking in front of the horse, she spoke soft and low, but even from where Annie sat she could hear the authority in her *schweschder's* voice.

It reminded her of what her *dat* had said—Charity was fine with horses. How would it translate to a man? She hadn't stopped to think of her *schweschder* marrying. Charity had always seemed like a little girl to her, but watching her walk back around and step up into the buggy, she realized that was no longer true.

In fact, she was guilty of the very same things she had been angry with Samuel about. She had neglected to notice Charity had grown up, exactly as Samuel had refused to acknowledge that she was no longer a young girl.

Charity clucked to Blaze, who moved out at a much steadier pace.

"How do you like working at the store with *Mamm*?"

"I don't mind it." Charity shrugged, then glanced at Annie curiously as if to determine what lurked behind the line of questioning.

"Which isn't the same as liking what you do every day."

"Didn't say I like it, said I don't mind it." Charity jerked on the reins when Blaze made to break into a faster trot.

"So would you like a different job?"

"No. I suspect any other job would be the same to me."

"I don't understand." Annie cornered herself in the buggy and studied her *schweschder*, now thoroughly curious.

"What's there to understand?" Charity looked at her with such an open expression that Annie immediately thought of her *bruder*. With Adam things were usually quite simple. Perhaps life was the same for Charity.

"What do you like about working in the store?"

"I need to work somewhere, and the store is interesting enough. I enjoy seeing different people every day, and the hours pass quickly."

"All right. And what don't you like about it?"

Charity reached up and adjusted her *kapp*. "I don't especially like being cooped up in one place all day long." She started to say more, but stopped herself, blushed slightly.

"What is it? What were you about to say?"

"You'll say I'm too young."

"Of course I won't. I was just thinking how you're no longer a girl. I hadn't realized how grown you've become."

Charity seemed to consider her confession as she focused on Blaze for a few seconds. "When the girls your age come in to the store, with their little *bopplin* or expecting one soon, then I know what I want to do."

"You mean—"

"*Ya*, that's exactly what I mean. And I know it's different for you. Because you have your nursing you love to do. I want a home of my own, though. It's all I've ever wanted." She settled back against the buggy seat, her voice losing some of its confidence. "I suppose I sound *gegisch*."

"You don't sound *gegisch* at all, Charity. Is there a special boy you have your eye on?"

"No. Of course not. You'd know if I was seeing someone."

"Is there someone you want to be seeing?" Annie tried to think back over the days since she'd been home. Had there been anyone her sister had paid special attention to?

"There isn't, but I have a lot of fun watching you and David."

"Charity Weaver."

"And you and Samuel."

"You're being ridiculous." Annie suddenly needed to push the blanket off her lap as heat flooded her cheeks.

"I don't know if I'm ready yet, but when I watch you, I think I want to be ready." Charity seemed oblivious to how embarrassed Annie had become. "And when I watch Adam and Leah, I know their relationship is the kind I want. I think it's worth waiting for too. Don't you?"

They were nearing Samuel's land, but Charity turned to Annie now, studied her, waited for her reply.

"Ya, I do think it's worth waiting for."

"I see how much Adam and Leah care for one another, see how they're willing to wait until the marrying season, wait until their home is ready and they can be together, and I know I can wait until the right person comes along."

Annie nodded, suddenly humbled by her little sister's wisdom.

Unfortunately, Blaze chose that moment to show off for the other horses. Throwing her head, she sidestepped, then attempted to speed toward Samuel's barn.

Charity took the reins firmly in hand, growled out a command that was incomprehensible to Annie, and saw them safely to the hitching post.

But not before more than a few of the neighbors had turned to stare at the Weaver girls.

14

*T*hough outside, the day remained briskly cold, warmth and people filled the inside of Samuel's barn as sunlight filled the day. In Samuel's work area, his potbellied stove heated what served as the waiting area.

But the activity of the thirty or so people gathered and the sun shining through the loft windows warmed even the stalls where he and Annie saw patients.

And they did see patients.

Working beside Samuel during the day, in the barn, was a completely new experience for Annie.

For one thing they were surrounded by people she'd known all her life.

For another, Charity kept popping in with bizarre questions and a teasing look in her eye.

"Should I separate the patients who are vomiting from the ones who aren't?"

"Are you two willing to look at a sick bird?"

And Annie's favorite, "This young man would like to bring his sheep with him into stall three. Should I allow it?"

The young man she referred to was four years old, and he had no intention of letting go of the sheep he'd turned into a pet—a sheep he referred to as Stank.

Charity was the one to discover that the boy didn't cry a bit as long as his right hand remained buried in Stank's somewhat foul-smelling wool. The boy, Luke, had clean rags completely swathed around his left hand.

"I'm so sorry." The young mother hurried over to where the boy stood with his sheep. She straightened the straw hat on the boy's head, explaining as she did so, "We have a large flock of sheep. For some reason Luke attached himself to this one. Every time I turn around he's out in that old pen with this sheep. I can't seem to keep him away from the animal."

"What's wrong with your hand, Luke?" Samuel knelt down next to Luke, since there would be no picking the animal up and setting him on the bench.

Annie stepped back as she watched Luke tilt his head. With wide, innocent blue eyes he carefully considered Samuel. After giving Stank's wool a final comforting tug, he touched his hurt hand with his well one. "Tripped while I was following my sheep. Bumped it against a nail."

Luke's frown became a smile as he remembered the most important part of his story. "Stank licked it for me, though, and *Mamm* bandaged it up."

The hand was bandaged to twice its normal size, so that it looked as if the boy wore a baseball mitt made of gauze. Annie was relieved to see that Luke could still move his arm well, which meant infection hadn't moved up his arm. He also didn't appear to have any fever.

Samuel's gaze traveled from the boy to the animal then back again. "Stank's a fine pet to take care of you, Luke."

"*Ya.*"

"And your *mamm* was smart to wrap it up."

The boy nodded, threading the fingers of his good hand back through Stank's wool.

"I need to unwrap the bandages, though, to take a look. Miss Annie's going to help me. Is that all right with you and Stank?"

Luke obviously wasn't happy with the arrangement, but his *mamm* cleared her throat, and he nodded his agreement.

Annie had clean bandages and disinfectant at Samuel's side before he had the hand unwrapped. The wound wasn't as bad as she feared, but it was definitely a puncture wound.

"Do you think it was a nail?" Samuel asked his mother.

"Probably. There's quite a bit of old lumber out that way. John has it all stacked and the nails out of it, but he might have missed one."

"You did a fine job cleaning it, Martha." Samuel swiped the wound again with disinfectant as Annie popped a sucker in Luke's mouth. "I'm afraid he is going to need a tetanus shot, though, and I'm not allowed to give those. You need to take him on to see Doc Stoltzfus."

Annie had the hand rebandaged by the time Samuel had written a note to the doctor.

"Give this to him. I don't think they'll need to reclean the wound, but I want Luke to have the tetanus shot today. It's valid for ten years, and I imagine Mr. Luke will be finding more rusty things to trip over by the time he's fourteen."

"*Ya*, I can hardly keep him in the house at all—even in the winter. *Danki*, Samuel. *Danki*, Annie."

"*Gem gschehne*," they both said, then smiled at each other as the words came out in near harmony.

There wasn't much time to dwell on the moment, though.

The morning had barely begun, and already every bench was filled with mothers and children. Men willing to brave the cold stood out in the yard, in the winter sunshine, talking of spring and crops.

It did not remind Annie of emergency room work—there was none of the violence and desperation she'd seen there. Instead, she kept thinking back to the six-week rotation she'd done with a general practitioner. The work had actually fascinated her.

This was very much like that old gentleman's office. As the sun warmed the barn to a comfortable temperature, and the snow on the trees began to melt and drip, they saw all manner of patients.

Old Mrs. Wagler presented with bowel problems. Samuel sat down, listened to her for five minutes, and had her lie on their one makeshift table so he could check her abdomen. After questioning her closely to be sure there'd been no blood in her bowels, he then asked her about her diet. Finally, she admitted that she'd had no green vegetables all winter, since her husband had passed. Her children had long ago moved to Ohio, and she'd put off following them there.

"Each year they visit, and each year they ask me to come, but I like it here, Samuel."

"Mrs. Wagler, I know your neighbors would be *froh* to bring you some of the vegetables they have put up for winter."

"Don't like the way they taste when they're not fresh."

"But your body needs them. I want you to start eating greens once a day, walk out to check on your spring plantings every morning—"

"They won't be up for another four months."

"I know they won't, but I want you to check on them nonetheless. I also want you to take a teaspoonful of this oil. One teaspoon per day."

He helped her off the table, and handed her the bottle of oil and the paper Annie had scribbled on. "Annie's written down everything I said. Follow those instructions, and come see me in two weeks if you're not feeling any better."

It continued in the same vein all morning.

They saw a half dozen people with the flu, all of whom Charity had managed to keep away from other folks who were waiting.

The owner of the livery stable in town had an ingrown nail so infected he could no longer put his shoe on. Samuel cut it out, disinfected it, and bandaged it up.

"Don't wait so long next time, Mark." Samuel shook the man's hand as he limped out toward his buggy.

"*Ya*. I meant to come in, but things have been busy this month."

"They'll be busier if you can't walk. Then you'll have to hire a few boys to do all your work."

Mark pushed his hat onto his head. "Wouldn't think a toe could cause so much trouble," he grumbled.

Annie was setting out clean tools when Samuel tugged on her hand. She looked up, startled at the touch of his fingers against her skin.

"Time for a break, Nurse Annie."

"But we're not done."

"Check the waiting room."

Annie stuck her head out of the stall and saw the area they'd set up with benches was miraculously empty. "Where'd they go? I counted six people waiting a few minutes ago. Lydia was here to have her stitches removed, and little baby Amos has a cold—"

"Stop."

"Stop?"

Samuel put both hands on her shoulders, and she feared she might melt right there—become a puddle in the middle of his barn. Why did his touch have such a strong effect on her? Before she could figure it out, he marched her to the door separating the work area from the larger part of the barn.

"Stop. It's lunchtime. Look," his voice whispered gently in her ear. "Everyone else has figured it out. Everyone but Miss Annie."

She turned then, pivoted in his arms so she could see his expression. "Oh, but we didn't . . . That is, I was so focused on bringing my things, I didn't think to bring—"

"Annie. Over here." Charity's voice broke through the cloud of confusion that had settled around her. Spinning again, she spied her sister sitting with one of the girls who worked with her at the store, on some crates stacked neatly under one of the barn's windows. Between them they'd set out the fixings of a thrown-together lunch.

Though most still wore their coats, sunlight poured down on them. Other families had similarly set up picnic areas.

Annie's stomach growled.

"Sounds like your *schweschder* has it covered." Samuel smiled broadly, angled her in the direction of Charity, then pushed her gently out of the workroom.

He'd had the oddest urge to kiss her on the little button of a nose that she'd turned up to him, which would of course have been entirely inappropriate. He stuck both of his hands in his pockets instead.

He watched her walk out into the larger room, then stepped back into the shadow of the workroom and took a deep breath, forced his heart rate back into a normal rhythm.

Samuel Yoder, confirmed bachelor and cranky old bear, was attracted to Annie Weaver. The truth hit him hard. What had happened?

When had it happened?

How had it happened?

His mind immediately thought of Mary, and he walked back to the examining stall, began tidying it, though everything lay in tip-top shape.

Mary. She would have wanted him to find another, would have expected him to move on with his life. It was the Amish way, what they were taught from a very young age—to give themselves up to whatever happened, accept all things as God's will.

But was what happened that December night God's will?

Or was it merely his mistake?

After eight years he still couldn't say. But even if he had been able to say, the point was an irrelevant one.

He straightened the last of the medical supplies, already in a row, and turned back to the main portion of his barn.

Truthfully, in the last eight years he hadn't been attracted to any other woman, and the letters he'd received from Rachel . . . Well, they had hardly sparked any feelings of attraction. They had inspired only guilt. While he cared for Mary's sister and wished her well, he had certainly never thought of her in any terms other than as a sister. Was that why her recent letters made him uncomfortable?

He could read between the lines to understand her meaning, but it hadn't been something he'd acknowledged, even to himself, until this moment.

Now it seemed as if he had awakened from a very long sleep.

Mary.

Little Annie Weaver.

They had been the only two women who stirred this place in his heart the same way a new dawn over his fields stirred his soul.

Running his fingers through his beard, he walked slowly out into the main portion of his barn. Perhaps some lunch would settle the ideas tumbling through his head.

He certainly needed to think more clearly.

Annie Weaver! She was ten years his junior, and she was his closest friend's daughter.

Blood pumped through his veins, causing him to feel as if he'd just run beside a buggy. Sweat trickled down the back of his neck, warm despite the coolness of the day. Samuel stepped over to the sink and began vigorously washing his hands. Ice-cold water poured into the basin as he scrubbed his hands, then splashed the water on his face.

"You cleaning up or taking a bath?"

Reaching for a hand towel, Samuel stopped at the sound of Bishop Levi's voice, turned, and nearly bumped into the older man.

"Levi, I didn't see you."

"Probably because I just arrived. You also seemed a bit distracted." Levi nodded at the water still pouring into the basin.

Samuel reached forward and turned off the faucet. When he'd finished drying his hands, he hung up the hand towel on a peg next to the sink. "*Ya*, I suppose I was. It's been a busy morning."

"So it seems by the number of buggies in your yard. You have quite a few people here." Levi smiled broadly, then rattled the brown paper bag in his hand. "I brought some lunch if you have time to take a few minutes and eat."

"I was washing up and headed inside to fix a quick meal. Looks like you saved me the trouble. What brings you so far out of town?"

"I needed to visit a few families, and I hoped to stop by and have a word with you. Knew it would be a busy day being third Saturday and all—so lunch would be my best chance."

Samuel led him over to an empty bench. "It's a *gut* plan, but I would have made time to see you without the food."

He accepted the sandwich Levi handed him, bit into the rye bread and pastrami, and closed his eyes as he savored the flavors. The rich meat and fresh bread tasted heavenly. He hadn't realized how much of an appetite he'd worked up.

"We have a situation over at the Smucker home," Levi said.

Samuel took another bite of the sandwich, waited.

"Youngest girl is expecting a child."

The words hung between them, along with all of the questions and complications they brought. Though young single mothers weren't unheard of in Amish communities, they were a rarity.

"Has she said who the father is?"

"Told her *mamm* he was an *Englischer*, someone passing through, and now he's gone."

Reaching for the lemonade Levi had brought, Samuel took a long drink. When he'd had his fill, he looked his bishop in the eye. He knew him to be a kind man, sometimes a strict leader—depending on what the situation demanded, but always compassionate.

"What would you have me do?" Samuel finally asked. "The girl needs prenatal care."

"Her parents would like the situation kept quiet for now."

"Belinda will be discreet."

Levi shook his head. "You know that won't work. Belinda is a fine midwife, but if her car starts going to their house twice a month, everyone will know why."

Samuel stood, suddenly ready to be done with this day's work. "People will know anyway, Levi. When the girl's condition begins to show, and when the child is born."

"*Ya*, and I said as much to the family. The girl, Sharon, is barely sixteen. She isn't a member of the church yet, so there's no need for a confession. I've counseled with her, and I'll continue to do so. But you know her father—"

"Phillip is a *gut* man."

"He is. He's taking this hard, though. We need to give him time."

"So you want me to go by and see her, instead of Belinda?"

"Someone should."

Samuel looked across his barn, over to where Charity and Annie were collecting their things together. One of the teenage boys had joined them and was helping to pack the hamper Charity's friend had brought. As the boy smiled and clowned, Samuel couldn't help feeling something akin to a pain in his stomach.

Annie was closer to the lad's age than his own.

She belonged with a boy her own age.

"So you'll go by and see her?" The bishop pressed.

"I didn't say I would, but I know someone who might be perfect for the job."

Levi followed his gaze. "Annie Weaver?"

"*Ya*. She helped me birth Faith Blauch's child the other night." He hesitated, then pushed on. "I spoke to her about becoming Belinda's apprentice."

Levi tugged on his graying beard, then nodded. "It would be an excellent thing for our district. What did she say?"

"She didn't, but I believe she's considering the idea. Helping Sharon Smucker might move her in that direction. She certainly has the training to handle the prenatal visits, and I'll see to it she has Belinda's contact information in case she has any questions."

"Are you sure Annie will do it?"

Samuel smiled, shook the older man's hand, and walked him outside, toward his buggy.

"There's not a lot I know about Annie Weaver, but I know she has trouble turning away a young one in need. She'll say yes."

The bishop climbed into his buggy, and Samuel made his way back into the barn. He knew the families behind him would begin filing back in toward the waiting room, knew he had another three hours of work ahead, but the idea of Annie by his side made the afternoon's work less bleak.

His earlier thoughts of courting her had been impetuous, of course. He could see that now.

But there was nothing wrong with thinking of her as a colleague—the girl had proven herself to have a calm head on her shoulders and solid training to boot.

Sharon Smucker would be in capable hands.

15

The afternoon passed even more quickly than the morning. Samuel looked up from his notation book, expecting to see another patient, and instead his gaze traveled once, twice, three times across the empty stall.

Where was his next patient?

Wondering what the problem might be, and hearing no one, he went in search of Annie, or Charity, or the next person who had managed to find a new and creative way to blunder into a farming instrument.

The place remained eerily quiet. Perhaps the girls had run into some problem. Maybe someone needed help with a buggy.

Or it could be Annie and Charity had found his new litter of border collie pups. Following the sound of their murmured exclamations, he found them in the back corner of his barn, pouring all their attention on the hounds.

"Are you telling me there are no people who deserve your astute medical skills more than these dogs do?"

"The people have all gone, Samuel. We're a fast team." Annie glanced up and smiled, as a puppy attempted to lick at her chin. "Why didn't you tell me you had pups? They're adorable."

Both girls sat cross-legged in the area he'd partitioned for the mother and six pups. The hound looked relieved to have someone else looking after her brood for a few minutes. She made her way over to the water dish and began to lap at it, then walked to a patch of afternoon sunlight, stretched, circled twice, and curled up in a ball.

The pups were out of the girls' laps in a split-second, falling over each other in their efforts to scamper across the stall and land on top of their mama.

"Imagine what Reba would do if she saw these," Charity said, her voice rising in excitement.

"She'd try to hide one in her pocket no doubt." Annie stood and began brushing straw off her dark blue dress. "How old are they?"

"Are they all spoken for?" Charity asked.

Samuel pulled at his beard, as if he were trying to remember. Both girls put their hands to their hips, and he began to laugh. "All right. As a matter of fact, I believe I might have an extra, if Reba is interested. Speak with her about them, and let me know what you all decide."

Annie and Charity exchanged a knowing look.

"She'll be interested all right," Charity said as she walked out of the stall. "The question is whether *Mamm* will tolerate another four legs around the place or not."

"We won't be asking Reba though. The pup will make an excellent Christmas present." Annie smiled up at him, and Samuel felt another piece of the ice around his heart melt and slide to the ground.

"Better than the scarf I've been knitting her," Charity admitted with a shake of her head.

Annie laughed as they all studied the pups. "She'll appreciate the scarf, but she'll probably use it to wrap up the pup."

"They'll be fine cattle dogs." Samuel ran his fingers through his beard. "I know your father is considering running dairy cows on the southern portion of his land."

"Would be a *gut* spring project for Reba, training one." Annie stooped down and ran her hand over the smallest pup, a black and white mix that had fallen fast asleep while the others nursed.

"I'm not sure Reba needs another project, but perhaps it would help her forget the rodents," Charity conceded. "If we're done here, I'll go and ready Blaze."

"Let me do that, Charity." Samuel moved to stop her.

"Nonsense. I've done nothing the last hour. I need to stretch my legs."

She'd walked out of sight before he could offer a *gut* argument.

"I appreciate you and your *schweschder* coming, Annie. Usually I'm not finished until near dark." Samuel glanced out at the afternoon sun. "I'll be able to put in a few hours of work still."

"Or you could rest." Annie's voice landed somewhere between teasing and scolding. "You do rest, Samuel. Right? You do remember what it means to find other activities to occupy your time?"

"*Ya*, I believe I heard someone speak about it at our last Sunday meeting."

She reached out and pushed at him playfully as she walked past.

He'd noticed that about her lately—the more comfortable she was around a person, the more she showed it with small touches.

Or maybe he was noticing because he'd been alone so long, but since Annie had returned he found himself seeking out her company. Being sociable seemed like a new thing to him, rather like wearing a new shirt. Part of him wanted to settle for what was old and comfortable, but another part couldn't resist her.

When she did a small thing, like touching him as she walked by, it breached his aloneness. It wasn't unpleasant at all, but it was startling.

This time, instead of letting her walk on by, he reached out and touched her arm, pulled her back into the shadow of the barn.

"There's something I'd like to talk to you about, Annie. If you can wait a minute longer."

❧

Annie looked down at Samuel's hand on her arm, heard the note of seriousness in his voice, and wondered what could possibly cause such a look of concern on his face.

The day had gone incredibly well, in her opinion.

Other than one young girl throwing up inside the waiting room, she couldn't think of a single incident that she'd change.

"What is it? *Was iss letz?*" She pulled her *kapp* strings back behind her shoulders and hoped he wasn't about to criticize her nursing. Now why would she worry about such a thing? He hadn't criticized her since she'd first come home. It seemed so long ago now.

"Nothing's wrong. Well, something is, but . . ." He pulled his straw hat off his head, then set it back down more firmly, causing his hair to stick out on the sides. "What I mean is, don't have such a worried look. You've done nothing wrong,

Annie. I was being truthful when I said you were a real help to me today."

He took a deep breath, looked to the pups, then continued. "I'd appreciate it if you'd consider coming back every Saturday when I have the medical side open. If you're not busy, that is. Folks generally come the weekends we don't have church meetings."

"Of course I will. I'd like to very much." A warm flush of embarrassment crept up her face at Samuel's praise. Then she realized he'd again taken off his hat. She moved closer, gazed up into his face, and realized he wasn't finished.

"That wasn't what I wanted to talk to you about, though. Bishop Levi stopped by earlier."

"I saw you eating lunch with him."

"He came to tell me about a special situation. It's a private matter, but a young girl in our district needs tending."

Annie tilted her head, trying to better discern the meaning behind his words. He suddenly looked everywhere but at her—out at his fields, toward Charity and the buggy, even back toward the pups.

"A young girl?"

"*Ya*. Well, I don't know why I feel awkward telling you this. I thought you would be the perfect person to check on her, but it's a confidential matter. That is to say, the family isn't ready to share with the congregation yet—"

Annie reached out and placed her hand on his arm. "Are you trying to say there's a young girl expecting a child?"

"That's exactly what I'm saying."

"And she's not married."

"Correct."

"I see." Annie let her hand slip away as she walked over to the curtained exam area and began gathering her supplies. "Well, of course I'll help, Samuel. But I haven't decided yet on what you asked me regarding the midwife apprenticeship. Belinda will be needing to see the girl."

"*Ya*. I suggested to Bishop Levi that Belinda should see the girl, but he doesn't think it's a *gut* idea. He says Sharon's father isn't ready yet—"

Not realizing how close he was, Annie nearly knocked him over when she turned around quickly. "Sharon Smucker?"

"*Ya*."

"She's only Charity's age."

"I know. Bishop Levi says he's meeting with the family, but they'd like to keep it quiet for a bit longer. I suggested you might be willing to go and do the prenatal visits for a while, in order to give the family a little time to adjust before everyone starts seeing Belinda's car stop at their house."

Annie picked up her quilted bag, walked out into the cold afternoon toward her buggy. She'd crossed half the distance when Samuel caught up with her. She suddenly needed the sun's warmth on her face, needed to be free of others' burdens for a little while.

When he caught up with her she stopped.

She felt him standing beside her, waiting, though they both knew there was nothing to wait for. There was no question as to whether she would help the girl.

"I'll be *froh* to visit Sharon, Samuel. We both realize, however, there's no keeping a baby secret."

He made to interrupt her, but she stopped him. "Babies shouldn't be secret, regardless the circumstances of their birth. I saw enough of such ways while I worked with the *Englischers*."

She looked across the field. In a few months they'd be green with crops, and Sharon's *boppli* would be born. "Not only does Sharon and the *boppli* need the love and support of her *freinden*, but our community needs Sharon and her baby. We're one family here, and it's part of what makes us special. It's part of what sets us apart."

Then she turned and joined Charity in the buggy.

She thought he might follow her, ask her to explain herself, but he didn't. He didn't need to, and they both knew it. In his heart he knew what she said made sense. Perhaps he hadn't had the time to think it through.

ᘓ᠑ᕲ

With all four grown children home, and Annie's *dat* still sporting casts on both legs, it was necessary to take two buggies to Deborah Umble's lunch the next day.

Often they stayed home on Sundays when there was no church meeting, but Deborah had invited them for a special Christmas celebration. Since the following weekend would be busy with church meetings on First Christmas, and family meals and gift-giving the day after, or Second Christmas as they called it, this would be their last chance to celebrate with friends.

Annie rode with Adam and Charity—leaving her mother to make sure Reba had no critters in her pockets. She'd volunteered to ride along and help with her *dat*, but Jacob had scowled and proceeded to lecture her as he clumsily worked his arm through his coat sleeve while leaning on his crutch.

"Won't be needing any help of that sort this morning. Believe I'm about ready to be shy of your professional skills, Annie girl." Then her father had bumped off, leaving her frowning at his back.

Adam pulled her toward his buggy as she started to remind him a second time to be careful. "Say another word, and he'll insist on driving," Adam cautioned.

"Why are men so stubborn?" Annie asked as Charity scooted over to make room for her.

"Don't ask me." Adam shut the buggy's door and walked around to his side. "I wouldn't know, since I'm the flexible, sensitive type of man."

"Those weren't exactly the words Leah used to describe you yesterday when mother ran into her at the store," Charity teased.

"Mother spoke with Leah at the store?" Adam giddy-upped to the mare he had re-shod yesterday.

"*Ya*, and I believe she called you stubborn and bullheaded." Charity elbowed Annie as she recounted the story.

"Leah told you he was stubborn?" Annie gave the question her best I'm-shocked-and-can't-believe-it tone.

Adam gave them both his best you-must-be-kidding stare. When they simply smiled back sweetly, he took the bait.

"And what would my bride-to-be have been referring to when she called me stubborn?"

"I wouldn't know for sure," Charity admitted. "I was at Samuel's all day, but according to *Mamm*, Leah seemed a bit upset."

"Upset?"

"*Ya*. She asked *Mamm* to stay, and they had two cups of tea in the café. Sounds fairly distressed to me."

"Over our *bruder*? Hard to believe; after all, he's flexible and sensitive." Annie coughed into her hand.

"Unlike our father," Charity added.

Adam pulled their buggy in line on the road behind Jacob and Rebekah's buggy. A smile now stretched completely across his face.

"*Mamm* must have been drinking tea with a different Leah King. My girl would never call me stubborn, let alone be frustrated about me enough to talk to her about it through two cups of tea."

"Your girl apparently asked *Mamm* if Annie would stop by this week."

"What?" Adam's voice rose like the gust of winter wind stirring the trees which lined the road. "You're not serious."

"I'm afraid so, dear *bruder*."

"*Mamm* didn't mention it to me, but then I went to bed early last night." Annie tapped Charity on the shoulder and mouthed, "Are you serious?"

Charity nodded yes, then shrugged.

"I stopped by her house last week." Adam scowled at the clouds building on the eastern horizon. "She wasn't upset about anything."

Annie cornered herself into the buggy and studied Adam. She was proud of him in every way. He'd grown into a fine young man. There were moments, though—like this one—when he still reminded her of the little boy but a year ahead of her in school, trying to puzzle out a particularly hard lesson.

"Someone was supposed to take her for a buggy ride yesterday." Charity looked at Annie and raised both eyebrows.

"He didn't cancel, did he?"

"*Ya.* Something about too much work, so he sent a message with his mother."

"Oh, Adam."

Both girls stared at him openly, waited for his response.

"Well, now, I had to see to this mare, didn't I?" Adam sat forward, shoulders hunched.

"I believe *Mamm* said the mare was re-shod by noon." Charity straightened her prayer *kapp* as they neared the Umble's home.

"True or false, Adam?"

"*Ya*, but I had planned to work on my and Leah's house in the morning. When I had to spend the morning on the mare, then I had to push the work on the house to afternoon."

"So you cancelled." Annie added a tsk-tsk as Adam whoaed the mare, pulled the buggy up into the row of buggies. Apparently, Deborah Umble had planned quite the Christmas party.

"Man has to finish his house if he expects to be married in the fall."

"Man better take his girl for an occasional ride on Saturday," Charity warned, "or she might become a bit *bedauerlich*."

Charity jumped out of the buggy after Annie, but Adam stopped her, a look of concern covering his face—all earlier playfulness now gone. "Was she upset about yesterday, Charity?"

"She misses seeing you, Adam. If the house isn't finished in time, the community will help. Spend some time with her today."

Adam nodded, then turned his attention to the horse.

Annie looked over to her *mamm* and *dat*. She'd planned on helping him into the Umbles' house, but they seemed to have it covered. In fact, he was leaning on Reba as she watched. So she stayed with Adam by the buggy and waited to go in with him.

"You don't have to worry about Leah, Adam. She cares about you very much."

"*Ya*, but we have less than ten months to finish the house. Plus there's my job over at the livery stable, and I'll need to plant spring crops and help *Dat*. It's a lot to accomplish, Annie."

"And Leah will help you. But you have to talk to her about all you need to finish, all your worries and what you're doing with your days. Find a quiet place today to speak with her. Tell her you're sorry you missed your time together yesterday. And ask her how you can make it up to her."

Adam's eyes searched hers. "You really think it's that simple?"

For some reason Annie's mind flashed back to yesterday afternoon, to the time she'd spent with Samuel in the barn, speaking with him as she'd held the pups.

"I'm fairly sure it is. A woman wants to know what's on your mind and your heart, then she'll help you as she can."

16

$\mathcal{A}$nnie and Adam climbed the steps of the two-story, clapboard house. It looked like so many other houses in their area—white picket fence, green tin roof, sweeping porch, and a red barn away and off to the side at least equal in size to the house.

The Umbles were neither wealthier nor poorer than any of the other families in their district. They did have a few more *kinner* than most.

Deborah Umble was a small woman. As Annie entered the house and moved over and among the women and children, she spotted her. Barely over five feet tall, certainly not weighing more than one hundred and ten pounds, she was probably nearing forty years old now.

How had she birthed eight children?

The thought was enough to make Annie want to lie down and take a nap.

Deborah's hair was covered with a prayer *kapp*, like all the other women's, but auburn wisps escaped as she bent to wipe the youngest girl's nose.

Annie had no trouble distinguishing the Umble children among the many in the house—though some had their father's burly build and some were slight like their *mamm*, all had Deborah's dark auburn hair. The youngest she carried on her hip. He looked to be almost a year old.

Food covered every inch of space on the kitchen counter, and tiny sprigs of evergreen decorated the table. Annie wondered where she should put the butter-squash casserole she held, but Charity whisked it out of her left hand and set it in the oven to warm.

"Desserts?" Annie asked with a smile.

"I've been put in charge of those." Samuel took the shoofly pie from her right hand even as he bent closer. "The dark green color looks attractive on you, Nurse Annie."

Then he was gone, standing across the room next to the long planks Stephen Umble had placed on sawhorses near the front windows. They were covered with pies, cakes, and Christmas cookies.

Candles perched on each windowsill, waiting for nightfall, and Annie noticed a few wrapped Christmas presents that had been stacked neatly and tucked under the end tables that flanked the couch in the living room. It all reminded her of how close Christmas was and how relieved she was to be here—to be home.

"Maybe you should step out of the kitchen, Annie. You look a bit flushed." Rebekah placed a hand lightly on her shoulder, offered her a cup of punch.

"Thanks, *Mamm*. I'm fine. What else can I do to help?" Annie turned from watching Samuel, but as she did she was sure she saw him smile at her and nod.

Now what was that about?

And why did her heart race every time he stood near?

Samuel accepted the plate of food from Rebekah Weaver. "*Danki.*"

"No need to thank me, Samuel. Though I'd appreciate it if you'd take an extra plate over to Annie. Maybe stay with her and see that she eats. She seems intent on hovering over her father. No doubt she'll set it down and walk away if you leave her for a minute."

Samuel followed her gaze and saw why she was worried.

Annie was attempting to find something Jacob could elevate his leg on. She kept trotting back to him with various-sized items—stools, small pillows from the couch, even a gift she'd found wrapped in bright red paper.

Jacob was having none of it.

He looked perfectly content sitting at the long table set up in the middle of the large open space straddling the kitchen and living room, and he wasn't going to move so he could elevate the leg with the larger cast.

The scene outside the windows revealed a world covered in snow, as the storm that had been building all morning had finally let loose.

Most of the children and even the single adults had filled their plates and gone to the barn to eat. No doubt even now a game of indoor volleyball had begun.

Annie had stayed behind.

"I'll take care of her," Samuel promised with a chuckle.

He accepted another plate of food and walked to where she was still trying to shove something under her father's foot.

"Leave a man alone, Annie." Jacob forked a piece of ham and pointed it at her. "My stomach is as important as my foot, and right now I'm hungry."

"But you've been on it all morning, and you should raise it up for a while."

"Is there a problem here?" Samuel spoke quietly, knowing she hadn't seen him walk up behind her.

She jumped, then scowled at them both. "Problem is he's stubborn as a mule."

"Hungry as one, too." Jacob looked up at Samuel with a smile. "I hope her mother sent you over here to rescue me."

"Actually, she did. Come with me, Annie. I need your help with something."

"Oh, well. All right, but I'll be back." Annie glowered at her father, but moved away with Samuel. "Is someone hurt? I saw all those children leaving for the barn. Did someone fall?"

Samuel nodded toward their coats, waited while she shrugged into hers. Then she took both plates, and he shrugged into his.

They hurried to the barn, through the falling snow. Once inside, amidst the noise of a volleyball game, a transistor radio, and several dozen kids and young adults ranging from four to twenty-four, he maneuvered her to the far side of the south wall.

Samuel set both plates down on a wooden crate that had been turned upside down.

"No one's hurt," he admitted.

"Then, what did you need me for?" She looked around, puzzled, as if she might find an emergency lurking under the closest hay bale.

"Because your mother wants you to eat, and your father wants to enjoy his lunch."

He watched the blush start at her neck and creep all the way up to her hairline. A man could grow used to watching such a beautiful sight.

"My father needs to elevate his foot."

"No, he needs to eat. Now, why don't you stop fussing over him and let the man be?"

"Samuel Yoder, I can't believe you'd say such a thing to me."

"I didn't say it first. Your *mamm* did. She also sent your plate and asked me to sit and eat with you."

If anything her face turned even redder.

She snatched the plate from his hand and plopped down on the hay bale next to the wooden crate. "Well, by all means don't feel like you have to stay because you promised my *mamm*."

"Actually, I was looking for you anyway." Samuel took a large bite of the casserole on his plate, decided he needed to eat the fresh bread before it grew completely cold, then wished he could wash it all down with a big drink of Deborah Umble's famous lemonade. "I see Charity brought out a jug of lemonade. Would you like me to bring you a cup?"

Annie rolled her eyes, but muttered, "*Ya*. Lemonade will make it all better."

He fetched the drinks, smiling as she took a big sip and squinted her eyes at the tartness. Sitting down beside her, he lowered his voice to a conspiratorial whisper. "It would have looked forward for me to seek you out. I got lucky when your *mamm* asked me to pull you away from your *dat*."

Annie had put the first bite of casserole into her mouth. At his confession, she swallowed wrong and began to choke.

Samuel set his own plate down and began patting her on the back. "Are you all right? Do I need to perform the Heimlich maneuver on you? Everyone's staring at us now, but I do know how to save a person who is choking. Learned it quite a few years ago, even had to perform the maneuver once on old Mr. Bender."

Annie grabbed her drink and swallowed half of it, holding up her hand to silence him. "I'm fine," she gasped. "Please don't Heimlich me. I don't want to give everyone another reason to stare."

Samuel laughed and sat back down. "You scared me for a minute there. Actually turned a little purple. Color matches nicely with your hair, but I prefer your normal complexion."

Annie picked up her fork, took one more bite, then set the plate down. "You're acting mighty strange, Samuel. Maybe you fell out of your buggy and hit your head."

"Nope. Just enjoying eating my Sunday lunch with a pretty girl. Can't blame a man for acting a little bit more friendly than normal."

Annie began to blush again, and Samuel decided he certainly did like it. He wouldn't mind thinking of more ways to make Annie Weaver blush.

"And you call this more friendly than normal?"

"More friendly than a bear."

"So you've been called a bear before?"

"I have, as a matter of fact."

They ate without talking, though Samuel liked to think it was a comfortable silence. Of course, the barn was hardly quiet, with so many young ones in it, and he didn't want to count the couples who were courting. There had been Sundays when sitting in the midst of so many people had made him feel lonely, but right now he couldn't remember why.

"Did you ask your mother about the pup?"

"I did, and she said Reba could have it—if you still have one you haven't given away."

Samuel grinned as he drank the last of his lemonade. "Seems the one you were so fond of is still looking for a home."

"*Wunderbaar.* She will love it. I can't think of a better Christmas present for Reba."

Suddenly Annie dropped her plate onto the crate and jumped up. He barely had time to understand what she'd seen and where she was headed.

He barely had time to stop her.

"Peace, Annie." He reached out, snagged her arm, pulled her back to where she'd been sitting. "Let your father be."

"But he's headed over toward the livestock. Do you realize what'll happen if he breaks his leg again?"

"Annie, look at me."

When she finally turned those dark brown eyes toward his, Samuel's heart rate kicked up a notch, and he realized he might be a bit more smitten with little Annie than he'd realized.

"Did you not listen to Bishop Levi at all last Sunday?"

She drew back as if she'd been slapped, and he thought she might walk away. Instead, all of the bluster went out of her. "*Ya*. I listened."

"Then finish your food. Make your *mamm froh*. I believe Charity's watching, and she'll probably report back."

Annie glanced over to where her *schweschder* was sitting, and Charity waved at them both. Samuel and Annie waved back, and Annie picked up her plate, moved the food around with her fork.

"I did listen to the bishop," she said a bit sheepishly.

"And?"

"And what?" She raised her eyes to his, clearly exasperated.

"Did you not believe him, or did you not understand what he said?"

Annie stared down at her plate, finally gave up playing with the food and the fork. "You'll laugh if I tell you the truth."

"'Course I won't laugh." Samuel had completely cleaned his plate. He set it aside, crossed his feet at the ankles and stretched his legs full-length. Hands crossed under his head, he leaned back against the wall. "Try me."

"It's just that while Bishop Levi was talking, it all made so much sense. I had this moment where everything seemed to click, and I thought—I want that. I want to be like that exactly—calm, peaceful, serene." She looked up at him then, a tentative smile playing at her lips.

"And I thought I had it," she continued. "Like when I'm holding one of Reba's kittens. Then, the service ended, and suddenly it vanished. *Dat* wouldn't behave himself, I started worrying he would fall, and I was going to be right there and unable to do anything about it. All the peacefulness slipped away . . . just like the kitten that scampered out of my hands."

He watched her play with the ties of her *kapp*, watched and waited to see if she would add anything else.

"I suppose I missed something." She released the ties, folded her hands in her lap.

"Why would you suppose that?"

"Because it didn't work. I didn't get it, obviously. Do I look serene to you?" Now her hands were spread out, gesturing.

Samuel couldn't have stopped the smile spreading across his face if a week's worth of crop depended on it.

"*Ach.* Never mind." Annie folded her arms tightly across her ribs and looked over at Adam and Leah, who were feeding Leah's youngest baby *schweschder.* "I don't know why I thought you'd understand."

"Actually, I think I do understand."

"You do?"

"It's not that you missed anything, Annie. It's that you care for your father very much—so it's natural to worry. But truth is he's fine, and you can trust him to act responsibly. You can also trust the Lord to look after him."

"*Ya*, but—"

"You know what else I think?"

"No, but—"

"I think you might be blaming yourself for your *dat's* accident in the first place. And his accident, Miss Annie, is not your fault."

"I don't blame myself." She scooted to the far side of her hay bale, turned sideways so she could look at him straight on. "Where would you get such an idea?"

"Well, I've been watching how you worry around him. Seems like you might be carrying a bit of guilt over his accident. Perhaps if you hadn't been away at the time, it wouldn't have happened—which isn't logical. Your father still would have been out that night, and the car still would have smashed into his buggy."

Annie pulled in her bottom lip, worried it a little, but didn't say anything.

"I suppose I guessed how you were feeling because I blamed myself for the longest time." Samuel sat up now, brushed the hay from his sleeves. "See, I asked him to come by my place and look at my fields, discuss a crop change with me. But neither you nor I hit his buggy. We're not to blame for his injury."

Annie straightened the apron covering her dress. "I hadn't thought of it the way you're saying. I do wish I'd been at the hospital when *Dat* was there. It took me a full day to make it home once I received the call—I know that haunts me."

Samuel leaned in, his face mere inches from hers. "You came, though. And you stayed."

Annie's smile should have stopped the snow, should have brought out the sun—it was that bright.

"*Ya*, I did."

"Most of us have trouble carrying the bishop's lessons out into the normal workweek," Samuel added. "It's not just you, Annie."

"Does it get any easier?"

"How would I know?"

"Well, you being older and all," she teased. "You've had years of trying. So much experience . . ."

Before he could think of a response, Reba had run up and was pulling Annie away, intent on showing her the Umbles' animal pens at the back of the barn.

He watched them walk away and wondered what he was doing.

Easy enough for him to talk about peacefulness.

He'd convinced himself yesterday that Annie Weaver was too young for him, and his best friend's daughter to boot.

Then there was the letter from Rachel waiting for him on the table at home.

Another letter from Rachel.

He hadn't even opened it.

He hadn't needed to—he knew what it said.

He'd still not decided how to answer her.

During last week's sermon, he too had experienced a deep sense of peace and calm—God's peace. Then Annie had walked into the Umbles, and his first thoughts had been of walking up behind her, touching her hand, catching the scent of soap on her skin.

Hard to resist one's heart's desire.

The thought came to him unbidden, and he wasn't sure what to do about it.

17

*M*onday, the blizzard continued, dropping over sixteen inches of snow across their fields and roads and fences. Adam, Rebekah, and Charity stayed home from work. Reba stayed home from school.

And Annie was not able to check on Sharon Smucker.

Monday night, a west wind blew the storm away from them toward New Jersey and out to the Atlantic. Annie found herself staring up into the same constellations she'd gazed at as a child, feeling every bit as lost in many ways, but trying to trust, seeking the peace she and Samuel had spoken of.

Tuesday, everyone bundled up and resumed their normal activities. Annie completed the housework in the morning, then fixed a late morning snack for David and her *dat* as she always did. They came in talking of spring and crops and warmer days that had no hope of arriving for quite some time.

She hadn't even argued with her father that morning when he declared he was going out to the barn. She was determined to practice peacefulness.

Scouring the entire downstairs had helped to work off her anxiety.

It had also kept her out of the barn, kept her from checking on him.

"Hello, Annie." David stopped at the front door to clean off his boots. "You're looking quite pretty today."

Annie looked down at the old apron she'd pulled on over her mother's most worn housedress—a dress at least four sizes too big for her. She hadn't wanted to soil the few dresses she had while she scrubbed floors, and she knew this was the one her *mamm* always wore to do heavy housework.

"*Danki*, David. Have you asked Samuel to check and see if you need glasses?"

David laughed as her father walked in from the bathroom.

"Did I miss a joke?"

"You certainly did," Annie said. "There's no time to explain it, though. I have a favor to ask David after you two eat."

"Anything for you, Annie."

"Don't be offering your services too quickly, David. Never volunteer with a woman before you hear what she needs." Jacob sat down at the table after kissing Annie on the cheek. "She could be about to ask you to clean out the chicken coop, or clean the upstairs windows from the outside. You don't want either of those jobs—save them for Adam."

Jacob laughed at his own joke and reached for warm bread to go with his hot *kaffi*.

Annie had reheated a bit of last night's ham. She had to admit, these two were easy to feed.

"Actually, I needed David to hitch up the buggy to the old mare—if he wouldn't mind."

"That's no problem at all, but the lanes are still covered high with snow this morning, Annie. Do you need me to drive you somewhere?"

"No!" Annie's spoon clattered in her saucer when she dropped it. "What I mean is, I'm sure the roads are fine. I heard the snowplows out on the main road earlier."

When both men stared at her she added, "One of the neighbors asked me to stop by and see them about a medical matter, so it would be best if I went alone."

"Should you wait until Adam comes home?" Jacob asked. "You know your *mamm* doesn't want you traveling on the road at night alone, and some of your calls tend to go a bit long."

"No. This will be a short visit." Annie stood, suddenly not hungry at all. "I do need to change clothes first, though. I can be ready in a half-hour."

"Not a problem at all." David smiled as he wolfed down another piece of the ham. Before she made it across the room, he couldn't help teasing her a little more, though. "Did you say you wanted me to hitch up Blaze for you?"

He nudged Jacob, and they both started laughing, heads bowed over their food.

Annie didn't even bother replying as she hurried up the stairs to her room.

Blaze, indeed.

She'd watched Adam take the mare out for a ride last week. It reminded her of a movie poster she'd seen in Philadelphia— one of the old westerns had been playing at the theater down by the hospital. Horse reared on its back legs, cowboy holding on to his hat, except in this case Adam had lost his.

No, she did not need to try and drive Blaze. Though she had to wonder how Charity had managed to do so when Adam had trouble handling the horse.

But then few animals or people had the nerve to give Charity trouble.

She changed out of the work dress and into her better Sunday one. She'd had little time for making new clothes, but she supposed she'd have to eventually.

The three dresses she had barely fit anymore. It wasn't that she'd gained weight exactly, but the weight she had had moved around somehow. She'd talked to her *mamm* about it the other night, and they'd had a nice laugh about it.

"You were a girl when I made those clothes, Annie. Now you're a young woman."

"Whatever the reason, I'm having some trouble fitting into them. I believe it might be owing more to your baking than anything else."

Her *mamm* had eyed her figure and shook her head no, then changed the subject.

At the house, she'd taken to wearing her mother's larger dresses—which was one of the ones David had commented on, but it was a little more difficult when she went out in public. They'd let out her one Sunday dress in the bosom, and Annie donned it quickly, covered it with a fresh apron, and put on a clean prayer *kapp*.

It was nearing ten thirty in the morning by the time she pulled up to the Smuckers' home. The drive had been slow and steady. The old mare was easy enough to control, but it was a good thing she hadn't been in a hurry.

She'd barely climbed down from the buggy when the front door of the single-story house opened.

Like most of the other farms in their area, the yard was clean, and the house whitewashed. A porch surrounded it on two sides. The barn was set a little farther back, and Annie noticed the place did seem to be a bit isolated—but then many of their homes were isolated. Farming was by nature a remote life.

Sharon's mother waited near the door as Annie walked up the stairs, her quilted bag in her hand.

"Hello, Mrs. Smucker. You might not remember me. I'm Annie Weaver. My younger *schweschder* is Charity. I believe she went to school with Sharon."

"I know who you are. I'd like to talk to you out here a minute. If you don't mind." She looked around, as if checking to be sure they remained alone. "Before you go inside to see Sharon."

"I don't mind at all." Annie pulled her coat more tightly against the December wind and followed her around to a sitting area on the side porch. Three rockers sat there and looked to the east, sheltered from the wind.

While Annie waited for Mrs. Smucker to begin, she studied her. Once-blonde hair had been pulled up into a tight bun— though a bit of it showed where she had severely parted her hair beneath her *kapp*. Light blue eyes reminded Annie of the color of a wildflower she'd often seen growing down by her *dat's* pond. She tried to think of the name of it but couldn't.

It eluded her as she watched this woman's grief-stricken eyes and waited.

Tonight, she'd ask her *mamm* the name of the flower, and when the weather grew warmer she'd walk down to the pond. The thought of spring and wildflowers helped to bolster her spirits.

Sadness hung heavy in the air here—like the snow clouds that had pressed down over their community on Sunday.

Like many farm wives, Mrs. Smucker had gained a few pounds over the years. She wasn't heavy but what Annie thought of as soft—motherly.

Annie could only imagine how at the moment this mother's heart ached.

"Mrs. Smucker—"

"Call me Ruth."

"All right. Ruth, I'd like to say I'm here because Samuel asked me, but I'm also here because I'd like to help Sharon. We want her to be as healthy as possible when the baby comes."

At the word baby, Ruth began to twist the dark apron covering her dress.

"Never thought this would happen to one of my girls."

"I'm sure it's quite a shock."

"Sharon's always been a respectable girl. Studied hard in school. Never gave us any trouble."

Annie reached out, covered the woman's hands with her own. She'd seen the Smucker family at the service last week— the mother, father, and younger children. They hadn't stayed for the meal, and Sharon hadn't been with them.

Looking around, she noticed no young ones, so they must be at school for the day. Nearest she could remember, the baby had been born a few years before she left for the city.

"My primary concern is Sharon's health," Annie reminded her gently. "It's important she still get out of the house, see her *freinden*, go to church."

Tears Ruth had been holding back tracked down her face. She raised her apron and vigorously rubbed them away. "*Ya*, I know. The bishop told Phillip the same thing, and I thought last week he'd let her go, but then when it came time he turned red in the face and told her to go to her room."

Annie waited, not knowing how to respond.

"He's a *gut* man, Phillip. Always kind to me and the children, but he's taking this real hard."

"No doubt." Annie patted her hand and stood. "We'll pray God softens his heart. I'm not a midwife, Ruth, and I won't be the one to deliver Sharon's baby. Belinda will need to be here for the birth or else Sharon will need to go to the *Englisch* hospital, whichever you decide."

"She'll be having the baby here, same as I did." Ruth stood, straightened her dress and apron.

On impulse, Annie leaned forward, wrapped her arms around the woman in a light embrace. "I know I'm young to be giving advice. I don't have any children of my own, and I've attended fewer than two dozen births. But I do know *bopplin* are a miracle—any *boppli* is a miracle. Sharon's *boppli* is a miracle."

Ruth nodded, returned the hug.

"How about we go and see your girl?"

Together, they turned and walked into the house.

⤫⤫

Sharon sat knitting in front of the stove.

Annie wasn't sure what she had expected. Perhaps a younger, just-as-tired version of Ruth.

The young girl with curly blonde hair peeking out of her prayer *kapp* and beautiful deep blue eyes somehow took her by surprise.

"Sharon, this is Miss Annie. She's going to check on you, check your *boppli*, and make sure everything is okay."

Sharon stopped rocking, set her knitting in a basket on the floor. "All right. What should I do?"

"Why don't we talk first? Ruth, could you make us some tea?"

"Sure thing."

When Ruth had moved off to the kitchen area, Annie took the seat nearest to Sharon.

"How are you feeling, Sharon?"

"Fine. A bit more tired than usual."

"That's normal. Your baby is growing, and he or she takes a lot of your energy. Has your stomach felt *naerfich*?"

"It did feel nervous—early in the mornings. But that's stopped."

Annie made a note in her patient book. "Do you remember when you had your last period?"

"*Ya*. It was in the summer. I remember because *Dat* had just bought the new bull, and he kept me awake making so much noise."

Annie wrote down "Five to six months?"

"What are you knitting?"

"Booties—yellow lined with green since I don't know if it's a boy or girl."

"Smart thinking." Annie smiled, hoping to put the girl at ease. She'd sat with her hand on her stomach the entire time they'd talked, but with the plain dress, the apron, and the way she sat, Annie couldn't possibly judge how far along she was in her pregnancy.

"Sharon, I need to measure your stomach and try to tell when your baby is due. I'd also like to take your blood pressure and your pulse to make sure your body is adjusting to carrying the baby as it should."

Sharon nodded, but her eyes started darting around the room nervously.

"Nothing I do is going to hurt, Sharon."

"Will I have to take my clothes off?"

"Nope. You can stay exactly as you are."

"Okay." The girl visibly relaxed. "I guess we can go in my room, then."

"Would you like your *mamm* to come with us?"

The girl shrugged, then pushed herself out of the rocker with her right hand. When she did, Annie saw what the girl's answers hadn't provided—she was easily closing in on her last trimester.

༄

Annie followed Sharon back to her room.

It was a small room, with two twin beds and a tiny window looking out over the fields.

"I share with my *schweschder*, Charity," Annie said.

"*Ya*, I share with Becca. Not sure where I'll put a crib for the baby, but we'll figure something out."

Sharon sat on the bed, then began fidgeting with the spread.

Instead of beginning the exam, Annie sat down across from her.

"Is something wrong, Sharon?"

"Never had an exam before. I've never been sick. Never even been to see Doc Samuel."

Annie knew many Amish people became anxious when faced with medical procedures, but warning bells began ringing in her ears. Something about Sharon's nervousness seemed out of place.

Looking out the single window, she prayed for a way to put Sharon at ease.

"I'd never been sick much either. But I'd seen Samuel help one of the *kind* at the schoolhouse."

Sharon nodded, but didn't interrupt.

"Then I went to stay with my *aenti* awhile, in the city."

"You lived with the *Englisch*?"

"For a few years. It was . . ." Annie paused, trying to think of how to sum up all that she'd experienced there. "It was a lonely time. I'm glad to be back now. But I learned a few things about helping people—like how to listen to your heart, and how to measure your baby."

Sharon had clasped her arms over her stomach and begun rocking at the word *Englisch.*

"Sharon? Are you okay?"

"Everything all right in here?" Ruth stuck her head in the door. "Tea's ready."

Seeing her mother, Sharon seemed to pull herself together, drew in a deep breath.

"We're almost done." Annie replied. She proceeded to show the purpose of each instrument before she used it—how the blood pressure cuff worked, why she wanted to measure the length and width of Sharon's stomach, the reason she needed to take her temperature.

Finally she pointed the stethoscope's rounded end toward her protruding stomach. "Sharon, I want to see if we can hear your *boppli's* heartbeat."

The girl's eyes grew wide, but she nodded.

"Remember, the scope is cold on the end. You'll probably feel it through your dress." Annie would have preferred to listen without the dress, but her instinct told her Sharon wasn't ready for that sort of exam.

She pressed the scope first at the top, then the side of Sharon's stomach, searching for the baby's heartbeat, listening closely. The doctors she'd worked with at Mercy had used a fetal stethoscope, but her acoustic scope would have to do.

When she found the rapid beat, she met the frightened girl's stare with a smile. "Want to hear?"

Sharon nodded hesitantly.

"Take the ear pieces from my ears and put them in yours. I don't want to lose the spot, as your *boppli* seems very active."

"*Ya,* he moves around a lot."

Sharon frowned as she adjusted the ear pieces. "All I hear is a loud rush, like a strong wind," she muttered.

Keeping her right hand firmly on the scope's round end, Annie reached up with her left—removed one side of the scope from Sharon's ears. "The windy sound is the fluid around the baby. Listen underneath the wind and you'll hear a soft beat. It's rather fast, like a buggy tire making a rhythmic sound as it turns on a road."

A look of wonder spread across the girl's face. "That's my *boppli's* heart?" Her voice faltered, cracked in disbelief. "Are you sure?"

"I'm very sure." Annie smiled into the girl's deep blue eyes, prayed she would relax and trust her.

They remained there for another minute, Annie's hand holding the round end of the scope to Sharon's stomach. Sharon's hand on top of Annie's, hope mingling with joy on her face.

Annie didn't know how this situation would resolve itself. How Sharon's father would learn to accept the grandchild in his home. What had happened to Sharon to make her so skittish.

But she did know a look of joy when she saw one.

18

Samuel read Rachel's letter one last time.

There was no mistaking her intent. How had he managed to ignore it for so long?

Rachel, Mary's *schweschder*.

Physically, the two looked very much alike—petite, blonde, and beautiful, but there the similarities ended.

His Mary had always been so gentle, and though she had a temper—a smile tugged as he remembered the time she'd threatened him with a skillet if he tracked mud across her kitchen again—overall, her words were usually kind.

Rachel was different.

The woman's spirit had always struck him as a bit harsh. She seemed to not think before she spoke, or if she did, it didn't concern her if her words bit like the cold winter wind.

Mary had often worried about her—worried first over how her attitude might keep her from marrying, and then how it might cause tension between her and her husband. She hadn't lived long enough to see Rachel become a widow, and for that Samuel was grateful.

Each fall, after the crops were in and when the marry-ing season was upon them, Samuel would take the bus over to Ohio—to visit Mary's family. Two years ago, his *bruder* Benjamin had made the trip with him, met a cousin of Mary's and fallen in love.

Samuel smiled to himself as he thought of Benjamin.

Then he glanced back down at the letter, reached for the cold mug of *kaffi*, and took a drink of it, though he knew how it would taste—bitter.

Exactly like the words in front of him.

He wished no ill for Rachel, which was why this letter hurt him so. As he read it slowly and carefully, praying for wisdom to understand her intent clearly, he could see her pain through her words, much as he could see infection in a wound.

But how to address her concerns? Certainly, it was time for him to do so.

Pushing the mug away, he read through it one last time.

Samuel,

My parents send their greetings, as do Ethan and Michael. You will be surprised how much the boys have grown when you visit this fall. They miss the guidance of having a daed *around, though your* bruder, *Benjamin, has helped when he can fit us into his schedule.*

It has been two years now since the passing of my husband, and my mourning period is long over. I am a practical woman, Samuel. I know how things were between you and Mary, and I don't pretend to be able to duplicate such a thing; however, I believe there is much we can offer each other as we grow older. It is not the Amish way to grow old alone. Moreover, Ethan and Michael would benefit from your presence.

Please consider the merit of my words.

Pray on them.

Discuss them with your bishop.

I have faith he will help you to understand your duty.

Rachel.

Samuel tapped the letter with his pen, then stood and poured the cold *kaffi* down the sink. Refilling his mug with the black brew he had reheated from breakfast, he sat down and pulled a clean sheet of paper toward him.

What bothered him most about the letter was not what she had said; it was what she had left unsaid.

There was no offer of love or even friendship. She might as well have been making a business proposal.

Were he to accept, would such a cold union be what Samuel would have to look forward to the rest of his years? An image of Annie flashed into his mind, and he pushed it away.

This wasn't about Annie.

This was about Rachel and family and obligations.

This was about what duty involved, and what it didn't.

He pulled the blank paper toward him and began to write.

⁓⊘⊱

Fifteen minutes later his reply was sealed in an envelope, the envelope was placed in his pocket, and his stomach was settled for having put the entire affair to rest.

He could leave it in his mailbox, but since he was headed into town anyway, he might as well drop it off at the post office.

The thought had barely formed when he looked up from hitching his mare to his buggy and saw Annie Weaver steering Jacob's old mare down the unmarked snow of his lane.

And was there a prettier sight than Annie wrapped up for a cold winter day?

He couldn't think of a single one.

Waiting until she'd pulled up beside his rig, he grabbed the horse's harness. "Annie, what brings you out this beautiful day?"

Her face rosy-red from the cold, a scarf wrapped around her neck, she climbed out of the buggy and smiled up into his face—but it was a smile tinged with concern.

"I've just been to check on Sharon Smucker. I was hoping to speak with you about her. This looks like a bad time, though."

"Actually, I'm headed into town to pick up a few supplies, then out to check on a few of the older folks. Any chance you could travel with me?"

Annie's smile widened, but then she looked back at her mare. "*Ya*, I'd like to, but I've got *dat's* mare . . ."

"Does he need her this afternoon?"

"No."

"Give me a minute then. I'll unhitch the buggy and settle her in my barn. Cover up with the blankets inside my buggy—climb inside while you wait, or you'll freeze to the ground."

～✑～

Annie waited inside Samuel's buggy, his blankets covering her lap and wrapped around her legs. He'd unhitched the old mare in half the time it would have taken her, and through the open barn door she saw him toss a handful of feed into its trough. Though she didn't mind doing these things herself, it struck her how much more naturally such chores came to a man.

Reba and Charity loved working with the horses, but she found the harnesses heavy and cumbersome—Samuel treated them as if he were removing a quilt from a bed and hanging it on a line for drying.

When he opened the door of his buggy, cold air rushed in. His dark eyes met hers, and an involuntary shiver worked its way up and through her body.

"Even with the sun out, the temperature isn't growing much warmer." Samuel reached behind her seat, his arm brushing against her shoulder as he did. "I keep this battery heater for days like this."

Smiling, he set it at her feet, turned it to full blast. Warm air filled the buggy quickly, as Samuel flicked the reins and they took off down the snowy lane.

"*Gut?*" His smile caught her off guard.

When would she grow used to the sight of Samuel Yoder smiling?

"*Ya*, I can almost feel my toes again."

"Be glad you aren't wearing those *Englisch* shoes you had on the first night you came home."

"Samuel." Annie's voice rose in mock-horror. "Do you mean to tell me you were staring at my feet as my *dat* lay in bed?"

"Might have noticed. Don't see shoes like those round here often."

A blush crawled up Annie's face, and she reached forward, turned down the little heater. "They happened to be the closest to Amish I could find in the city, *danki*."

Samuel allowed their banter to rest between them as they drove through the early afternoon. Though snow still remained piled high beside the road, several buggies passed them headed in the opposite direction. It had been this way as long as Annie could remember—a big snow, snuggling inside with her family, then a collective sigh as people began to unbury after their time of being cooped up.

As usual, they shared the roads with their *Englisch* neighbors. The occasional automobile chugged along behind them.

Annie noticed Samuel pulled Smokey to the right where the snow plows had cleared extra room, so the motor cars could pass. Where there wasn't an extra lane cleared, though, he let the *Englischers* wait.

"You're not fussing about the *Englisch* drivers."

Samuel cocked an eye her direction, tugged on his beard. "Fuss about a thing like rude drivers, I'm going to be fussing every day."

"Some men do, though," she teased.

"You don't say? Men, but never women?" Samuel pulled over to let a large black truck zoom by. Teenagers filled the cab, and though the windows were closed, loud music spilled from the vehicle.

"Okay. You have a point. Charity probably would have fought with the truck over who had the right of way, but she's still young and stubborn."

"No use causing a buggy accident, or a vehicle one for that matter." He paused, glanced at her, then pushed forward. "Do you miss the city, Annie? Do you ever wish you could go back there? Or are you content here now?"

She knew his questions were more than casual queries to pass the time. Samuel wanted to know, and her answer mattered. Small lines appeared between his eyes, the way they did when he was truly focusing—she'd seen the same expression when they'd delivered Faith's baby and again when she'd worked with him on Saturday.

Did her answer matter so much to him?

She looked out at the farms they passed as they drew closer to town.

"Mifflin County is my home. It's where I belong." She sighed, adjusted the blanket on her lap. "I won't say I wish I'd never left."

"Because of the nursing?"

"*Ya*, the nursing is what I think the Lord wants me to do, and I'm pleased the bishop is going to allow it. But being with the *Englisch* also helped me understand our people in a different way. Am I making any sense?"

Annie noticed his hand travel to his coat pocket, as if to check whether he'd forgotten something. "It does make sense. I travel to Ohio each fall, where my *bruder* Benjamin lives—and where Mary's family lives. When I come home, I have a better understanding and a new appreciation for our community."

It was the first time Samuel had mentioned Mary to her, and Annie wondered if they'd crossed another barrier.

"'Course I miss my *schweschder*-in-law's cooking when I come back here—back to my bachelor life—but I'd still rather be home." Samuel slowed Smokey for the increased traffic as they entered town. "You'd think I'd learn to cook better, but it's the one skill I haven't mastered well in all these years."

Annie smiled, both because of his teasing and because she noticed that even more Christmas decorations had popped up in the store windows. "I missed my *mamm's* cooking a lot while I was gone. I know how to make the identical meals she makes, but it's not the same preparing food for yourself, eating alone. I made a friend in the city, several friends actually. But one girl in particular, Jenny, would always cook for me when I became homesick."

"I'm glad you had someone there who looked after you." Samuel reached out and touched her arm as he pulled the buggy to a stop in front of her *mamm's* shop. "But I'm more glad you're back where you belong."

"I am too. I won't lie to you. I miss the *kinner*, especially Kiptyn."

"A little boy. I heard you mention him to the bishop at church."

"*Ya.*" Annie reached into her bag, pulled out a letter she had written to him the evening before. "I had a letter from him and another from his parents last week, though. He's still improving. It's really a miracle."

"That's *gut*. I'm very glad to hear it."

"His parents are the nicest *Englischers* I've met. They might bring him for a visit in the spring—if he's well enough."

She looked out at the storefront windows in front of her, thought about Christmas and all the promise it held.

She thought of how it held promises for Kiptyn too.

Samuel reached out, touched her shoulder. "I'll pray he continues to improve."

"*Danki.*"

"Did you eat lunch at Sharon's house?"

"No. Why?" Annie tried to catch up, confused by the change in topic, more confused by the touch of his hand on her shoulder.

"Because it's half past twelve, and I had finished mine when you drove up. Perhaps you should grab a bite at the store where your *mamm* works while I take care of a few errands."

"Do I have enough time?"

"Sure. I could stand to reorder some supplies while I'm here."

"All right. First I'll drop off my letter to Kiptyn, then stop and tell *Mamm* we're going on a few house calls."

"And eat," he reminded her.

"And eat," she agreed.

Samuel's hand again traveled to his coat pocket. "I'll order my medical supplies, then go over to the feed store and the hardware store to check on some work I left there. Why don't we meet back here in an hour?"

Annie folded his lap blanket, then reached down and turned off the battery heater. By the time she'd opened her door of the buggy, Samuel was there, offering his hand to help her, being sure she didn't slip on the icy road.

She meant to smile at him properly and look away, but she couldn't.

Something about his gaze drew hers—until it seemed it was only the two of them standing there on the busy snowy avenue.

Her heart beat faster, her hands began to sweat inside of her gloves, and for the first time since she'd come home she allowed herself to wonder what promises Christmas might hold for her.

19

$\mathcal{A}$nnie dropped off her letter in the post office box on the corner, then walked slowly back toward her *mamm's*. On the way, she stopped to study the displays in the various store windows, admired the evergreen boughs, the red ribbons, the occasional nativity scenes.

Amish wares lay interspersed among the holiday decorations, and she was sure she recognized the handmade quilts of some of her friends. There was a time when Amish folk made a living solely off the land, but more and more they sold their handicrafts in town in the stores.

She'd heard her parents discussing it several times since returning home. Quilts and canning provided a decent extra income, especially for years when crops failed due to bad weather or insects. The general store was a perfect example of a place where they could sell their wares and purchase the items they needed.

In other words, as a community they still depended on it to survive.

Thinking about how so much had stayed the same even as the small things had changed, Annie opened the door to the general store and walked straight into her *Onkel* Eli.

"Annie. I haven't seen you in town since you've been home. How are you?"

"I'm fine, *Onkel*. How are you?"

They stepped aside to allow a pair of *Englisch* tourists by, and Eli ran his fingers under his suspenders, lowered his voice.

"I'm a little worried, since you asked."

Annie tugged on his arm, pulled him over to a bench in front of the general store window. Oddly her *onkel* was not really so old—her father's younger *bruder*, she thought he'd recently turned forty.

Why was it he'd never married?

He wasn't a bad-looking fellow, and he had the sweetest temperament of any man she'd ever known. In fact, this was the most worried she'd ever seen him.

"What's happened? Why are you upset?"

"Remember the toys I sell here in the general store?"

"'Course I do. You sent me one for Kiptyn, when I was in the city." The second mention of Kiptyn in the last hour stirred an ache in Annie's heart.

She missed the little guy more than she'd realized—seeing Eli, remembering the small horse she had given the boy and the way it had lifted his spirits, all combined to bring back the last time she'd seen Kiptyn with remarkable clarity.

Eli's eyes brightened. "The boy you met while staying with your *aenti*? How is Kiptyn?"

"I had another letter this week. He's still gaining ground with the new medicines." Annie patted his hand. "But back to your story. What has happened with your toys?"

"Well, nothing happened with them. I'm still making them, and *Englischers* still love them."

"Plain folk love them too," Annie pointed out.

"*Ya*, you're right. Well anyway, I just found out old Mr. Bontrager is selling the store."

"It's for sale?" Annie turned around to check the window. "I don't see a FOR SALE sign."

"Which is the oddest part." Eli pushed his thumbs under his suspenders, rubbed them up and down as if doing so could produce a better answer. "Bontrager's being real quiet about it. Says he's been thinking about moving to Ohio where his kids settled. He went there a month ago to visit. While he was there, he mentioned he might want to sell, and someone offered to buy the place."

"Just like that?" Annie's voice went up in disbelief.

"Just like that." Eli sat back against the bench, stared out at Main Street, and continued to worry his suspenders.

"All right. I suppose such news would come as a shock, but it's not so bad. Not like the store is closing." She reached out and patted his knee, determined to help him see the bright side of things. Change was hard on older folk—

The idea had barely slipped through her mind when she realized Samuel was almost halfway between Eli's age and her own—not so old after all.

"You're not understanding. The new owner sent along a message."

Annie pulled her mind away from Samuel and back toward the conversation at hand. "What kind of message?"

"A message to all the people currently selling merchandise."

Eli reached into his shirt pocket and pulled out the folded sheet of paper. It was typed on half a sheet—who sent a formal notice on half a sheet?—and still it didn't take up more than a small portion of it.

Upon my arrival I will determine whose merchandise will continue to be sold in The General Store of Mifflin County and at what rate of commission. Until such time you may continue to sell your wares there if you choose, or you may seek business opportunities elsewhere. Management.

Annie read the note again, as if it would make more sense the second time. It didn't.

"Mr. Bontrager gave you this?"

"*Ya*. He gave one to everyone."

"Did he explain it?"

"Nope. He said he was moving in January and the new management would be here then. Any questions we had we could take up with them."

Annie tugged on the strings of her prayer *kapp*. "It's a little odd."

"Indeed it is."

"Do you have a contract with Bontrager?"

"Never needed one. We always had a verbal understanding."

Annie spied Samuel walking into the feed store. "You might want to talk to my *dat* about it."

"*Ya*. That's a *gut* idea."

"I should finish with my shopping." Annie rose and hugged Eli. "I'm sure things will work out for the best."

"Let's hope so." Eli suddenly brightened. "The Lord has a plan in all things. Maybe things will work out even better than they are now."

"Maybe so," Annie agreed, but something about the notice didn't set right with her. It had been too terse, too impersonal. Why hadn't the person at least signed his name?

She pushed into the store, distracted by the jingle of bells and sound of Christmas carols and bumped right into Charity. When she did, all thoughts of Eli's problems flew from her head.

Her *schweschder* was clutching a large package, and Annie saw three bundles of cloth peeking out of the top at the same instant Charity attempted to hide the bag under her coat.

"What are you doing here, Annie?"

"I came into town with Samuel. What's in the bag?"

"What bag?"

Their eyes locked, and Annie was sure Charity would never have given an inch, but suddenly the sales clerk rushed up, bubbling and breathless. "Charity, you nearly forgot the matching thread for your *schweschder's* . . ."

As the girl's face turned a red darker than the ribbon decorating the counter, both Annie and Charity burst into laughter.

"I spoiled a Christmas gift, didn't I?"

"It's no problem," Annie said. "*Danki* for the thread."

Accepting the spool of thread from the girl, Annie linked her arm with Charity's and turned her toward the door.

"We almost surprised you," Charity muttered.

"Indeed you did. Now tell me everything."

⤳☙

Five minutes later they sat at a table in her *mamm's* store, the material spread out between them.

"Three new dresses?" Annie ran her fingers over the cloth, then hugged Charity. "I can't wait to start sewing."

Rebekah poked her head between Charity and Annie with some effort—the two girls hovered over the new material as if they'd found a treasure hidden near a rainbow.

"*Mamm!*" Annie turned and engulfed her mother in a hug.

"I take it that means you're *froh.*" Rebekah laughed, then stepped back and smoothed down her dress. "By the way, what are you doing in town?"

"I came with Samuel. He asked me to go with him to see some patients. I was hoping you could let *Dat* know I might be returning his buggy a little late."

Charity and Rebekah exchanged a knowing look.

Rebekah beamed as if she'd been given an early Christmas gift herself, then patted Annie's shoulder. "No problem, dear. Take as long as you need. Now about these dresses—"

"I think three is too many. Two would have been fine."

"Have you seen yourself in *Mamm's* old clothes?" Charity rolled her eyes. "You look worse than ridiculous. You look as if you've had some illness that left nothing but an old dress and a few bones. No offense, *Mamm*."

"None taken. Charity's right, and I should have thought of new clothes earlier. I didn't realize how poorly your old ones fit. You've grown since you went to the city." Rebekah beamed at her girls. "How long do you think it will take us to sew these up?"

"Not long with the three of us working on them." Annie sat back and shot an amused look at them both. "Charity bought everything we need from the General Store."

The words had no sooner flown from her mouth than she remembered her conversation with Eli. Her smile slid away as she told her *mamm* and Charity what she'd learned.

"I'd heard there was a new buyer from two of the ladies who sell their quilts there." Rebekah straightened a place setting on the table. "Stay here while I bring us some tea. I'll pay for it out of my tips, and I haven't had my break this afternoon yet."

"Your boss doesn't mind you taking breaks at the same time?" Annie asked.

Charity shook her head. "Store's quiet right now, so Mr. Eby prefers we take our break while there are no customers."

Rebekah returned with the tea, cheeses, and some of yesterday's unsold breads. "I heated them up a bit. They'll taste as fresh as if they came straight from the oven. Now, tell me again exactly what the note said, Annie."

When she did, Charity tapped her fingers against the table. "Maybe an *Englischer* is buying the store."

"Possibly. The note didn't say."

"I've known Efram Bontrager all my life." Rebekah sipped from her tea. "I have a hard time picturing him selling to a complete stranger, and if there's one thing I'm certain of it's that Efram would prefer to sell to someone within our faith."

"It was more than the fact that the note didn't give a name. The tone of the note was a bit unfriendly." Annie looked up as the little bell over the door chimed, indicating a customer.

"Belinda Strong." Rebekah jumped up from her chair, hurried over, and embraced the older woman who had entered.

Short, thin, and at least sixty years old, she wore her gray hair in a stylish bob. There was no doubt she was an *Englischer*, but Annie had to smile when she heard the woman utter a nice strong, "*Gudemariye*, Rebekah. How are you this fine December day?"

Annie hadn't seen the midwife in quite a few years, but there was no mistaking her for anyone else.

Few people managed to completely bridge the gap between Amish and *Englisch*, fit into their society as well as Belinda had. She was not only welcome in all their homes, but Annie had overheard families mention "our Belinda" in passing, as if she were in fact an integral part of their community.

And perhaps she was.

She had birthed more of their children than the local hospital, including all of the Weaver children.

"Charity and Annie?" Belinda hugged them both, then held Annie at arm's length. "I was about to say you've grown, but it's something more. Do you have time to tell me about it?"

"Actually, Charity and I need to be getting back to work." Rebekah herded them back toward the table. "I'll bring you some fresh tea—I remember exactly the kind you like, and I'll put a wedge of lemon on the side."

"You're *gut* to me, Rebekah. It was nice seeing you too, Charity. You're even prettier than the last time I was in—you look so much like your mother."

Charity blushed and excused herself.

"You have a few minutes?" Belinda asked, now all business.

"*Ya.* I'm supposed to meet Samuel soon, but—"

"But not yet. Tell me about your training. What did you think of the *Englisch*? What did you think of Mercy Hospital?"

"So you know?" Annie asked.

"What the bishop speaks of spreads quickly through the entire Amish community, and what the Amish know, I know." Belinda reached across the table, squeezed her hand, then patted it twice. "Now tell me everything."

And so they talked medicine. Heads together, as the sun continued to melt the snow outside the window, customers now coming and going, Annie poured her heart out to Belinda.

When she saw Samuel begin to load feed into the back of his buggy across the street, she thought of staying, waiting until her mother went home later in the afternoon.

"Don't worry, dear. I need to be going as well. Two prenatal visits on the east side, and a wee one probably due before morning." Belinda stood and pulled her heavy coat more tightly around her, wrapped her scarf snuggly around her neck, and tugged on her gloves. "There was a time I didn't need all of this to stay warm, but age changes things. Now I'm still cold in April."

They said their goodbyes to her *mamm* and Charity, then walked out into the afternoon sunshine.

"Samuel said you were planning to look in on the Smucker girl."

"*Ya,* I did this morning. I'll give him all my notes, but Belinda, there's something bothering me about her case."

Belinda had been fiddling with her scarf, but now she stopped, put both her hands on Annie's shoulders, looked straight in her eyes, though she had to look up a bit to do so. "When you're feeling there's something different about a case—something more than what they're telling you—usually there is."

A sadness entered her eyes then, and Annie wondered what all she'd seen in her twenty-plus years of birthing. "Trust your instincts, that's what I'm saying. God gave them to you, and they're as valuable as what you learned in school."

Annie waved at Samuel to let him know she was coming, then turned back to Belinda. "It's that Sharon is so skittish. She'd barely let me touch her, and I didn't dare suggest a vaginal exam, though she should have one."

"Do you think she was raped?"

Annie stared down at her shoes. "I honestly don't know. She hasn't talked to me about the father of her baby at all."

Belinda looped arms with her, walked her toward Samuel's buggy. "Watch her for signs of depression, and tell her I'll be out in the next two weeks—regardless what her father or the bishop says. We shouldn't risk the health of the girl or the baby because someone might be embarrassed."

"All right."

"And think about the apprenticeship. I could use your help."

"I'll pray about it," Annie agreed.

"Do that, too."

Belinda waved at Samuel, then continued down Main Street.

Annie climbed into the buggy, clutching her packages from the General Store. She was still *eiferich* about the new material, but somehow it didn't bring her quite as much happiness as it had an hour before.

Belinda had given voice to her gravest fears about Sharon, and there was little she could do about it.

20

Samuel knew he should stay away the next day.

He thought he could wear himself out working on his pastures' fences.

He convinced himself he would not drive to Annie's house.

Walking inside, he looked around the kitchen, spied the still unmailed letter to Rachel he had placed on his desk when he returned home from town. He should take it to the post office, mail it today. But then it would arrive directly after Christmas.

Better to wait a few days after the holiday.

He didn't need to go to town, and he couldn't think of a single excuse for going to Annie's.

When he found himself hitching up his buggy, he drove in the opposite direction—toward the Umbles' farm. Stephen had not come in on Saturday, and no doubt his hand needed checking. Or that was the story he invented as he directed the mare.

Point was, the trip kept him busy for the better part of the afternoon.

By the time he made it back to the road that cut off to his farm, he should have been exhausted. He should have pulled in and gone home.

But he didn't.

Instead he murmured to his mare and directed it down the road that led to Annie Weaver's house.

"She's too young," he muttered, even as he allowed the mare a steady trot. "I've no business courting a girl her age."

The mare offered no answer, and neither did the fields, which lay quiet in the December afternoon. The weather remained pleasant, considering the amount of snow dumped on them less than forty-eight hours earlier. He could actually feel his toes as he rode along in the buggy.

Muttering to no one, he admitted, "Thought I'd grown used to being alone."

And no one answered him, but a hawk soared above— dipping once, then settling out to ride on the currents of air Samuel couldn't even see.

He knew faith resembled the currents—something that he couldn't see but that existed in his life nonetheless. It would hold him up, just as the air currents supported the hawk.

And he could trust his heart to tell him the correct thing to do regarding one Miss Annie Weaver.

❦

Thirty minutes later he pulled into Jacob's lane—feeling a bit foolish, but set on his course.

When a man has made up his mind, when he's prayed things through and decided to risk his pride and heart one more time—well, it gives him a fresh perspective on things.

Jacob's fields appeared well-tended.

And David Hostetler looked a tad less gangly as he made his way down the lane—possibly owing to the fact he was leaving for the day. If he'd been staying, Samuel might have had more trouble waving and smiling at the lad.

Past.

Any jealously he might have felt toward David was past.

He'd make his intentions plain to Jacob and then Annie tonight. Then they could move into the future, or at least the present.

"Are you here for dinner, Samuel?" Reba stood in the doorway, smiling at him, holding a kitten in her arms.

"Let Samuel in and take the kitten to the barn, Reba Weaver."

"I will, *Mamm*." Reba slid past him, broke into a run when her feet hit the last porch step.

As usual, the house teemed with conversation and energy. Smells of freshly baked bread and some homemade soup he couldn't identify filled the air.

Then there were the decorations of Christmas that had been steadily increasing each time he'd stopped by—a small smattering of gifts wrapped in brown paper, tied with red ribbon, and stacked under the table holding the gas reading lamp. The smell of evergreen boughs—Adam must have cut some and brought them in as Annie had been asking him to. Battery-operated candles had been placed in each window, waiting for someone to switch them on once night had completely fallen.

Jacob sat in the living room while the women busied themselves preparing the meal.

"Samuel, nice to see you. I just sat down with *The Budget*." Jacob made to push himself out of the chair with the help of his cane, but Samuel stopped him.

"Don't get up. I was in the area—" Samuel hesitated over the excuse that usually explained why he stopped by. "Actually, I came over because I wanted to talk to you about something."

Rebekah, Charity, and Annie were working on the far side of the kitchen. He didn't think they could hear him, but he wasn't sure—and he certainly didn't want to be interrupted.

"I'm suspecting this is something of a private nature?"

"*Ya*, actually. It is."

"Can it wait until after supper?"

Samuel smiled, sat down in the chair Jacob indicated. "Actually, it can."

"Rebekah, Samuel's staying for dinner."

"We were hoping he might."

Jacob pulled the paper apart, passed half of it to Samuel.

Samuel had read it already, but he didn't mind looking over the upcoming auction again, especially since it gave him a chance to listen to the chatter in the other room. Something about the General Store, new clothes, and *Onkel* Eli.

The women's voices flowed over him like a fresh spring breeze, and he found himself relaxing for the first time all day.

Why had he resisted coming here?

Why had he resisted Annie?

Fifteen minutes flew by, and then Adam came in with Leah and Reba in tow. Extra chairs were pulled up to the table, heads were bowed in silent prayer, then large bowls of potato soup and platters of fresh, hot bread were passed around.

"Annie, your new dress turned out very nice," Leah said, accepting the platter of bread.

"*Danki*." Annie blushed a rosy pink, and Samuel had the sudden desire to tease her more. Instead, he waited for her to raise her eyes to his.

When she did, he smiled, held her gaze.

"You must have sewed all day," Leah continued.

"*Ya*, and Charity didn't work today, so she was able to help me."

She must have expected him to say something, because his silence seemed to confuse her. She picked up her spoon, then set it back down. Finally reaching for her glass of iced tea, she took a sip from it.

When had he first noticed how beautiful she was? The night she came home to help her father?

Conversation swirled around them. He tried to answer when spoken to, attempted to participate so no one would think he'd gone completely daft, but the meal seemed to stretch on twice as long as normal.

Finally, Jacob pushed back from the table.

"Rebekah, I'd like to show Samuel something in the barn if we're done here."

"*Ya*. You men go on outside."

"I can help with the dishes," Leah said.

"No. Adam will be taking you home before it's too late. Already the sun is beginning to set." Rebekah embraced the young woman. "I'm glad he brought you over for dinner, though. Man needs to find time for the girl he loves."

Adam had pulled his hat from the peg by the door. Pushing it down on his head, he tried to look put out with both of them. "If I didn't know better, I'd think you two had been talking about me again."

"Of course we have," Rebekah confessed. "We talk about what a sweet boy you are. Now take her home, and be careful on the main road."

Samuel watched as Adam helped Leah into her coat. They seemed so natural together. Something about being around the two of them reminded him of when he was young.

When he was with Mary.

The memory remained precious to him, but for some reason it no longer hurt like it once did. He didn't miss her any less, didn't expect he'd ever miss her any less, but he now knew God intended for him to live in the present, not the past.

He held the front door open as Jacob grabbed his cane and hobbled through it.

"How are your legs feeling?" he asked, more out of habit than any real concern.

"*Gut.* Feels *gut.* Both itch like crazy. Had Reba find me a long stick so I could scratch down inside of the casts last night."

"Means they're healing, Jacob. That's an excellent sign."

They walked into the night, their steps crunching over the snow as they moved toward the barn. Somehow speaking in the barn seemed appropriate too. Samuel had always been more comfortable there—with the animals, close to the earth.

"How do you expect the spring planting to be?"

"We've had plenty of snow, as you know, so I expect planting will be fine, but I doubt you wanted to talk to me about crops." Jacob smiled as he picked up an old piece of wood he'd been working with and began sanding.

"You're right." Samuel cleared his throat, tried to think of where to begin. "Actually, what I came to talk to you about . . . That is, what I'd like your permission on . . ."

Samuel stopped, wiped his sweaty palms on his trousers. "I feel like a school boy."

"You're doing fine," Jacob said, now watching him with a smile on his face.

"What I wanted to ask is for your permission to court Annie."

Jacob stood and slapped him on the back. "I knew you could get that out if I gave you long enough; however, you know it's not necessary to ask my permission. You're free to see Annie if you'd like to do so—and if she's willing."

"True, but our situation is different. We're not youngsters—well, what I mean is I'm not a young man like Adam."

"You're not exactly old either." Jacob studied him, a smile creasing his face as he waited for him to continue.

"*Ya.* The way I reasoned it out, though, it seems appropriate that in this situation I would come to you first, speak to you about it first, and ask your permission—though I know it's not necessary."

"And my answer is of course you can." Jacob grabbed his hand, shook it firmly.

"Just like that?" Samuel returned the man's handshake, feeling a bit dazed. He hadn't realized how worried he'd been that Jacob might refuse him.

"Just like that."

"Don't you have any questions for me?"

"I've known you as long as I've known Annie, son. What would you expect me to ask?"

Samuel sat down on the workbench, picked up a discarded piece of wood, and studied it. "I don't know. I expected there'd be questions."

"Maybe you'd like to ask me something."

"No. No, I've puzzled this out for quite some time. Resisted it, too. But I believe Annie's the girl for me. I believe God might have brought her back home for me."

Jacob chuckled softly. "You have seemed a bit smitten."

"I have?"

Retrieving the long block of wood, Jacob began sanding it again. "I could see it. A man can tell."

"Our age difference worried me a bit," Samuel confided. "I thought she might be better off with someone her own age. Someone like David."

Jacob nodded. "Age difference can be a problem, but it can be a help at times too."

"*Ya*, I see your point. In the beginning, when you were first injured, when Annie first came back, it stirred up quite a few memories of Mary."

Jacob's hand paused on the block of wood, and he looked Samuel in the eye. "I know those years were a hard time for you, son."

"*Ya*, but I don't believe God would have me live in the past. I can still honor her and move on with my life."

"I believe you can."

"All this talk, and I don't even know how Annie feels about me. I haven't even asked."

"There's one way to find out." Jacob nodded toward the house.

"You wouldn't mind if I—"

"I'd be disappointed if you didn't."

⁂

Annie watched Samuel walk across from the barn, past the nativity scene, and toward the house. In the fading light, she couldn't make out his expression. What had he been talking to her *dat* about? The way Samuel had gazed at her during dinner—it had sent fireflies skittering around her stomach.

Now, as he paused at the bottom step of the porch, she had the certain feeling something was about to change.

Excitement surged through her heart—parts of her heart.

But other parts held back, wanted to run upstairs to the bed she'd slept in since she was a little girl, pull the covers over her head, and insist everything remain the same.

What if he said something that crushed her dreams?

He certainly looked serious.

"Evening, Annie."

"Evening, Samuel."

He joined her at the porch railing. "Cold out tonight."

"*Ya*, but I like looking for the stars as they begin to appear."

They stood that way a minute, staring up as the last of the light faded from the sky, until Samuel finally broke the silence. "Leah was right, you know."

She cocked her head, waited.

"About your dress. It's very pretty."

The warmth started deep within her and rose up into her cheeks, until Annie felt as if her face was on fire like the western sky in front of them.

"Samuel Yoder, I never know what is going to come out of your mouth."

"I was hoping we could talk for a few minutes—if you're not too cold." He motioned toward the oak rocking chairs.

Annie's thoughts immediately conjured up that other evening when she'd first come home. "Why don't we walk instead?" She pulled her coat more snugly around her midsection, though she could hardly feel the chill in the air with Samuel so close by her side.

"All right. Sure."

Annie followed her natural path, the one she took most evenings, the one that led to the vegetable garden behind the house. Though snow still covered the rows, she could now imagine it as they'd planned it for spring. She'd spent hours with Charity and her *mamm* looking at seed catalogs.

"How do you feel about me, Annie?"

His question caught her completely off guard. She'd wrestled with it so many times, but she'd never expected to be asked and certainly never by him.

"You know how I feel, Samuel." When he didn't rescue her by agreeing, she swallowed and pushed on. "I respect you very much. You have excellent doctoring skills—and of course I realize you're not a doctor. You're very kind to the people in our community, and you give to them selflessly. You've done so for a long time. I admire that about you."

"I didn't ask for a professional reference." He leaned back against the fence post, blocking her way into the garden. "But *danki* for the kind words."

"*Gem gschehne.*" Samuel's words confused her, but his smile made her pulse jump in a *gut* way. So why was she so light-headed all of a sudden? Perhaps she had caught something from one of the patients with fever on Saturday.

Was this conversation actually happening?

"How do you feel about me, Annie?" This time he reached out and tucked a stray curl into her prayer *kapp*. The touch sent a shiver all the way to her toes, even though she could barely feel her toes—the night's cold had fallen around them like a blanket of ice.

"I . . . I like you, Samuel." As an afterthought she added, "Now."

His laughter pierced the night.

"Oh, Annie. You are a delight, do you realize that?"

She slapped his arm and pushed past him into the garden, though it now lay cloaked in near-darkness. Suddenly, she needed to be there, needed to be among the rows where she would plant seedlings in a few months.

"I don't know why you're teasing me. You know yourself how hard you were to be around when I first came—and I certainly didn't like you then. You growled every time I stepped into the room. Do you even remember the conversation on my own front porch? You practically threw me out of my parents' home."

"I did, didn't I?" Instead of sounding defensive, he actually sounded amused.

"*Ya*, you did." She wanted to stomp her foot, wanted to wipe the smile off his face, though she could barely see it in the gathering dusk. She could hear it, though. What had gotten into him? Why was he behaving so oddly?

And then he said the words she hadn't ever expected to hear. "I was a little frightened the evening you came home, Annie. I didn't know what to think of you. When you arrived, breathless and worried, in your *dat's* room, you weren't what I expected. You still aren't what I expect, and that has me confused—I'll be honest."

"So what are you saying?"

"I'm saying I enjoy your company, on many levels." His shoulder brushed against hers as they turned and began walking back toward the house, back toward the glow of the gas lamps in the kitchen and living room, back toward the windows lighted with Christmas candles.

"I spoke with your father earlier this evening, asked him if it would be all right for me to come calling. Would you mind if I came calling, Annie?"

"I . . . I don't know what to say," she stammered, her heart now beating faster, but she slowed her steps. She wasn't ready to be back on the porch yet.

"Say yes. Say you'd like to spend time with me. Say I don't have to keep pretending to be checking on your father's leg when I stop by."

Her laughter bubbled up, surprising them both.

"I'd sort of figured that was a ruse."

"Oh, you had, had you?"

"*Ya.*"

"Ruse—is that another *Englisch* word you learned?"

They continued up the porch steps, but he stopped her before they entered the house.

"You'll think on what I've said?" he asked softly.

"Of course I will."

"*Danki.*" Then he opened the door for her.

The evening had taken on an unreal quality to Annie, but she didn't mind one bit. In fact, it might be something she could grow to like.

21

The next day was Thursday, December twenty-third. How had the month passed so quickly? It seemed only yesterday Annie had been trudging down the city sidewalks to her job at the hospital, wishing for the quietness of home, the simplicity of Christmas among her family.

Now Christmas waited—only two days away.

She busied herself with housework in the morning, and before lunch she put the finishing stitches into Leah and Adam's gift.

Then a few moments before noon, Charity, Reba, and her *mamm* came home early—full of news about the school pageant, which would be the next evening, more rumors about the General Store, and excitement over the approaching holiday.

Reba dashed off to the barn as soon as she'd grabbed a piece of fruit out of the bowl on the table.

"By the way, Annie, someone dropped off a note for you today." Charity smiled as she hung her coat on a peg near the door.

"A note for me?"

"*Ya.*" Rebekah teased. "I hope I didn't leave it there. I thought I put it in my apron, but now I'm worried I lost it."

"You didn't lose it. I have it." Charity smiled, held up the folded sheet of paper.

Annie glanced from one to the other. "Anyone want to tell me who wrote this mysterious note?"

Both shook their heads.

"Guess I'll have to read it then." Snatching it from Charity's hand, she plopped down into her father's chair and unfolded the sheet.

"Well, what does it say?" Charity demanded.

"Now, Charity. Could be private. Leave your *schweschder* alone and come help me with dinner."

"We know it's from Samuel, *Mamm.* It would be cruel for her not to read it to us."

"Cruel?" Annie asked as she continued to stare at the single sheet of paper. "Cruel, like not telling someone who wrote the note in the first place?"

"Sorry, dear." Her mother pulled out the fixings for chicken and potato casserole. "We couldn't resist having a little fun with you. Samuel reminded me of a schoolboy when he asked us to bring it home to you. What are the two of you cooking up, anyway?"

Annie joined them in the kitchen, unable to temper the smile on her face.

"Love, could be love is what they're cooking up." Charity selected several potatoes from the bowl and began washing and peeling them.

"Don't tease, Charity."

"Look at her, she's read it three times now, and still she's staring at the paper with moon eyes. Wouldn't you call that look love?"

"Love is more than a look, dear."

"Still, she does have moon eyes. You can't deny it, and she is staring."

"I am not staring at it with moon eyes, and don't talk about me as if I'm not sitting right here." Annie smoothed the note out with the palm of her hand. "I think he's sweet is all. I'm not sure I ever received a note from a man before today."

"Does Samuel need your help with another patient?" Rebekah asked.

Charity and Annie exchanged looks, and Charity mouthed, "Tell her."

"Did *Dat* not speak to you last night when he came in from the barn?" Annie asked.

"Your father fell asleep before I even managed to climb into bed. I wanted to talk to him about Reba and the puppy you two talked me into, but I didn't have a chance." Rebekah stopped grating cheese and stared at both girls. "What am I missing here? Obviously, you two know something I don't."

When Annie and Charity continued to grin at each other, Rebekah grated the cheese more slowly and played along. "You asked me if your father spoke with me, I said no . . . what would he have talked to me about last night?"

"Samuel wants to court Annie," Charity blurted.

Annie rolled her eyes, but smiled at her *schweschder*.

"You don't say." Rebekah wiped her hands on a dishtowel and moved around the table, wrapped Annie in a hug. "What do you think about the idea, dear?"

"I'm not sure what I think about it, or how I feel."

"She's certainly smiling about the note." Charity dropped the potato she'd peeled into the casserole dish and scooted around next to Annie where she could read the words he'd written.

Dearest Annie,

Would you care to join me, Adam, and Leah for a ride out to their new home this afternoon? They want to show us what

progress they've made, and then we'll go to dinner in town. Adam and I have worked out the details if you're interested.
Affectionately,
Samuel

"Doesn't hardly sound like the same man," Charity said.

"Love softens their edges." Rebekah went back to the end of the table and resumed grating the cheese. "I suppose this is what you and Samuel talked about last night when you went for your walk."

"It is, but I thought perhaps I'd imagined the whole thing."

"Apparently not." Charity plopped another potato into the dish and set the paring knife down, propped her chin on her hand, and stared out the window. "A weekday buggy ride, dinner in town—and not a sick person around. That'll be a new experience for the two of you."

"*Ya*, it will," Annie agreed, and something told her she was going to like it.

⟡

It was a different experience all right.

The afternoon was clear, bright, and incredibly cold. But Adam wasn't about to let chilly winter temperatures deter his plans. They bundled up with extra scarves, coats, and gloves, and stacked blankets in the buggy.

Then Adam decided if Charity could handle Blaze then he could too.

They picked Leah up first, and circled around to pick up Samuel.

Annie had decided on her new blue dress. The material was a heavy-weight cotton that both added some extra warmth and would hold up through years of washing. Truthfully, it was heavenly to wear something not too tight across the bosom.

She'd bleached her aprons, so they appeared brand new as well.

She felt like a schoolgirl, ready for the first day of lessons.

She had expected Leah to move to the back of the buggy when they picked up Samuel, but instead he jumped agilely into the back, Adam clucked to Blaze, and they were off like a comet streaking across the sky.

"Can't you slow her down?" Annie hollered, steadying the extra blankets stacked on the seat between them.

Samuel leaned closer, eyes twinkling, as he tucked his battery-operated heater near their feet. "I wouldn't worry. Odds are you and I wouldn't both be hurt, so one of us could patch everyone else up. That's probably why they agreed to let us come along."

Leah began to laugh, then reached forward to grasp the front rail along the buggy. When she did, she let go of the dish towel covering the chocolate oatmeal cookies she'd brought in case they wanted a snack before dinner. The red-checkered towel flew out the window, out into the road, and she laughed even harder, gasping now and pointing at the towel—trying to draw Adam's attention to it.

"Whoa there, Blaze." Adam pulled on the reins, slowing and finally stopping the mare, which tossed her head but obeyed.

"First casualty of the day—one dish towel." Samuel smiled broadly, then hopped out of the buggy before anyone could ask where he was going.

They all turned and stared as he jogged back down the roadside, waited for two *Englisch* cars to pass, then retrieved the towel, which had caught in the branches of a bush. As he hustled back—clutching his coat with one hand and his hat with the other, a car of teenagers zoomed by, honking their horn and waving.

"You made quite the impression," Adam noted as Samuel handed the towel to Leah.

"*Ya*. Probably my jaunty clothes caught them by surprise."

"Jaunty?" Annie asked.

"It could have been my handsome mare." Adam flicked the reins and Blaze started off again, this time at a slightly more controlled pace.

Annie shook her head in disbelief. "I think you two need to eat one of Leah's cookies now."

"Why would you think that, Annie girl?" Samuel placed his arm across the back of the seat.

"Those *Englischers* were not honking at Samuel's clothing or your horse. They slowed down enough to smell Leah's cookies and wished to buy some of her Amish cooking once they arrived in town."

Leah shared a smile with her as they turned down the lane to their new home.

Annie hadn't been there since Adam had started building. She'd meant to stop by but hadn't found the time. Or perhaps she'd been putting off the inevitable.

She stared at the frame of their home and a pang suddenly seized her—Adam would be moving away. What would their home be like without him?

Adam pulled the buggy to a stop in front of the house.

They all sat there, considering what still needed to be done, and what would be here in a few short months.

Annie blinked back the tears pooling in her eyes.

Her big *bruder* was moving off—starting a family of his own. She'd known it, but it hadn't been real to her until this moment. Of course, he'd only be a little way down the road, but still it wouldn't be the same. She was so used to having his curly head and smiling face around.

Samuel must have sensed her change in mood, because he reached over, covered her hand with his, and said, "Adam told me he's been working on this since last fall."

The reminder worked. She focused on Leah and Adam's future, the family they were looking forward to building here, not the ways her own life would change.

"You've done a *gut* job, Adam. Between your job in town and helping *dat* around the farm, I don't understand how you've managed to complete so much on your own."

"Some days I stop by on my way home from work—they let me off early if I work through lunch. I can get in an hour or two each day that way, and it's amazing what I can do on a full Saturday."

"When you're not picnicking," Leah teased him.

"A man has to eat," Adam answered, lacing his fingers with hers. "Now come and let me show you where the living room will be."

The two exited the buggy, huddling together as they made a dash for the part of the house that would offer shelter from the wind—Adam carrying a jug of tea and a checkered cloth he'd stowed on the buggy's floor, Leah still holding the plate of cookies.

Annie told herself she should follow, felt the winter breeze gently rock the buggy, but still her feet didn't want to move.

"He won't be so far away." Samuel's voice—soft, gentle—slowed the anxiousness crawling up her spine.

"*Ya*, you're right. Seeing his home makes it seem very real is all—took me by surprise. He's going to be married. He and Leah will have children, and then he'll be a father."

Samuel's laugh was a deep, resonant sound. He reached out and took her hand in his as he helped her out of the buggy. When he did, goose bumps ran from her fingers up her arm.

"Which is usually how it works. A man marries, then has children, and becomes a father—but then you'd know the process, being a nurse."

His teasing eased the knot of worry that had begun forming a headache along the back of her neck. And of course he was right. What Leah and Adam were doing was a natural and proper thing.

In their community sons often stayed on their father's land and built a home adjacent to the main house—like the Blauchs had done. But Adam had worked since he'd left school, saved his money, and bought a nice piece of land. He was lucky to be able to purchase it when it came up for sale. Tillable farming land was becoming increasingly hard to find.

What if he'd decided to move to Ohio as several in their community had done?

No, she'd be satisfied he was a few miles down the road, halfway between her parents' home and Leah's.

She'd be satisfied any *bopplin* would be a short buggy ride away, and should she decide to be an apprentice to Belinda, she might be the one to help deliver them.

The thought stopped her cold.

"Something wrong?" Samuel asked.

"No." She tried to wrap her mind around the idea of being an *aenti*, of delivering her own nieces and nephews, as she watched Adam and Leah spread the large checkered cloth in the middle of their home, between two walls that had been partially framed. They'd be protected from the north breeze but still able to enjoy the afternoon sun.

"Are you sure? Because you've turned awfully pale." Samuel laced his fingers in hers, rubbed his thumb over the back of her hand. Raising his other hand he nodded at the little heater. "Maybe you should sit down near this—get warm."

Annie shook her head, forced herself away from the future and into the present.

"I'm fine, but a glass of tea would be *gut*." She reversed directions back toward the buggy, found the bag of cups and napkins she'd brought.

As they joined Adam and Leah, she thought back on the bishop's lesson the previous week—how he'd spoken to them about *gelassenheit*. It had sounded so simple then—peacefulness, composure, calm.

Yet it seemed at every turn, her emotions galloped off toward what might happen, bringing turbulence not peace. She let the conversation flow around her and tried to rein in her worries.

It was a beautiful winter day. It wasn't nearly as cold with the blankets spread over their laps, sitting in the shelter of Adam's walls, the heater on, and the sun shining down—though it was definitely the oddest picnic she'd ever been on.

Annie knew the sunny weather wouldn't last. The clouds would come again—rain and snow would force them to return inside for another two months.

This day shone like a blessed reprieve. It sparkled like a gift.

She was on her first date, and Samuel was being a surprisingly attentive companion—no grumpy bear in sight. Come to think of it, she hadn't seen the ill-tempered side of him in quite some time.

Samuel sitting at her side.

Her family was well and near to her.

And she had found a way to use her medical skills, plus Samuel had offered her a way to participate in the community in an even more meaningful way should she decide to take the apprenticeship.

She hadn't realized when the call had come into the nurses' station less than a month ago that she'd be taking the first few steps toward a long journey home, but it would seem she had.

Looking around at Adam, Leah, and Samuel, she couldn't help thinking that life indeed was a gift, and she had much to be grateful for—friends, family, and health.

What more could a girl want?

22

*D*ecember twenty-fourth was a Friday.

Normally Christmas Eve was a regular workday, but since the school program was that evening, Rebekah and Charity had arranged to go in at noon and work until six. It would make for one less trip into town.

School wasn't starting until noon since the students would be staying for the evening, so Reba could ride into town when her *mamm* went to work.

Annie woke to the smell of pies cooking downstairs.

"What do you think *mamm's* doing?" she mumbled into her pillow.

"Best guess? We're going to be sent on missions of mercy." Charity burrowed deeper under her covers.

"With pies?"

"*Ya.* They won't be cool for another hour. Go back to sleep."

But Annie was already awake—awake and thinking of yesterday. She'd never go back to sleep.

Samuel had been the perfect gentleman. If anything his attentiveness had flustered her. She wasn't accustomed to seeing a pleasant and carefree side of him. It was something she could grow used to—and she didn't know what to do with that thought.

She was growing to care for Samuel more than she had expected she would, in ways she hadn't experienced before.

Then there had been the problem of Adam and Leah. Watching those two together had stirred a restlessness in her soul. They had reminded her that most girls her age were married by now, married and expecting children of their own.

The day had been pleasant, exciting, and unsettling all in one.

Slipping into her clothes, she tiptoed out of the room and down the stairs.

"*Dat's* already outside?" she asked with a yawn.

"You'll have trouble catching him still now," her mother admitted with a smile. "He's learned to move around with that crutch as fast as he did without it."

"When is his next appointment to see Dr. Stoltzfus?"

"We had scheduled for next Thursday, but you know your father. He wants to be here to help David when the new cattle arrive."

"So he cancelled?" Annie's voice squeaked as she reached for a mug and the kettle of hot water.

"Not exactly. He changed it to the following Saturday. Fortunately Dr. Stoltzfus still has Saturday morning hours once a month, and it happens to be next weekend."

"If not, *Dat* would be in the barn trying to break the cast off with a hacksaw."

"Probably he would, but at least it proves he's feeling well."

"*Ya*, and I'm thankful for that." Annie sat at the table and studied the pies, which covered nearly every inch. "*Mamm*, are you planning on starting your own bakery?"

Rebekah's laughter mixed with Reba's squeal as she chased something through the front room. Annie didn't want to see exactly what, at least not until she'd had her first cup of tea.

"I did get carried away a bit, didn't I? Once I started rolling out dough it seemed simpler to keep rolling." Rebekah sat and studied her work with a smile. "Christmas hits me this way sometimes. I start thinking on how fortunate I am to have all my children here, under my roof . . ."

"And then?"

"Well, then I think about your *Onkel* Eli." Rebekah reached out, patted her hand, then stood and began washing dishes.

"*Mamm*, do you expect *Onkel* Eli to eat all of those pies?"

"'Course not, but after I made him two, I thought I might as well make one for Samuel. Then I remembered what you said about Mrs. Wagler not eating well."

Annie reached for a piece of breakfast bread and made herself another cup of tea. "All right, you've accounted for four, I suppose. What about the rest?"

"Two I made for us. You don't think I could make pies and not save some for your *dat*? And the last two . . ." Rebekah stopped, a look of confusion replacing her smile.

"Hooleys'." Reba said, sliding into a chair beside Annie. "You said you thought Annie should check on the Hooley family."

"*Ya*, you're right." Rebekah's eyes narrowed in a look of concern. "I probably should have made a few for the Smucker family too."

"Mrs. Smucker lives in the opposite direction of the others," Annie pointed out. "And she can cook just fine. I'm sure she'd enjoy a visit from you without pies."

"Excellent point. Charity and I will go see Mrs. Smucker, then go on in to work. You can take Reba with you to deliver pies to the Hooleys and Samuel, then drop her off at the school-house, if you don't mind."

"Then I can see the puppies!" Reba tossed her straight dark hair back behind her shoulder. "I've asked for one for Christmas, but *Dat* hasn't said yet. I talked to him again this morning. He reminded me I'd have to care for it and train it."

Reba lay her head down on the table, traced the wood's grain with one finger. "I hope Samuel has one available. I hope *Dat* agrees I can have one."

Annie smiled at her enthusiasm. Had there ever been a time when a dog had made life perfect for her?

"So you're going with me?" Annie asked.

"Absolutely. Plus you'll look more official delivering pies if I go along, since I've been working an hour after school in the bakery and all."

"Well, I certainly want to look official."

"I'll go wash up then." Reba launched herself off her chair and headed for the bathroom.

Watching her, some of the weight eased from Annie's shoulders. Perhaps she took life a tad too seriously. Perhaps it was as simple as delivering pies and training puppies.

"She's a special one," Rebekah said, sitting down again at the table.

"I have trouble believing she's fourteen."

"In some ways she still acts much younger. I've stopped by the bakery a few times, and she's always proper. You would scarcely recognize her. Once she's home, though, she turns into the Reba we know—full of energy and still a bit of a child."

"I envy those things about her, though. I'm not sure a puppy ever solved the problems of the world for me."

"Well, you were always my serious child, Annie." Rebekah reached out, ran a hand down her arm. "Want to talk about yesterday?"

"I enjoyed it. Samuel is not at all what I expected."

"How so?"

"He's different when he's away from his work, or maybe I finally had a chance to see another side of him."

"It seems to me men remain very focused when they're working. They take what they do seriously, and for an understandable reason—it's how they provide for their family."

"We care about our work too."

"Of course we do, but there's less intensity involved for us. Wouldn't you agree?"

"*Ya*. Maybe so. Maybe that's why *Dat* can't stay in bed even when he knows he should."

"Perhaps, and I won't argue with him about it. He works as hard as he does to provide for me and you and your *bruder* and *schweschders*. I'm sure it's the same with Samuel."

"But he has no family." The words popped out of Annie's mouth before she could consider how they'd sound, and then she couldn't pull them back.

"True." Rebekah turned one of the pies, studied its crust. "He did once, though. I suppose he couldn't merely stop when he lost them. And maybe he hopes to have a family again someday."

"Is that what I would be? His second family?"

"I don't know, sweetheart. If you and Samuel were to decide to marry, I'm sure Samuel would love you as he did Mary. He couldn't love you less. Same as how I don't love you less than I love Adam or Charity or Reba."

Annie nodded, then stood and threw her arms around her mother.

"What's that for?"

"Always being there. Being a *gut* mother. Making excellent pies." Annie swiped at her tears and laughed lightly. "Pick a reason."

⤫

An hour later she and Reba were on their way, six pies safely tucked into a box in the back of the buggy, the old mare safely hitched to the front.

"Would you like me to drive?" Reba asked.

"*Danki*, but I think I need the experience."

They stopped first at Mrs. Wagler's home. Rebekah had decided to send three jars of canned vegetables along with the pie.

Annie was relieved to see that the older woman seemed to be moving around easily, with few physical problems. She questioned her in a roundabout way and learned she was following Samuel's instructions to the letter—her bowel problems had improved considerably.

"You still need to eat these vegetables, Mrs. Wagler."

"I'll have my own by spring—the garden always grows fine." Mrs. Wagler waved a wrinkled hand at her as they climbed back into their buggy.

"Before spring you'll be back at Samuel's. Now promise me you'll eat the vegetables."

"*Ya*, I'll eat them. Wouldn't want to hurt Rebekah's feelings. Did your mother tell you I once taught her when she was a small girl?"

"No, she didn't."

"It's true. The teacher had to be out due to a terrible cold for a few weeks, and I filled in. Rebekah was around seven at the time, but I still remember her being the smartest in the class. You can tell her I said so."

"I will, Mrs. Wagler."

"Little girl, you tell the bakery owner he's putting too much cinnamon in his apple pies. He'd do better to make them like your *mamm* does."

"Yes, Mrs. Wagler." Reba's eyes were large, but she nodded in agreement as Annie turned the buggy and the mare clip-clopped off.

"I can't tell Mr. Bender that, Annie." Reba's voice bordered on panic. "It would be rude. Besides, our pies from the bakery taste great. We sell out every day."

"It's all right. You can tell him Mrs. Wagler requested a light cinnamon pie—old people have different tastes. If he started a new line of pies for older folks, he could increase his sales even more. That way you're not lying to Mrs. Wagler, but you're not insulting Mr. Bender's pies either."

"Hadn't thought of that. Great idea." Reba studied the road as they headed toward Samuel's.

"I wish I was like you," she declared. "I'm great with animals, and I'm fair with food—which is why I do okay at the bakery. I don't manage quite as well with people, though. They befuddle me sometimes."

Annie nodded as they moved to the side of the road so a car could pass them. "Every one of us has skills, Reba. Be glad you know yours. As far as understanding people—it becomes a little easier as you grow older, but some people are more difficult to understand—"

"I know a few of those at school."

"And others seem difficult to get along with, no matter how you try." Annie's mind drifted back to some of her more difficult patients at Mercy Hospital.

"I used to find Samuel kind of frightening. He didn't smile much, and he looked kind of sad all the time. He's changed, though. I like it when he comes to visit now."

"You do, do you?"

"*Ya.*"

"Doesn't have anything to do with those border collies?"

"Nope. I'd like him anyway."

"Hunh. Nice to know—in case they're all gone."

Reba squinted up at her anxiously, and Annie felt a little bad for teasing her. Not bad enough to tell her Samuel had reminded her last night there was still one left.

Waiting was half the fun of receiving.

And they were almost to Samuel's place. She turned down his lane and giddy-upped to the mare.

By the time they pulled up to the house, Samuel stood on the porch steps, smiling at them.

"This is a surprise—two of my favorite people on Christmas Eve morning."

"*Mamm* sent you pies, and my *dat* is still thinking about whether I can have one of the puppies for Christmas—if you have one left that is. Are there any left? Annie said they might be all gone, and that's okay if they are, but I sure hope you have at least one still needing a home." Reba stood below the steps, shuffling from foot to foot, staring up at him hopefully.

Samuel glanced over at Annie and almost broke into a smile, but somehow he resisted.

"Let me see, I did give away a few since Annie was here Saturday, but I think . . ." He pulled on his beard, scanned out across the clear blue sky, then looked back at Reba with a smile. "Why, yes, I'm sure of it. There's one little male left, waiting in the back corner of the barn with his mother."

"The pie's apple," Reba said shoving it into his hands, then she was gone—tearing off around the corner of the house to the barn.

"I think she's a bit *eiferich*." Samuel motioned toward the house with the pie. "Would you like to come in while I put this up?"

"Oh. Sure." Annie followed him inside. "I don't know why she's so thrilled about a pup. Well, I do know why. She gets this way about animals. It's not that we haven't ever had a dog before, because we have. But the last one lived to be so old, and then we weren't ready to replace him and there was really no need since we had no cattle."

She heard herself rambling as she followed him through the house to the kitchen.

What had she expected his home to look like?

A place that was all male, completely devoid of feminine touches?

A place that was a shrine to his *gschtarewe fraa*?

Samuel's house was neither. Obviously, it was a man's house, as some of the softer touches she noticed about her mother's home were missing.

No basket of knitting sat by the chair.

No shawl hung on the peg by the door.

No smells of baking filled the air.

But neither was his house depressingly devoid of personality. Amish homes were by nature modestly decorated—counters without knickknacks or clutter, windows covered with shades rather than curtains, no proliferation of throw pillows on the couch.

Annie wouldn't have expected those things, and she didn't find them.

Samuel had kept the house freshly painted, though, and clean—which she would expect from a man in the medical profession.

"Does it meet your approval, Miss Weaver?"

"What?" She turned, found him standing in the doorway between the kitchen and the living room, watching her. "I'm sorry. I didn't mean to stare. It's just that I've never been in your home, and you've been in mine so many times."

"Is it what you expected?"

"I don't know. I don't know what I expected."

"It's only a house, Annie—walls and a roof. What matters is the people who live inside—that's what makes a place a home. That's what makes your parents' place so welcoming."

"*Ya*, I know what you're saying is right." She followed him into the kitchen, stood by the small table as he put the pie into the refrigerator. "When I stayed with my *aenti*, I never could get used to all the things she had lying around. Made me feel crowded."

"I believe your experience there changed you—and for the better." He closed the distance between them, touched her face. When he did, it seemed as if the sun had pierced through the window, warmed the room. "What I mean is, I think it made you appreciate things here more."

"Maybe so." She had trouble pushing the words out. She had trouble concentrating with his dark eyes staring into hers. "I know I think about home differently now."

"And?"

Annie stepped away, moved back into the living room. "And I'm glad we don't have all those knickknacks. Makes for a lot of dusting."

Samuel laughed and followed her out onto the porch.

"We best go check on Reba," he said. "Where are you girls headed next?"

"The Hooleys', then *Onkel* Eli's."

"I had some wood I wanted to send to Eli. I think he could use it for the toys he makes. Would you mind taking it with you?"

"'Course not." Annie also didn't mind when he reached for her hand, closed his fingers around hers.

"I'll bring the pup by this evening, before the Christmas presentation at the school. Would you like to ride with me this evening?"

"*Ya*, I would. *Danki*."

They slowed their pace, still holding hands, as they moved toward the barn in the bright morning sunshine.

23

$\mathcal{A}$nnie delivered the pies from her mother to the Hooleys.

Next stop—*Onkel* Eli's. He was thrilled with the pie, but his face glowed when he saw the maple wood.

She delivered Reba to the one-room schoolhouse. Then she drove the buggy home, arriving there well before noon.

And she began to grow restless.

She'd finished all of the laundry.

Every last present had been completed and wrapped—and though the stack was small by her *Englisch freinden* standards, she knew Second Christmas would bring smiles from her family.

Still, she had six hours to kill before she needed to be ready for tonight. How was she to occupy herself?

Why was she looking for ways to occupy herself?

She should be working. She should have a job.

She thought of scrubbing the floors one last time, but it would require changing out of her new dress, then changing back again for this evening. She picked up some darning her mother had begun, but each stitch she sewed somehow added to her impatience.

What to do?

Looking over at the basket beside her mother's chair, she spied the baby blanket. Had she mentioned it was for Sharon Smucker? Yes, and when Annie had stopped by the store, she'd told her their visit had gone well.

She'd also said Sharon's mother appeared calmer, and Mr. Smucker hadn't hidden in the barn when she'd arrived. Perhaps it would be a *gut* time for her to go over and talk to them again about the midwife.

Annie hurried to the kitchen, set out a cold lunch for her *dat* and David, then grabbed her coat from the hook by the door and headed toward the barn.

A ride in the buggy might also temper the impatience in her soul.

Rehearsing how she might broach the subject of Belinda Strong with the Smucker family, Annie nearly ran right into David.

"Hello, David."

"*Gudemariye.*" David smiled, pushed down on his straw hat.

"It's nearly afternoon actually. How's your work in the barn going?"

"Very well. I know your *dat* will be *froh* to be able to do more himself once the smaller cast is removed next week."

Annie followed him into the barn. "I'm not sure what he's told you, David. But because the cast is removed doesn't mean he'll be able to run this farm by himself right away."

"*Ya*, he mentioned you would say as much." David offered his usual smile and some of her anxiousness fell away. She'd noticed that around David it was impossible to feel *naerfich*.

"You always act as if everything is going to be all right."

"It usually is, isn't it?" Gentle eyes smiled at her as they entered the barn together.

"I suppose, but I tend to worry nonetheless."

"Perhaps because you're a caretaker, Annie. It's *wunderbaar* the way you look after your father, and don't worry about the farmwork. I'll still be here half days for awhile. Your *mamm* has already talked to me about the spring planting schedule."

Annie felt a burden she didn't realize she'd been carrying lift off her shoulders as she reached for the old mare's harness.

"I'll be taking that for you." David arms reached around her. "You need Ginger harnessed to the rig?"

Annie blushed slightly, but released the harness without argument. "I do. I wanted to go and visit one of our neighbors. Oh and I've set out lunch already in the kitchen."

"I appreciate it, but your father and I could find lunch for ourselves if you're too busy, Annie."

"I'm not too busy." She ran a hand over her father's workbench. "Some days I barely know how to fill my time," she continued, her voice taking on the tone of someone revealing something they'd rather not own up to.

David nodded. "We're in those in-between years, when we don't have our own place yet, an apprenticeship of sorts that isn't as much work as real life will be. That's how I like to think of it."

Annie glanced up quickly. It was as if he'd been struggling with the very same things she had, but surely David was so busy he didn't know which pasture he needed to till next.

"Your *dat's* in the near pasture working on the gate latch. Why don't you go and have a word with him while I tend to this?"

"*Danki.*"

"No need to thank me, but *gem gschehne.*"

Annie knew he meant rigging up the horse. She could have let the misunderstanding go, but something about his mild-mannered ways had calmed her this morning.

David had reached the barn door and pushed it open. Sunlight splashed into the work area, filling even the darkest corners.

She spoke anyway—knowing he would stop. "I meant to thank you for everything you've done for my family. Thank you for being here, for dividing your attention between your parents' farm and my parents'. Mostly thank you for doing so in a considerate way."

David tilted his head, and she had the thought his straw hat might fall off on to the ground.

He turned, moved back into the workroom. When he stopped beside her, she had to scrunch her neck to see up into his eyes. It struck her then how much he reminded her of Adam, and how her feelings for him mirrored those she felt for her *bruder*.

"It's what we do, Annie. You know that—it's what we've always done for one another." He reached forward, swiped at some straw clinging to the sleeve of her dress. "You'd do the same for us."

She nodded in agreement, almost stopped the words that wanted to push out. "Do you remember when you asked me to go for a buggy ride with you?"

"*Ya.*"

"I don't know if you are aware of it, but I'm seeing Samuel now."

"I know."

"I wanted to say how much your friendship means to me, and how much I appreciate your kindness. You've been a *gut* friend to me since the day I came home."

"I'm glad you've found someone, Annie. God has someone for each of us." Grinning sheepishly, he added, "No one can have too many friends."

As if that last thought explained it all, he turned to walk back outside. She started to walk out with him, but as she stepped forward her foot caught on the corner of the workbench.

She let out a squeak, and David turned, jumped to catch her as she fell into a bale of hay he'd been using to stack old rope on top of.

Annie grabbed at him, trying not to fall, but instead of steadying herself she succeeded in pulling David off balance. They both went down in one giant cloud of hay dust.

Seeing the look on David's face, and the hay in his hair, Annie started laughing and couldn't stop.

"It's funny now," David said, standing and brushing off his clothes. "We'll see who's laughing when the laundry has to be redone."

He reached for her hand to pull her out of the hay when suddenly the light was blotted by someone standing in the doorway.

Annie's hand went to her chest, her heart rate doubling. She must have made a sound, for David's hand curled around hers and he pulled her to her feet, placed a steadying hand on her elbow.

"It's only Samuel," David said.

"You scared the breath out of me," Annie sputtered. "I didn't hear your buggy drive up."

"Apparently you didn't," Samuel said in a voice colder than the morning frost.

Instead of stepping into the barn, he remained in the doorway.

Annie shielded her eyes but still couldn't make out his expression with the sun blazing behind him.

"I'll have the buggy ready for you in a few minutes, Annie. Unless you'd rather wait now." David put a few steps between them, and Annie had the most absurd idea he did it in order to put Samuel at ease.

"*Danki*. I'm not sure if I'll be going right away or not—"

"Don't change your plans for me." Now a clear edge sharpened Samuel's voice.

"Of course I can change my plans." Annie stepped toward him, was finally able to make out the frozen expression on his face. "It's just I wasn't expecting you."

"Obviously."

Annie shook her head, as if she could clear it, could make sense of his mood or his words. "I don't know what you mean. I don't understand . . ."

She looked to David for an explanation, but he merely shrugged as he picked up the harness and carried it toward Ginger's stall.

When she turned back toward Samuel, he was gone.

Gone? Where could he have possibly gone?

She hurried through the door and caught up with him as he opened the door to climb into his buggy.

⁓

Samuel didn't know what he'd seen in the barn between Annie and David, and he sure didn't want her explaining it. Not now.

He needed to go home, needed to get back to work, needed to get his life back on track.

"Samuel, where are you going?"

"I'm going back home."

"But, why did you come by?"

He reached into the back of the buggy, pulled out the pup, and dropped it into her arms.

"I wanted to bring you this. I'm needed on the far side of the district to check on a sick family."

"Would you like me to go with you?" Annie's arms curled around the pup, and her eyes went from it to him, imploring him to explain, but he didn't fall for her supposed confusion.

He knew what he'd witnessed.

He was a man of science after all, and facts were facts. He was man enough to face up to them.

"Samuel? Would you like me to come with you to help?"

"No, Annie. I wouldn't." He picked up the reins, stared out over Smokey's ears, out past Jacob's fields.

"*Was iss letz*? Why are you angry?"

He closed his eyes for a moment. What he wanted most was to go back in time, to go back four weeks and not allow his heart to unthaw. Then he wouldn't be feeling this pain, and he wouldn't have to explain to her what had happened, what he'd seen.

But he'd worked in medicine too long to allow something to fester—best to get it over and done with.

"I'm leaving because I saw how it is between you and David."

"How . . . what?"

"Annie." Suddenly he ached with fatigue, doubted whether he could drive the rig home. How had he thought he could find the energy to start over, to be the husband she would need?

"Come down out of the rig. Talk to me."

He allowed his eyes to linger on her then. Though her voice had landed somewhere between anger and scolding, her bottom lip trembled and she pulled it in between her teeth and worried it as she waited.

"No. Don't you see, Annie? David's what you need. I knew that. Somewhere inside I suppose I've always known. Then when I walked into the barn and saw the two of you . . ."

"We were only talking." She clenched her arms around the puppy at the same moment a single tear escaped from her right eye.

Both tore at his heart, but he knew he was right.

He couldn't turn back now.

"*Ya*, but can't you see? David is young like you are. David doesn't have . . ." His hand went out in front of him, took in the fields that held no crops. "He doesn't have the history I have. David and you have more in common than we do."

"Don't I have a say in this? Two nights ago you stood in the garden and asked me, you asked me if I'd like to have you come calling."

"Well I'm un-asking now."

"And I have no say in it?"

"You said it all with the way you were looking at him."

"You're being unfair. I don't know what think you saw, but you're wrong."

He shook his head, gathered the reins more tightly in his hands. "No, I'm not. You need someone like David. You deserve him, and I deserve—"

He bit off the words even as the image of Rachel popped into his mind.

Why hadn't he realized it earlier?

Of course, his duties lay in Ohio.

And it was the reason he hadn't mailed the letter he'd written.

The reason it still sat on his desk at home.

Annie's voice pulled him back. "You deserve who, Samuel? Look at me. I have a right to know."

He considered not telling her but knew if he didn't then she wouldn't go on with her life.

David pulled Jacob's mare, hitched to the buggy, out of the barn. He was a good man, David. He would be a good husband to her.

The best way to show Annie how much he cared about her would be to help her move on, help her move in the direction of what was best for her.

He could accomplish it by telling her about Rachel.

"Who do you deserve?" Her question was a whisper, a broken promise waiting to be heard.

"Mary's *schweschder* has been asking me to move to Ohio. She has two small boys who need a *daed*." He refused to look away until the weight of his words had sank in, had registered fully. "Her name is Rachel."

Annie stepped back away from his buggy, hopped back—as if she'd been slapped. "You've never mentioned her before."

"I know I haven't. I didn't want to move. Didn't want to accept . . ." he swallowed, pushed the words out past the lump forming in his throat. "Didn't want to acknowledge my obligations."

He glanced at her once more.

Arms crossed, clutching the puppy to herself as if she might fly to pieces. She continued to stare at him, as tears ran in rivulets down her face.

Stared at him as if he were someone she didn't know.

And perhaps that was the truth.

So he murmured to his mare and drove away.

24

$\mathcal{A}$nnie stared down at the squirming pup in her arms.

She glanced up when the sound of Samuel's buggy, retreating down their lane, registered in her heart.

"Would you like me to take the hound?" David's voice was quiet, and he stood a few feet from her, still back and toward the barn.

Annie turned slowly, after she'd brushed at the tears with the heels of her hands. She knew her face must look a mess, but there was nothing she could do about it now.

"*Ya*, please."

He accepted the warm bundle from her arms, and the little hound immediately began licking him on the chin. Still, David didn't smile. He did pet the pup, attempting to calm it, and studied her with a concerned look.

He didn't say anything, or ask anything.

He simply waited—like a friend or *bruder* would.

"What just happened, David?"

"I believe maybe Samuel misunderstood what he saw."

She nodded in agreement, pulled in a deep steadying breath as they returned to the barn.

"But I tried to explain. He wouldn't even listen. He . . ." Her words fell away. Perhaps it wasn't proper to be discussing this with David. She should wait. Speak with her *mamm* tonight, but that was hours away, and she had a weight on her heart threatening to crush her.

"Samuel walked in at the worst possible moment, Annie. I wouldn't be too hard on him. Maybe if you give him time to reflect on what he saw, he'll reconsider. Or maybe if I go and speak with him—"

"No." She reached out, touched his arm. "You've been a *gut* friend to me, but this isn't between you and Samuel. If he can misinterpret such a small thing, if he won't even hear me out, then perhaps he isn't the man I thought he was."

David frowned as he tucked the puppy into a wooden kennel they'd made for him, made and hidden in her *dat's* office portion of the barn—a portion Reba didn't enter without permission. "I've never known Samuel to be the jealous type, though. Or hasty in his judgment. Something else must be at work here."

Annie thought back over his words, about her deserving someone younger, about his obligations to Rachel. But she couldn't explain that to David—not without the tears spilling again.

Instead, she reached forward and caressed the pup. "He'll be all right here?"

"*Ya*, it's plenty warm, and Reba won't be able to hear him from the main part of the barn. It'll be a nice surprise."

"*Danki*," Annie said softly, then stood and stumbled out into the December day. It seemed less bright now, though of course it wasn't. The sun still shone in the sky.

Christmas Eve.

Where had all the hope and joy of Christmas gone?

Climbing up into the buggy, she headed down the lane, toward the Smuckers. If she could do nothing here, perhaps she could do some small good there.

꒰ꑌ꒱

This time, when Annie pulled up in front of the Smucker home, no one stepped out on the front porch to greet her.

Actually, it looked like no one was in the house, though laundry did hang from the line.

She also noticed Mr. Smucker working out beside the barn.

Might as well knock on the door, though. She'd driven this far.

Sharon answered the door after her second knock. The girl appeared to have gained a bit of weight in the short time since Annie had seen her.

"Annie, I didn't expect you to come by today."

"I was thinking of you," Annie replied honestly. "May I come in?"

"Of course." Sharon opened the door wider, then stood there as if unsure what to say next.

Finally she offered, "My *mamm* went into town to pick up a few last-minute things for Christmas."

"That's all right. Maybe you and I could visit a little while."

"Would you be needing to examine me again?" A look of concern passed over the young girl's face, and Annie wondered again why the exams bothered her so.

"No, Sharon. Not unless you're feeling differently."

"Feel about the same—though my *boppli* seems to grow each day." She placed her hand on top of her protruding stomach. "Don't remember my *mamm* being so big with my little *bruder*."

Annie smiled, trying to put her at ease. "It's different with everyone. Some women carry their babies to the front, so the stomach looks and feels larger. Other women carry their babies more to the back. They look smaller, but with the smallness comes more of a backache."

A genuine smile crossed Sharon's face for the first time. "I'll take the big stomach, then. What with the gas and the going to the bathroom so much, I don't need a backache too."

They stood there for a moment, afternoon sunshine spilling into the living room, when the sound of a teakettle pierced the silence. "I was just making some hot tea. Can I make you a cup?"

"That would be *gut*." Annie followed her into the kitchen and resisted the urge to take out her patient book and start making notes. Sharon's color was *gut*, she was moving around easily, and the gas and increased urination sounded normal enough.

They settled across the table from one another, each holding a mug of hot tea.

"How's the knitting coming?"

Sharon beamed at her now. "*Wunderbaar.* I had knitted before, but only scarves and small things. Since I haven't . . ." she stumbled, pushed on, "left the house, I've had a lot of time to learn how to make booties, caps, even little sweaters. I'm actually becoming quite talented with the knitting needles."

Annie's temper rose toward Mr. Smucker for not allowing Sharon to leave the house. She tamped it down and focused on Sharon. "It's *gut* you're using your time well. The baby will be here before you know it."

"*Ya.*" The young girl gazed down into her tea, took a tentative sip. "That's where *Mamm* is now. In town buying more yarn . . . and things." She pulled her bottom lip in, worried it, then glanced out the window at the bright sunny day. When the tears began to spill over, she pushed away from the table, mumbled "Excuse me," and fled.

Annie waited for a few minutes, then rose and rinsed out the glasses. When Sharon still didn't return, she became concerned and went in search of her.

She walked back to the room she'd examined her in, stopped at the door standing slightly ajar. Soft sobs from the other side tore at her heart.

She knocked lightly, then pushed the door open.

Sharon lay on her side, facing the wall.

"May I come in? I don't want to intrude, but I'd like to make sure you're all right before I leave."

"I'm fine," Sharon mumbled.

Annie entered the room, sat on the side of the bed. "It's normal to be emotional while you're pregnant. Faith Blauch told me she cried enough to fill up a milking pail the two weeks before little Noah was born."

Sharon sniffled, rubbed her nose against the arm of her dress. "What would Faith have to cry about? Faith has a husband."

Reaching forward and pulling Sharon's hair back away from her face, Annie wondered how to answer that—she recognized it for what it was.

A heart's cry.

"Is that what this is about? You having no husband?"

Sharon didn't answer, but her crying lessened a bit.

"I don't know your situation, Sharon. I don't know how you arrived at this point or what happened before today, but I do know one thing. The *boppli* growing inside you is a miracle— one I'm *eiferich* about. One you will love and your family will love."

Still sniffling, Sharon sat up, her back against the headboard, her legs—which Annie could now see were a bit swollen—propped up on the mattress. "Do you truly believe that?"

"I do, every word of it."

Sharon stared at her a minute, and Annie knew she was being sized up, realized Sharon was making a decision. Finally she sighed, reached for a handkerchief on the little table between the two beds, and said, "I didn't imagine it being this way."

"Being pregnant?"

She shook her head, then waved her hand at the bassinet sitting at the foot of her bed. "This. Life. When I started seeing Keith, he said he loved me. He acted different from Amish boys—exciting and different."

Plucking at the bedspread, she didn't look up for a few seconds. When she did, Annie thought the tears pooling in her eyes would spill again. Instead, she raised her chin, stared out into the hall. Something like a shiver passed over her.

"What are you thinking of now, Sharon?"

"It's nothing." Her voice grew smaller. "It doesn't matter."

"It might make you feel better if you told someone, though, and if you asked I would keep it between the two of us."

Sharon looked at her then as though Annie might offer the one road back to a place she longed to be. "I didn't want to. He said it wouldn't hurt, said all the *Englisch* girls did. He said if I cared about him I would."

Annie waited, her heart hammering. Waited though she knew what Sharon's next words would be.

"Still I couldn't, because it's against our ways. Seeing an *Englisch* boy was one thing, but being with one in such a way—I knew it was wrong." The tears spilled now, but just two of them, as if a sacrifice of two tears to his memory was plenty.

"Then he went away for a time. He said it was with his work, but I think he meant to punish me. When he came back, I wanted him to stay. Wanted to show him I did care about him, so I . . . I did what he asked." She rubbed her stomach, not really talking to Annie any longer. "Only twice, but I suppose that's all it took."

Annie reached out, covered Sharon's hand with her own.

"When he went away the second time, he didn't come back." Sharon glanced down, her gaze locking on Annie's hand over hers. When she looked up, the tears were gone. "And you know what?"

"What, Sharon?"

"I don't want to see him either. I can do this. I can do this on my own."

"But you don't have to do this on your own, sweetie. Because you're surrounded by people who care about you."

"Even my father?" Her words were sharp like a stone.

"Even your father. Our *dats* might have a hard time accepting some things, and they might have difficulty when life curves away from the road Amish normally take, but Sharon, never doubt your father loves you. Give him time. Pray for him. I know this is going to work out fine."

She enfolded the girl in a hug, left her there to nap, then quietly left the house.

Annie had the maturity to walk away and let things be, but Phillip Smucker picked that moment to walk from his barn to his house.

He looked up, saw her, and stopped.

Annie thought for a moment he might turn and walk back into the barn, but he didn't. He nodded once and kept walking toward the house. "Annie," he said.

"Mr. Smucker." She waited there by her buggy, thinking he would pause at least to inquire why she was there. When he headed toward the porch steps instead, she moved in front of him. "I'd like to talk to you about Sharon."

"I've nothing to say." He met her gaze when he said it, then looked away.

Knowing she needed to maintain control of her anger, Annie pulled in a deep breath, fought to keep her voice low, and said clearly, "You might not have anything to say, but I do."

"Best say it to Ruth then. She'll be back from town directly, I expect."

"It's not Ruth I need to speak with."

Phillip jerked his gaze back toward her. "I don't understand—"

"I know you don't," Annie said softly. "I'm not sure I understand completely, but I do know there's a young lady in there who needs her *dat's* love and acceptance."

"I don't expect you to be telling me what my daughter needs."

He started walking away, but Annie hurried to catch up with him. "Apparently someone needs to, and I believe you and your *fraa* asked me to come out and look after Sharon's medical condition. Or you asked Bishop Levi to find someone, and he found me. So you either trust him or you don't."

"Is this about Sharon's health?" Phillip turned on her, frustration edging his voice.

"As a matter of fact, it is, Mr. Smucker."

He stormed away from her then, didn't stop until he'd reached the nearest tree and stood studying it. When he turned back, Annie saw some of the struggle had gone out of him—much of the pain remained, but a bit of the resistance he'd been carrying was gone.

"The girl seemed fine this morning. Is she sick?"

"She's not sick, Mr. Smucker. She's pregnant."

He flinched at the word.

"Your grandchild will be born soon, probably in this very house—the same house Sharon was born in, but I can't assist that birth alone. Belinda needs to come and see her."

He shook his head. "I'm not ready yet—"

"This *boppli* will come whether you're ready for it or not. I'm worried about Sharon's emotional state, which could affect the *boppli's* health."

Phillip studied her now, concern replacing the look of stubbornness.

"I've always looked forward to being a *grossdaddi*. Sharon's child will be my first."

"And you wouldn't want anything to happen to him or her?"

He stood up straighter now, taken aback by her comment. "Of course not."

Annie moved closer, bridging the gap between them. "I understand you might be upset with Sharon, but she needs to see the midwife."

"It's early yet—"

"She needs to get out of this house. Let her go into town. Certainly allow her to attend the school presentation tonight and the Christmas service tomorrow. Sharon needs to feel the love and support of her *freinden*."

Phillip didn't agree or disagree with her.

"Don't doubt our community will care for Sharon and her baby." When he remained silent, Annie thought back to what David had said to her a few hours before, found herself echoing his same words. "It's what we've always done for one another—and you'd do the same for them."

She waited until he nodded slightly, then she walked to her buggy and drove away.

Her heart still ached over Samuel, over the loss of a relationship that had come to mean so much to her in such a short time. To think she'd begun to care for him, begun to love him.

Did she love Samuel Yoder?

What caused men like him and Phillip Smucker to insist on carrying life's burdens alone?

But then Samuel hadn't spoken of carrying his alone. He had spoken of a woman named Rachel. A woman Annie had never heard of before.

A woman he didn't seem to care for very much.

Annie pulled on the reins and turned her buggy toward home, toward her family, toward something that might make sense.

In a few hours the *kinner* would present the school Christmas presentation.

Would Samuel be there? If he was, what would she say to him? What would she say to her family?

She didn't have any answers, so she prayed the entire drive home. She prayed both Samuel and Phillip would have a change of heart. Prayed Sharon would heal from the hurtful time she'd been through. And she prayed the baby would arrive safely into a family that had learned to accept it and make room for it, and was willing to love it.

25

*A*s Samuel drove home from the district's far side, drove home from the family that had a solid case of the flu but nothing worse, he felt like a man who had stepped into one of those carnival rides he'd once watched in an *Englisch* town.

He'd never actually ridden a carnival ride, of course, but he had studied them a few years back. Returning from a trip to visit his *bruder* in Ohio, the bus he'd been traveling in had pulled over for a thirty-minute rest stop. After purchasing a dinner he still would rather forget, he'd gone outside to enjoy the afternoon's sunset.

The large gasoline/travel station was surrounded by what had to be an acre of concrete parking space, and it shared one side with a large discount store.

As he sat eating what they'd advertised as a bologna sandwich and drinking a small carton of milk, Samuel watched families come and go with the packages of goods they'd purchased—more goods than he could imagine carting into his home.

The carnival had been set up in front of the discount store. As the day gave way to evening, the lights of the various rides came on, pulsing with each turn as they slung the *Englischers* round and round. He'd stood there, watching, slightly amused by the distractions of a world so near and yet so foreign.

Then he'd caught sight of the giant wheel rising into the night.

"It's a Ferris wheel," Charles said. The elderly gentleman who'd come to stand beside him had been his seatmate for most of the ride from Ohio.

"*Ya.* I've seen them when they come to our discount store in Mifflin County." He sized up Charles, finally smiled. "It's just we're not usually out at night—because of the buggies and all. I've never seen one lit up."

The wheel continued to rise into the sky, turning round, moving toward the ground and then rising again.

"Took my granddaughter on one two years ago. Thought I might lose my dinner." Charles laughed. "You've ten minutes left, if you want to try it."

Samuel stuck his hands into his pockets, turned with Charles and walked back toward their bus. "Think I'll stay on the ground, *danki.* It's a sight though, isn't it?"

As their bus had pulled away, his gaze had been drawn to the lights of the Ferris wheel again, rising up into the night.

Driving through town—his town that was now completely closed up for Christmas Eve—he realized this was truly his home, and he had no desire to leave.

He'd never had an urge to try the *Englisch* world, never wanted to sample what they had to give—from what he could see, nothing they offered made up for what he would lose by leaving behind the life of his *dat* and *grossdaddi.*

No, Samuel was completely content in his life, other than the loneliness, which sometimes bit into his soul.

And most days he accepted that as a part of *Gotte's wille.*

Then Annie had dropped into his life, and he'd begun to wonder if his aloneness had been God's will or his own pridefulness. Perhaps he'd been too immersed in his own aloneness to let anyone else into his life.

A white truck passed him on the road, spewing snow and slush.

Were he honest, he understood he'd been selfish all along pursuing Annie. He'd been guilty of claiming the very best for himself. And he had watched David, knowing David would make a better husband for her.

David was younger. David would be home more often, not traveling around the county every time a *boppli* fell ill.

David wasn't damaged.

Samuel knew that as much as he tried to cover it up he would always be somehow damaged.

He understood by the stricken look on Annie's face that what he'd seen in the barn between the two of them had been innocent enough. What she didn't understand was the look on her face, the laughter in her voice, the second before she'd realized he was there.

The scene remained frozen in Samuel's mind.

Playing round and round like the carousel.

Annie—young, carefree, happy.

Annie as she should be, not as she was with him.

He flicked the reins lightly, moved past the schoolhouse where buggies were hitched all the way from the doorway to the road.

Best he didn't stop tonight.

Seeing her wouldn't help.

Besides, he should write to Rachel. Tell her he'd come in the spring, as soon as he found a buyer for his farm. It was long past time he joined his *bruder* Benjamin there.

But he kept thinking of the *Englisch* Ferris wheel, twirling round and round.

Up, up, up, and then over.

Morning sunlight poured in the window of the Hostetlers' living room windows. The brightness hurt Annie's eyes.

The fact it was Christmas morning hurt her heart.

She stared down at her folded hands, stared at the row of top stitches so recently sewn on her new midnight blue dress, stared anywhere but across the room into Samuel's eyes.

She tried to concentrate on Bishop Levi's words.

"We all know Christmas is about the Infant Child, what he brings to our lives, what he offers to our hearts. We know this, but we live as if he hadn't even been born in that manger so long ago. We live as if the Christ child hadn't exchanged heaven for a manger—for you and for me."

Tears blurred her vision, and the top stitches became a single white line.

Annie was guilty of all those things Bishop Levi spoke of and more. It seemed whether she lived in the *Englisch* world or the Amish one, she insisted on putting her own needs first.

It seemed Christmas wasn't so simple after all.

When would she learn?

When would she stop acting like the *kinner* who waited for Second Christmas and gave so little thought to the true meaning?

She didn't realize the tears were tracking down her cheeks until Charity pressed a handkerchief into her hand.

"*Danki*," she whispered.

Instead of replying, Charity turned and hushed Reba.

"I want to know why she's *bedauerlich* on First Christmas," Reba mumbled.

Annie looked up to see if Bishop Levi was nearing the end of his sermon. Though he had stepped back toward the center of the living room, he hadn't closed his Bible, and he didn't look as if he was ready to sit for the final Christmas hymn.

She stared back down at her hands, at the handkerchief stitched by Charity. If she could calm her pounding heart, stop the river of tears, she'd be able to make it to the end of the service.

Rebekah sat directly behind her. Annie's mind drifted away from Bishop Levi's sermon and back to her conversation with her *mamm* the night before.

She remembered little of it, since she'd spent most of the time sobbing in her arms. It was so unlike her—she'd always prided herself in having some semblance of control over her emotions.

Her cheeks warmed at the memory, and almost against her will her gaze went up, over and across the room—found Samuel, who continued to watch her.

Bowing her head, she forced her mind back to the bishop's words. "It *is* simple, though. Christmas is a time of grace, and all we need do is accept His grace."

"Give him grace, Annie."

"I think I love him, *Mamm*. Is that even possible?"

"Of course it is."

"But I've been home less than a month."

"Love doesn't take time, dear. It takes giving of yourself."

"Then why would he walk away? Why wouldn't he listen?"

"We don't know what Samuel is struggling with, what burden he carries. Give him time and give him grace."

The bishop's words and her *mamm's* intersected in her mind and in her heart, wove together until she feared they would tie her stomach into knots.

Professionally, she understood the signs of a panic attack, realized she needed to relax.

Physically, she seemed powerless to stop the trembling claiming her body, heart, and soul—stealing her very breath.

Suddenly the room's warmth and the closeness of the women around her pressed down on Annie. She needed to be outside, in the snow, in the fresh air, away from sympathetic but well-meaning looks like Reba's.

She glanced up, but instead of finding the bishop, her gaze again locked with Samuel. Her heart slammed into her throat, and she worried it would stop beating.

As if, even across the room and across the dozens of people who sat between them, she could feel his love for her.

She knew then.

She finally understood. Not all of it, but enough.

And the knowing hurt her nearly as much as all that had come before.

Pulling in a shaky breath, she turned to Charity. "I need to use the facilities," she whispered.

Charity nodded, scooted her chair to the side to make room for her to pass through, and again hushed Reba.

Samuel watched Annie rise and push past the row of chairs.

He had not slept much the night before, but he had prayed—prayed and read through his parents' Bible. It had the family tree written in front, a tree marked by love and commitment, not obligation. Working his ways through the pages, he had found many answers.

Meeting privately with the bishop before the services, he had found more. Levi had helped him to see that his insecurities were coloring his judgment, much as the clouds on a summer day could tint the fields behind his home. He should have trusted Annie, should have listened to her explanation, and he should have believed what was in his heart.

Rising from his seat, he knew that now was the moment to ask her forgiveness.

Actually, he had two questions he needed to ask her.

⁓♊︎

Once free of the rows of chairs, free of the overly stuffy room, Annie pushed through the door at the back of the kitchen.

She hadn't lied.

She did need to use the bathroom, but she needed air more. She gulped it in as if it were water, relished in the feel of it in her lungs, even as the cold brushed her face, bit at her fingers and nose.

Fresh snow lay on the Hostetlers' fields, on the fences, and of course on the nativity scene the *kinner* had set up in front of the barn.

Annie moved hesitantly toward it, studied the wooden figures of Mary and Joseph. In front of them was a feed trough, filled with hay and holding a baby doll swaddled in a blanket.

The holy family.

She reached out, touched the babe, closed her eyes, and prayed.

Prayed for peace.

Prayed for compassion.

Prayed for understanding.

It was exactly as Bishop Levi had said, and she'd been foolish to focus on other things. She was here, home, where she belonged. The Lord had allowed her to come back and be surrounded by family and *freinden* who cared for her.

She drew in a shaky breath.

A winter finch hopped from a nearby bush to the ground, and from the ground to the trough where the baby lay.

Perhaps she could resolve to be like the finch.

The finch wasn't an eagle, soaring across the morning sky. It hopped and twitted, making its way from one spot to the next, until it reached its destination.

She could survive as the finch did—day by day, one small step at a time.

It wasn't the life she had envisioned, but life in any form was a gift.

Isn't that what the bishop had been trying to say?

Isn't that what she'd learned from Kiptyn?

If she were honest with herself, she'd admit she had been lucky to know Samuel before he'd needed to move on—she would count the little time they'd shared together as a gift, and she'd always treasure the memory of this Christmas season.

"I brought your coat."

His voice caused her heart to beat faster.

She waited until he moved beside her, accepted the coat he placed over her shoulders with a tentative smile, though another part of her heart trembled at the sight and smell and closeness of him.

It will get easier, she thought. *I don't know how, but I do know it will get easier.*

"You're not angry anymore." He loosened her *kapp* strings that had become entangled beneath the collar of her coat.

When she reached up to help pull them free, their hands touched, and she thought she might lose her composure then, turn into a sobbing, puddling heap, but she remembered the finch and drew a steadying breath.

"No, Samuel, I'm not angry anymore."

"Why?"

"I was wrong to be angry with you earlier. You're doing what you think is best for your family—for your *schweschder-in-law*. I see that now, and I'm sorry."

"You're sorry?" His voice rose higher in disbelief, even as her stomach tossed and pitched.

"*Ya.* I wasn't being fair to you."

Samuel reached for the bale of hay nearest the wooden Joseph and sank down on it, looking as if he might collapse into the feeding trough if he didn't. "Annie, you owe me no apology. I promised you—"

"You promised me nothing." She met his eyes then, even as her chin went up and a fraction of her old spark return. "We went out a few times, that's all. We were not promised, Samuel. I won't be having people saying we were."

"That's not what I meant." He pulled at his beard and peered out toward the buggies as children began pouring from the house. "I know there was no formal question asked or answer given. I almost wish, that is . . . if I had."

Annie waited, her heart hammering so loudly she thought surely he would hear and think she was having a stroke.

Suddenly he was beside her, entwining her fingers in his and pulling her toward the barn's back side. "I want to show you something, Annie."

"Where are we going?"

"This will take no more than a few minutes."

"But my family will be leaving now that the service is ended."

"No one ever leaves that quickly, and I can't talk to you with twenty or thirty *kinner* crawling all over us amidst the manger scene."

Tugging on her hand, he pulled her past the barn, back toward the pond to the south of the main house.

There, beneath the bare limbs of a giant oak tree sat a bench built into the shelter of a stand of trees. They were protected from the wind, and when they'd reached it, when they'd sat and nothing could interrupt them but the sound of the birds and the ice cracking out on the pond, he turned to her and reached into his pocket.

"I'm sorry about yesterday," he began tentatively, then added, "about what happened at the barn."

"There's no need to apologize."

"*Ya*, there is. Maybe I was afraid."

"Afraid of what, Samuel?"

Instead of answering her, he stared out over the pond. "The day we returned from delivering Faith's baby, we stopped at the top of the hill overlooking your *dat's* place."

"I remember."

"The farms stretched out, reminding me of a quilt my *mamm* had made—a quilt I hadn't seen in quite some time." He pulled out a finely crocheted bookmark, with a cradle at the top and a cross at the bottom. Placing it in her hand, he explained, "Last night I found myself wanting, needing to read the Christmas story from my *mamm* and *dat's* old family Bible. I keep it wrapped in that quilt, in an old cedar chest my *dat* made."

His fingers caressed the bookmark's delicate threads. "I unfolded the quilt and pulled out the Bible, and I came across this. I remember the year my *mamm* made it, how I used to keep it in my Bible, but I don't remember why I stopped."

"Samuel—"

"Maybe somewhere along the way, maybe after Mary and Hannah died, I stopped believing in God's goodness. Maybe I stopped believing in the gift of Christmas, or that God had any *gut* thing left for me."

Annie reached out and touched his face. "Samuel, that's not true."

"*Ya*, I know that now." He smiled, and his smile did much to mend her heart. "I think I knew it last night when I found this old gift from my *mamm*. Maybe I knew it the first night I laid eyes on you, when you rushed into your *dat's* room."

"I don't—"

"But I *know* I understood the goodness of God when Bishop Levi started preaching this morning, when he preached about grace and our need to accept it and offer it to each other."

Annie sat frozen, her eyes darting back and forth from the cross in her hand to Samuel, trying to understand.

Samuel took her hand in his, gently placed the bookmark there, and closed her fingers around it.

"Do you remember when you told me Faith's baby reminded you of the Christ child and the cross?"

She nodded, her tears now spilling.

"First Christmas isn't our day for gift-giving," she whispered.

"Let's make an exception."

Annie stared down at the bookmark, trying to make sense of all he was saying.

"So you're giving this to me as a gift?"

"*Ya*, but I can't be letting it out of my family."

"Out of your family?"

Samuel smiled, reached forward and kissed her lightly on the lips. Annie thought she might have heard snow fall softly around them, or it might have been the brush of angels' wings.

Or perhaps her heart took flight.

"I'm asking you to marry me, Annie Weaver."

"What about—"

"Say yes or no. We'll work out the rest later."

"But—"

"Say what's in your heart, Annie."

"You're in my heart, Samuel."

He kissed her again, sent her heart rate into a quick double rhythm.

"Are you saying yes?"

"I'm saying yes."

Samuel closed his hands around hers, which still held the crocheted heirloom, still held the cross. "Then you can keep the gift."

Glossary

Ach—oh
Aenti—aunt
Bedauerlich—sad
Boppli—baby
Bopplin—babies
Bruder—brother
Daed—dad
Danki—thank you
Dat—father
Dietsch—Pennsylvania Dutch
Dochdern—daughters
Eiferich—excited
Englisch/Englischer—non-Amish person
Fraa—wife
Freinden—friends
Froh—happy
Gegisch—silly
Gelassenheit—calmness, composure, placidity
Gem gschehne—you're welcome
Gotte's wille—God's will
Grandkinner—grandchildren

Grossdaddi—grandfather

Grossdochdern—granddaughters

Grossmammi—grandmother

Gschtarewe—dead

Gudemariye—good morning

Gut—good

In lieb—in love

Kaffi—coffee

Kapp—prayer covering

Kind—child

Kinner—children

Mamm—mom

Naerfich—nervous

Onkel—uncle

Rumschpringe—running around; time before an Amish young person has officially joined the church, provides a bridge between childhood and adulthood.

Schweschder—sister

Was iss letz—what's wrong

Wunderbaar—wonderful

Ya—yes

Discussion Questions

1. When the Christmas season begins, Annie realizes how homesick she is. How do you feel when Christmas songs and decorations begin popping up the day after Thanksgiving? Do you think it honors God or detracts from the meaning of Christmas?

2. By the end of the third chapter, we see that God is going to use Annie's skills, which she acquired during her period of rebellion, to minister to her family and her community. How does this coincide with the Bible's teachings of grace?

3. At the end of chapter 9, Annie's mother reminds her of the Scripture found in Matthew 7:12—to treat others as we'd want to be treated. Annie's claims that she knows the Scripture, to which Rebekah replies, "I expect you do. Most of us know it. The knowing is easy. It's the doing that gives us trouble." What response did you have to this conversation?

4. Chapter 11 is one of my favorite scenes, where Aaron and Faith have their child at home. My mother was born at home, so I very much enjoyed writing this. What was your reaction to this scene, and what are your thoughts on home-birthing in our age of modern medical technological advancements?

5. Samuel learns a young girl in their community, Sharon Smucker, is pregnant and will be needing medical care. Even the Amish community occasionally needs to deal with issues such as single mothers. What did you think about how this aspect of the story developed?

6. In chapter 16, Annie confesses to Samuel that she understood Bishop Levi's sermon, even thought she'd taken it to heart, but then a few hours later all the peace

had melted away. Have you ever had trouble holding on to a special, spiritual moment?

7. The Amish believe strongly in accepting *Gotte's wille* and moving on with your life, even when tragedy strikes. Samuel has a bit of trouble with this, but he finally comes to the conclusion that he can honor Mary and still love Annie. What are some ways that we can honor those who have gone on to be with the Lord?

8. Samuel overreacts to what he thinks he sees in the barn when he encounters Annie and David there. His reaction was emotional, not logical, and reflected past hurts and present insecurities. In the end, God uses this misunderstanding to bring him closer to Annie. What is necessary for God to use our mistakes for our own good?

9. Annie wonders if she can really love Samuel, when they've only been re-acquainted for less than a month. What do you think? Does true love take time?

10. One of the themes of the book is forgiveness. Discuss a situation in your life where you have given, received, or need to offer forgiveness.

Dear Readers,

Are you part of a reading group or book club? I adore meeting my readers. If you'd like to set up a book chat, or if you'd just like me to respond to some of your questions, email me at VannettaChapman@gmail.com. I can also be reached via my website http://www.vannettachapman.com, or you're welcome to come and blog with me at http://vannettachapman.wordpress.com.

An Interview with Author Vannetta Chapman

Q: What inspired you to create the story of *A Simple Amish Christmas*?

Vannetta: Two things really. First, the idea that while there are many differences between the Amish community and the one where I live, there are also many things we share in common. I wanted to explore one of those commonalities—the need to fit into a community you love and find a way to use your God-given talents. Second, the more I learn about the Amish and the more Amish people I meet, the more I am inspired by their ability to keep the main thing the main thing—that being family and faith. What better way to discuss that than with a Christmas story?

Q: Are there any elements that readers may be able to relate to?

Vannetta: I think we can all relate to the need to slow down, simplify our lives, and spend time with the people we love. Whether it's Christmas or summer vacation, life speeds by in the blink of an eye. Annie's story reminds us that time doesn't stand still, and we aren't guaranteed to have those we love around us forever, so it's important to appreciate every day.

Q: How do you as the author connect with your characters?

Vannetta: It's very crowded in my little office with all of these characters milling around! Seriously though, I connect with my characters easily because they represent real people with real hurts and dreams. When I write a story, it might be shelved as fiction but it's nonfiction to me in that I draw from past experience—both my own and that of other people. Then it's only a matter of coloring in the details with my imagination.

Q: What do you think readers will enjoy most about the love story between Annie and Samuel?

Vannetta: What I enjoyed the most as Annie and Samuel's story unfolded was the fact that they weren't the "perfect" couple. They didn't get along in every scene, and their relationship didn't progress smoothly at every turn. Instead, like most of us, they had to work at it in a few places. They had to seek the advice of others, and they had to pray about what was the best direction to take. In the end, they had to trust their hearts and trust the Lord. I love this, because it's a true life romance. In my opinion, those are the very best kind.

Q: Even though this is a seasonal story would you say that *A Simple Amish Christmas* can be enjoyed year round?

Vannetta: Absolutely! Now you knew I'd say that. Honestly, I think this story is less about a certain holiday than it is about a way of life and the paths of two people. When their paths cross, they have a few decisions to make, and it will change their lives as well as the lives of their families. Christmas is part of the setting, and it's a fun element of the story, but Annie and Samuel's story began before December 1, and it will continue past the new year. I think readers can enjoy it all year long as well!

Want to learn more about author
Vannetta Chapman and check out other great
fiction from Abingdon Press?

Sign up for our fiction newsletter at
www.AbingdonPress.com
to read interviews with your favorite authors, find tips
for starting a reading group, and stay posted on what
new titles are on the horizon. It's a place to connect
with other fiction readers or post a
comment about this book.

Be sure to visit Vannetta online!

http://www.vannettachapman.com
http://vannettachapman.wordpresscom

What they're saying about...

Gone to Green, by Judy Christie

"...Refreshingly realistic religious fiction, this novel is unafraid to address the injustices of sexism, racism, and corruption as well as the spiritual devastation that often accompanies the loss of loved ones. Yet these darker narrative tones beautifully highlight the novel's message of friendship, community, and God's reassuring and transformative love." —*Publishers Weekly* **starred review**

The Call of Zulina, by Kay Marshall Strom

"This compelling drama will challenge readers to remember slavery's brutal history, and its heroic characters will inspire them. Highly recommended." —*Library Journal* **starred review**

Surrender the Wind, by Rita Gerlach

"I am purely a romance reader, and yet you hooked me in with a war scene, of all things! I would have never believed it. You set the mood beautifully and have a clean, strong, lyrical way with words. You have done your research well enough to transport me back to the war-torn period of colonial times." —Julie Lessman, **author of** *The Daughters of Boston* **series**

One Imperfect Christmas, by Myra Johnson

"Debut novelist Myra Johnson ushers us into the Christmas season with a fresh and exciting story that will give you a chuckle and a special warmth." —DiAnn Mills, **author of** *Awaken My Heart* **and** *Breach of Trust*

The Prayers of Agnes Sparrow, by Joyce Magnin

"Beware of *The Prayers of Agnes Sparrow*. Just when you have become fully enchanted by its marvelous quirky zaniness, you will suddenly be taken to your knees by its poignant truth-telling about what it means to be divinely human. I'm convinced that 'on our knees' is exactly where Joyce Magnin planned for us to land all along." —Nancy Rue, **co-author of** *Healing Waters* **(***Sullivan Crisp* **Series)** 2009 Novel of the Year

The Fence My Father Built, by Linda S. Clare

"...Linda Clare reminds us with her writing that is wise, funny, and heartbreaking, that what matters most in life are the people we love and the One who gave them to us."—Gina Ochsner, **Dark Horse Literary, winner of the Oregon Book Award and the Flannery O'Connor Award for Short Fiction**

eye of the god, by Ariel Allison

"Filled with action on three continents, *eye of the god* is a riveting fast-paced thriller, but it is Abby—who, in spite of another letdown by a man, remains filled with hope—who makes Ariel Allison's tale a super read."—**Harriet Klausner**